... of New South ... has appeared in a number of films and TV commercials but prefers to concentrate on a career as a writer. He is the author of twenty-one books, including *Goodoo Goodoo*, *The Wind and the Monkey*, *Leaving Bondi*, *The Ultimate Aphrodisiac*, *Mystery Bay Blues*, *Rosa-Marie's Baby* and *The Tesla Legacy*.

To find out more about Bob and his books
visit these websites:
www.robertgbarrett.com.au
or
www.harpercollins.com.au/robertgbarrett

CRIME SCENE CESSNOCK

CRIME SCENE CESSNOCK

ROBERT G. BARRETT

HarperCollins*Publishers*

Tai chi prayer quoted on page 219–220 reproduced by kind
permission of The Golden Door Health Retreat Elysia

HarperCollinsPublishers

First published in Australia in 2005
This edition published in 2006
by HarperCollinsPublishers Australia Pty Limited
ABN 36 009 913 517
www.harpercollins.com.au

HarperCollinsPublishers

25 Ryde Road, Pymble, Sydney NSW 2073, Australia
31 View Road, Glenfield, Auckland 10, New Zealand
77–85 Fulham Palace Road, London W6 8JB, United Kingdom
2 Bloor Street East, 20th floor, Toronto, Ontario M4W 1A8, Canada
10 East 53rd Street, New York NY 10022, USA

National Library of Australia Cataloguing-in-Publication data:

Barrett, Robert G.
   Crime scene Cessnock.
   2nd ed.
   ISBN 13: 978 0 7322 8212 7.
   ISBN 10: 0 7322 8212 8.
   1. Pokolbin Region (N.S.W.) – Fiction. I. Title.
A823.3

Cover design by Darren Holt, HarperCollins Design Studio
Cover image: Robert G. Barrett (sunset); Getty Images (silhouette)
Typeset in 11/15pt Minion by Kirby Jones
Printed and bound in Australia by Griffin Press.

50gsm Bulky News used by HarperCollinsPublishers is a natural, recyclable
product made from wood grown in sustainable plantation forests. The
manufacturing processes conform to the environmental regulations in the
country of origin, New Zealand.

DEDICATION

The author would like to thank the following people for their help in writing this book:

The management and staff at the Golden Door Health Retreat, Elysia, in the Pokolbin Valley, New South Wales.

Dr Frank Vella, FRACGP, MBBS, at the Terrigal Medical Centre, New South Wales.

This book is dedicated to the Australian military personnel who lost their lives helping others in the tsunami disaster, and their families.

A percentage of the royalties from this book is being donated to the Calga Springs Wildlife Sanctuary, New South Wales, and to Avoca Surf Club.

A MESSAGE FROM THE AUTHOR

Firstly, I have to thank all those people who have written to me. I do my level best to answer every letter, but I just found a stack got lost while I wrote this book, so some of you have missed out. For that I am sorry. But I read and truly appreciate every letter. Even the ones abusing me for not writing a book last year. But I got webbed up in film scripts and all sorts of other things and got distracted.

Everyone wants to know what's going on with the movie of *You Wouldn't Be Dead For Quids*. All I can say is, it's a longer and slower process than I imagined. But some progress is being made. I've also given a bloke an option to make *The Ultimate Aphrodisiac* into an animated feature film. The bloke's an old waxhead like me and very talented. And if he gets it up, I guarantee it will be the best movie ever made in Australia. I'm about to update my website so check things out when I can elaborate more on the matter. I might even have something special coming up that might interest some people.

As for the T-shirts and caps, we've re-stocked, but the medium sizes are about finished. However, due to unprecedented demand, I got a run of *Mystery Bay Blues* T-shirts with that nutty little bear on the front. Through no fault of my own, they're not Australian-made T-shirts, but they still look good. So all T-shirts are now $30.00 delivered. Check the website or just send a money order to Psycho Possum Productions, PO Box 382, Terrigal NSW 2260. And don't forget to include your phone number in case there's a glitch.

That's about it. I'm sure you'll like this book. And Les turns out to be a good bloke again. When doesn't he? See you in the next book.

Robert G. Barrett

CRIME SCENE CESSNOCK

For a sparkling summer afternoon on Bondi Beach at the beginning of February, it wasn't too punishingly hot, and wearing a grey T-shirt hanging out over a pair of Levi's shorts, Les Norton was smiling happily as he walked from North Bondi RSL Club in Ramsgate Avenue back to North Bondi Surf Club. After an easy Friday night at the pickle factory, he'd met Billy Dunne down the beach earlier for a training session with two off-duty army boys they'd become friends with. Nothing spectacular, just a lazy six laps' jog on the soft sand, followed by a four-lap paddle on the skis, swim a lap, then walk back to the north end. Some days they'd put the pressure on, most days they opted to do it slow but steady. Today was one of those days. After they all got cleaned up, the two diggers went their way, leaving Les and Billy to enjoy a steak lunch at the 'rissole' washed down with mineral water and coffee. Billy's wife Lyndy had picked Billy up outside the RSL, leaving Les with a short stroll back to the surf club where he'd left his latest pride and joy chained to the white fence running along the north side of the surf club.

The apple of Norton's eye was an old blue Europa ten-speed pushbike with cow-horn handlebars he'd found when he was driving past a garage sale in Coogee. After paying a bloke even older than the bike thirty dollars for it, Les took the old Europa to a bike shop at Clovelly where, for another seventy dollars, he got the handlebars changed, the brakes tightened, and had the cheese-cutter seat swapped for one more suited to his ample backside. So for a hundred dollars, Les finished up with a fairly good ten-speed that suited him down to the ground. Parking along Bondi Beach, if you could find a spot, cost an arm and a leg, and the moment your meter ran out, the rangers were on you like flies on shit. Subsequently, Les left his car at home most of the time and walked. And even though the fifteen-minute walk from Chez Norton down to North Bondi wasn't Heartbreak Hill, it was much quicker by bike with an easy pedal home via Roscoe Street. And if he was ever unlucky enough to get his bike stolen, although it would be a pain in the arse, Les was only out a hundred bucks. Nevertheless, Norton always chained his bike up securely, just in case there happened to be a citizen out there who needed it to ride back and forth between Waverley Courthouse and the nearest methadone centre more than Les needed it to ride down to the beach and back.

So besides starting off well, Saturday was turning out to be an excellent day all round. In fact, Les was in that good a mood as he got ready to ride home for an afternoon nap, he was actually looking forward to work that night so he could renew a spirited conversation he'd been having with Billy about the coming football season. Bloody Billy, smiled Les. How could you live in the Eastern Suburbs and follow St George?

After crossing the grass, Les was still smiling and whistling happily out of tune as he walked up the side of the surf club. But the smile on his face evaporated as fast as the whistling stopped when he got to his bike. It was still standing where he'd left it all right, and his green helmet was still attached to the handlebars. However, the front tyre was flat. Flat on the ground.

'Ahh, fuck it,' groaned Les. 'Wouldn't that give you the shits.' Norton's eyes narrowed. 'And you can bet some smartarse has let the bloody thing down too.'

Les lifted the front wheel of his bike and spun it slowly around. Just near the valve, a small piece of rusty nail was stuck in the tyre.

'Bugger it,' scowled Les. He plucked the piece of nail out of the tyre, looked at it for a second then tossed it onto the grass. 'Just my bloody luck.'

Now what to do? Les pondered. He didn't have a puncture kit, and if he had he wouldn't know what to do with it. Pushing his bike home wouldn't be much joy either; as well as looking and feeling like a dill, he'd probably bugger up the rim. No. The only answer was to leave the bike where it was, walk home, come back with his car, then put the bike in the boot and take it over to the bike shop in Clovelly before it closed. With a bit of luck they'd have the tyre repaired by tomorrow. After adjusting his cap and sunglasses and shrugging his backpack more comfortably across his shoulders, Norton headed for Campbell Parade.

For a Saturday afternoon there wasn't all that much traffic or many people around and Les was thinking lightly about this and that as he strolled along in the sun. He'd missed out on a huge earn in Torquay. But the money did go to a good cause: the orphanage. However, Les felt Mrs Setree could have given him some sort of a guernsey on the front page of the Melbourne *Age* instead of saying she and her daughter had found the paintings. On the upside, Roxy had rung him from WA saying she'd almost finished researching her book there and was thinking of calling into Sydney for a few days before she left for the Northern Territory. And Amazing Grace had invited him down to Narooma for a bit of R and R, as soon as she got back from Melbourne where she was lining up a chain of shops to sell her T-shirts. Yes, boss, smiled Les, winking up at the sky as he came to the roundabout at the corner of Wairoa Avenue and Bondi Beach Public School, I can't complain too much. Things are bumping along all right.

And talking about things bumping along. Who should Les suddenly see bumping past the school in his battered white Ford Laser but Benny the Beak, his old Jewish landlord. There was no mistaking Benny's bald head barely poking up behind the wheel and if there was a worse driver in Sydney, nobody knew who it was, but Benny would be right behind him in a tight, photo finish. Being a rotten driver wasn't Benny's only attribute. He rarely wore his seat-belt, hardly ever used his blinkers and was too stuck in his ways to buy a car with an automatic gear shift. Subsequently, Benny was always stalling the engine or sending other drivers wild with his erratic turns. Benny should have lost his licence years ago. But Benny's God smiled on him and somehow Benny never got so much as a parking ticket.

Oddly enough, even though Les had taken Benny to the cleaners over a flat he once rented from him, Les finished up on friendly terms with Benny, and if ever they spotted each other at the Hakoah Club in Hall Street and Benny was on his own, they'd join each other for their meal or coffee. Les would tell Benny about things at Kings Cross and Benny would regale Les with tales about when the Russians invaded Hungary. Like the time he got shot in the leg throwing a Molotov cocktail at a Russian tank. Now here was Benny bumping merrily along and sure enough, he stalled the car when he slowed down for the roundabout. Les was about to yell out at Benny and ask him what he was doing driving a car on Saturday, when he noticed a silver Ford Falcon right up Benny's rear, booming out American gangsta rap. Inside were four westie hoons of Middle Eastern appearance wearing black tracksuits with their baseball caps on back to front; the driver bipping his horn impatiently for Benny to move. But the more the driver bipped his horn, the more flustered Benny became till finally he flooded the motor.

'Come on, you cunt,' bipped the hoon driving. 'Move your fuckin arse.'

'Yeah. Move your arse, man,' the hoon sitting behind the driver shouted out from his window.

Benny kept trying to start the engine. But the more the driver behind tooted his horn, the more exasperated Benny became. Les watched on with amusement at Benny's predicament and disgust at the hoons' attitude. Then Benny put his arm out the window and waved for the hoons to go round him. But with Benny's pudgy little hands it didn't look that way to the hoon behind the wheel.

'Hey!' he yelled. 'Don't give me the finger, you cunt, or I'll break your fuckin arm.' Benny waved another gesture for the driver to go round. 'What? Fuck you!' yelled the hoon behind the wheel, slipping off his seat-belt and getting out of the car.

With the other hoons egging him on, the driver stormed up to Benny's old Laser then wrenched the door open and dragged little Benny out by the collar of his crumpled white shirt. After shoving Benny up against the front mudguard he then punched him flush in the face with a hard right.

Benny didn't know what hit him. He tumbled back across the bonnet then fell down and hit the back of his head on the road, knocking himself unconscious. As blood started oozing out from under Benny's head, the hoon walked round and, to the cheers of his friends in the Ford, started kicking the motionless Benny in the ribs. Les could hardly believe what he was seeing.

'Hey. Piss off, you idiot,' he shouted. Dodging traffic, Les ran across the road and pulled the hoon off Benny. 'What the fuck do you think you're doing? You fuckin hero.'

The hoon glared at Les. 'Fuck off, cunt. This has got nothing to do with you.' The hoon gave Les a shove in the chest. 'Piss off.'

Les glowered. 'What? Fuck you. You would-be homeboy prick.'

Les stepped back and belted the hoon in the face with a wicked short right that busted his mouth open and knocked out two of the hoon's front teeth. The hoon's eyes rolled back and he fell over the bonnet, then slid down the front, hitting his head on the bumper bar and landing next to Benny out cold.

A rage of cursing and shouting erupted from inside the Falcon and the other three hoons jumped out to get at Les. Les spun around to face the one that had been sitting behind the driver. But his backpack, with a big wet towel, a bottle of water and other odds and ends inside it, caused him to overbalance and twist his right knee. This didn't stop him, however, from poking out a quick left jab which the hoon walked straight into, stopping him dead in his tracks and knocking off his black baseball cap. Gaining his balance, Les hooked hard off the jab and the instant Norton's big fist hit him in the face, the second hoon toppled down on the road, blood bubbling out of his broken nose. When the two remaining hoons quickly realised they had a horrible snag on their hands, they stopped and turned to each other.

'Fuck this cunt,' said the hoon who had been sitting next to the driver. 'See how he goes with a few bullets in him.'

The third hoon ran back to the passenger-side door and reached into the glove box. Before he could get it open, Les sprinted round the front of the car and slammed the door on his arm, dislocating his shoulder.

'Ohh, shit! My fuckin arm,' howled the hoon. Les slammed the door on the hoon's arm again, this time breaking his elbow. 'Ohh, fuck. Fuck!' yelped the hoon, clutching his shattered arm as he fell back against the car.

Les turned, the last hoon and gave him a sinister smile. 'Okay, homeboy. This just leaves you and me.'

The remaining hoon stood his ground then snarled and pointed a finger at Les. 'I know you, cunt. You work at that club up the Cross. I've seen you there.' The hoon made trigger pulling gestures with his right index finger. 'You're dead meat, cunt. Dead fuckin meat.'

'Yeah?' replied Les, moving towards the last hoon. 'Well, you're barbecued.'

By this time a small crowd had gathered round to watch the action. At the same time what should come cruising down Wairoa Avenue but a white Commodore with two young cops in the front seat. Then seemingly from out of nowhere, a paddy wagon came cruising along Campbell Parade with three more of New South Wales's finest crammed in the front: two men and a dumpy blonde woman. The Commodore hit the siren and accelerated in the wrong side of the roundabout, the paddy wagon screeched to a stop alongside the two cars and Les suddenly found himself surrounded by uniformed police.

'Righto. What's going on here?' demanded the oldest cop, a florid-faced sergeant who'd been sitting in the wagon.

'We weren't doing nothing,' yelled the fourth hoon, pointing at Les. 'We stopped for this old guy in the Laser. And this cunt started punching into us. He's fuckin crazy, man.'

'Yeah,' groaned the third hoon, still slumped up against the passenger-side door clutching his right arm. 'He's fuckin nuts. Look at my fuckin arm. He just broke it. Ohh fuck! Get me an ambulance.'

'Bullshit!' yelled Les, indicating to the front of Benny's Laser. 'That big prick in the black tracksuit was kicking into the old bloke. I ran over to stop him. The old bloke's Benny Rabinski. He's a friend of mine.'

'It didn't look that way to us, sir,' said one of the young cops who'd got out of the Commodore. 'As we turned the corner, you were slamming the door against this man's arm.'

'Yeah.' Les nodded to the Ford. 'Because there's a gun in there. He was going to shoot me. Have a look in the glove box.'

The young cop reached inside the Ford and opened the glove box. Sitting under some papers was a silver .32 automatic.

'He's right, sarge,' said the young cop. 'There is a gun in here.'

'That's what I told you,' said Les.

'Yeah. Cause this big cunt put it there,' yelled the fourth hoon. 'He's trying to set us up.'

'What? Ohh, don't give me the shits.'

Les momentarily lost his temper and moved towards the fourth hoon. The hoon feigned terror and moved back.

'I want him charged with assault,' whined the hoon with the broken arm.

'Yeah. Keep him away from me,' said the fourth hoon. 'Lock the cunt up. He's fuckin crazy, man.'

'Crazy,' hissed Les. 'I'll show you crazy. You lying prick.'

'Stay where you are,' ordered the sergeant.

'Ohh, balls!' said Les.

'That's it. You're under arrest,' said the sergeant.

'Under arrest? What for?' howled Les. 'I was trying to help Benny. Are you nuts?'

'I'm arresting you for assault.' The sergeant turned to one of the cops from the Commodore. 'Matty. Ring for an ambulance. Dan. Put this man in the back of the Holden.'

'Ohh, bullshit,' said Les. 'I don't believe this.'

'Sir. Put your hands behind your back,' ordered the woman cop tersely.

'You gotta be kidding,' protested Les.

The woman cop took out a can of capsicum spray. 'I said, put your hands behind your back.'

Les closed his eyes and shook his head in despair. 'Shit!' he cursed, totally unable to believe his rotten luck.

Before Les knew it, he was handcuffed, bundled through the crowd and sitting uncomfortably in the back seat of the Commodore; outside he could sense people peering into the car at him. Les felt like telling them all to piss off. Instead he stared blankly at the floor of the car in stunned disbelief. One minute he'd been walking along Campbell Parade, minding his own business, the next he was handcuffed and sitting in the back of a police car under arrest for assault. And all for stopping to save an old bloke from getting bashed. Les stared balefully out the car window and up at the sky. Did I say something earlier about not being able to complain? Yeah. Thanks, boss. When you dump on me, you sure do it a-la-carte, don't you?

The crowd quickly increased. Three ambulances with sirens wailing pulled up and one of the cops started diverting traffic. Les didn't bother watching all the action. Instead he kept staring at the floor, wondering what was he going to tell Price. Wondering what he was going to tell Warren. And most of all, fucked if he knew how was he going to get out of all this Eliot. If Benny died or finished in a coma, Les was gone. It was his word against four others. And he'd pretty much been found holding a smoking gun. Or in this case, a broken arm.

Eventually the front door of the Commodore opened and the two young cops piled inside. The one on the passenger side picked up the two-way.

'Waverley. This is 104. We're coming in with a prisoner.'

'Copy that, 104.'

The young cop replaced the receiver as the Commodore turned into Campbell Parade and proceeded on to Bondi Road.

'This is all bullshit, you know,' Les maintained from the back seat.

The cop driving looked at Les in the rear-view mirror. 'Save it till we get to the station.'

'Yeah, righto,' replied Les glumly.

Before Les knew it the police car had pulled up in Bronte Road outside his home away from home: Waverley Police Station. Les was led inside to the front desk where he was processed and charged with Assault to Occasion Actual Bodily Harm and Affray. With the preliminaries out off the way, Les was relieved of his backpack and it was searched while he was led up to the detectives' room and told to wait there for a detective who would take a written statement from him.

Just like old times, mused Les, staring around the detectives' room at the same blue-grey carpet, the same grey filing cabinets and the same dusty windows with the same shitty view. About the only difference from his last visit there was that the pot-plant in the corner looked like it was now ready to throw the towel in and amongst the dog-eared posters on the wall was another one saying COPS ARE TOPS. Yeah, nodded Les. So are the hairs round my arse. Les opted not to ring Price for the time being, instead he just sat there brooding for what seemed like hours before the door opened behind him and he heard a familiar voice.

'Hello, Les,' the voice said cheerfully. 'And how are you on this delightful summer's afternoon?'

Les looked up as a detective with short dark hair wearing a brown check sports coat and matching trousers sat down at the desk in front of him. Despite his predicament, Norton was able to muster a brief smile.

'Well, well, well. If it isn't my old mate Detective Caccano. How's things?'

'Very good, thank you, Les.' Detective Caccano looked at the charge sheet in front of him and smiled. 'My goodness, Les. Haven't you been a busy boy today.' The detective fixed his eyes directly on Les. 'Care to tell me about it?'

'You really want to fuckin know?' answered a disgruntled Les.

The detective looked impassively at Norton. 'I didn't come in here to play noughts and crosses.'

Les stared back at Detective Caccano for a moment, sucked in some air and snorted it out. 'I got a flat tyre on my bike.'

Les proceeded to tell Detective Caccano everything that happened that day, from the minute he met Billy outside the surf club, till the minute he was left in the detectives' room.

'And that, I might add,' concluded Les, 'is the truth, the whole truth, and nothing but the fuckin truth. So help me God. Or Buddha or Allah or any other deity you care to name.'

Detective Caccano looked at Les for a moment then smiled. 'You know something, Les? I tend to believe you.'

'Good,' enthused Norton. 'So how about letting me go?'

Detective Caccano shook his head. 'It's not quite as simple as that, old mate. Four people are in hospital. One young gentleman of Middle Eastern appearance has even got a broken arm.'

'He was going to shoot me.'

'So you say, Les.'

'There was a gun in the glove box.'

'He claims you put it there.'

'Ohh, bollocks!'

'It's their word against yours, old mate. A good lawyer would have you on toast.'

'So what was I supposed to do?' said Les. 'Just stand back and let that big mug kick poor little Benny half to death?'

'Well, you're not really supposed to break someone's arm in a car door, Les,' said Detective Caccano.

'Hey, how is Benny anyway?'

The detective looked at the charge sheet. 'Mr ... Rabinski is in hospital with a hairline fracture of the skull and a broken rib. He's still unconscious. But he should be all right before too long.'

Les felt relieved. 'Well that's good to know. He'll clear me.'

'Possibly. But the person whose arm you broke has charged you with assault. So have the others.'

'I should have broken his back,' snorted Les.

The detective smiled. 'I tend to agree with you, Les. But you know the law. Those smartarses are allowed to abuse you. Rob you. Assault you. Whatever their little hearts desire. And you're only allowed to react with a minimum or equal amount of force. Then ring for the police.'

'And they'll get there in about two hours.'

'If they've got nothing else on and there's no traffic. My oath they will.'

'What if you haven't got a phone?'

'Stiff shit.'

'Maybe I should have counselled them,' Les suggested sarcastically.

'Even better,' nodded Detective Caccano.

'That's fucked,' said Les.

'I agree with you, mate. But it's also the law.'

'Bloody hell!'

'Look,' said Detective Caccano, 'we could be here all night going over this crap. But I believe what you said. And I'll see that you get bail. Then you're going to have to sort it all out through the proper channels.'

'Fair enough,' replied Les.

Detective Caccano gave Les a wink. 'I'm certain your friend Mr Galese will arrange something.'

'Yeah,' nodded Les. 'I don't know what. But I sure hope so.'

Detective Caccano looked directly at Norton. 'I'll tell you something though, Les. If that little shit said he knows you from the Cross, and you're dead meat, I wouldn't go to work tonight. They'll organise a drive-by for sure. And if they don't get you there, they'll find out where you live and have another go.' The detective shook his head. 'And there's not much we can do about it.'

'Shit!'

'To be honest, I'd disappear for a while if I were you. At least till this all cools down a bit.'

Les thought for a moment. 'Yeah. You could be right, I suppose.'

Detective Caccano looked at Les. 'I'll tell you something else, Les. But you didn't get this from me. Okay?'

'Sure,' nodded Les.

'The bloke you claimed was kicking Mr Rabinski is a low-life named Assad Derbas. He's got a rap sheet longer than the straight at Randwick and he comes from Condell Park. That might help you.'

'Okay. Thanks a lot.'

The detective rose from the table. 'All right. Stay there for a while and I'll sort your bail out. Then you can hit the toe.'

'Righto.' Les watched as the detective walked over and opened the door. 'Hey, Detective Caccano. Thanks for that. I dead set owe you one.'

The detective gave Les a wink from the door. 'Don't worry about it.'

It was getting dark when Les limped out of Waverley Police Station with his backpack. But

Detective Caccano was as good as his word and Les was granted bail of his own recognisance to appear back at Waverley Courthouse in a month for a committal hearing on charges of assault and affray. Well, I suppose the first thing I have to do, thought Les, hailing a passing taxi, is get home and give Price the good news. The taxi pulled up and Les climbed in the back. No. The first thing I have to do is go and get my bloody bike.

The taxi pulled up outside Chez Norton in Cox Avenue. Les paid the driver then got straight into his green Berlina and drove to North Bondi. When he walked up the side of the surf club, his bike was still there. But somebody needed Norton's helmet more than Les did. What a day, scowled Les as he wheeled his bike up to the car. First I get buckled for assault. Now I get my good helmet nicked. Les looked up at the evening sky now peppered lightly with stars. There's no mercy, is there, eh. No bloody mercy. Les pushed the bike into the boot of his car and headed home.

Once he had his pushbike sitting safely on the back verandah, Les put the kettle on and walked over to the telephone. The answering service was blinking and he had four messages.

'Les. It's Price. What's going on, mate? I just heard your name on the radio. Ring me back.'

'Les. It's Billy. I just heard your name come over the radio. You've been arrested over some road rage incident. When I left you, you were going to get your bike. What's going on? Give us a ring.'

'Les. It's Eddie. Are you in some sort of strife? Let me know what's going on. I'll be here till nine.'

'You fuckin big idiot. What have you done now, you moron? Fair dinkum. It's not safe to be out on the street with dills like you around. I'll ring you back about seven. Hey. I see they're still referring to you as a waiter. You couldn't wait in line, you dope.'

Les shook his head. 'Fuckin Warren,' he grunted. Where's the cunt again? Shooting a wine commercial. Les walked into the kitchen. Fancy that little pisshead shooting a wine commercial. It'd be like Dracula shooting an ad for the blood bank. Les made a cup of coffee and rang Price.

'Price. It's Les. How are you?'

'Well, I'm all right,' answered Price. 'What have you been up to? I was home listening to the races and your name bobbed up on the news. What's going on?'

Les took a sip of coffee. 'It's not real good, Price, I can tell you that.'

Les told his boss everything that had happened, including getting the name of one of the hoons. Price listened intently and didn't say anything till Les had finished.

'Shit! What a drama,' said Price. 'And you say this flip Derbas comes from Condell Park?'

'So I was told,' replied Les.

'Sounds like they're Lebanese.' Price thought for a moment. 'Look. Don't worry too much. Eddie's got a strong connection with the Lebs. He should be able to work something out. But take the night off. I'll get Danny to fill in for you.'

'Righto,' nodded Les.

'I can't see anything happening tonight if you're not there. But I'll tell the boys to keep an eye out. Just in case.'

'Okay.'

'In fact it might be an idea if you do what that cop said and get out of town for a while.'

'If you say so, Price. But Jesus. It gives me the shits, having to piss off because four fuckin wogs from the Western Suburbs have got their noses out of joint.'

Price chuckled. 'According to the news, they've got a bit more out of joint than just their noses. One's got a broken jaw. Another's got his arm broken in two places. Shit. You don't muck around, do you?'

'Ohh, you should have seen what this big prick was doing to Benny the Beak. Benny's about as big as a penguin.'

'Yeah. Fair enough. All right. Don't worry too much. Just take it easy. And I'll probably see you tomorrow. Don't bother ringing the others. I'll sort all that out tonight. But Eddie will get in touch with you tomorrow. Okay?'

'Righto. I'll hear from you and Eddie tomorrow. See you, Price.'

'See you, Les.'

Les hung up and looked at the phone. Well, I suppose that's a bit better. At least there's a chance Eddie might be able to do something. But what a pain in the arse. Those mugs tried to four out me. And got a bit of smack for their trouble. Christ! Why can't they cop it sweet? Les was deliberating on this when the phone rang again.

'Les. Are you there? It's Warren. Pick up the phone, you big sheila.'

Les picked up the phone. 'Hello, Warren. How are you … mate?'

'Better than you by the sound of things. What happened? I was listening to the cricket and your name came up on the news. I can't wait to see the papers tomorrow.' Warren laughed out loud. 'You've done it again. You're a legend.'

'Thanks,' grunted Les. 'So where are you ringing from?'

'Beautiful downtown Cessnock. We're still shooting this commercial for Bogenhuber Chardonnay. We'll have it wrapped tomorrow morning.'

'Lucky you.'

'So what happened? Tell me. I've a need to know.'

Les shook his head. 'Ohh, what the fuck do you think happened?'

Les told Warren pretty much what he could over the phone about the afternoon's events. Excluding what he knew about the hoon from Condell Park.

'So that's about it, Woz,' said Les. 'I was in the wrong place at the wrong time. All because I got a flat tyre on my bike. Ohh. And when I went back to get it, some prick's knocked off my helmet.'

Warren shook his head at the other end of the line. 'Fair dinkum. That's unbelievable.'

'Yeah,' agreed Les. 'The thing is though, Warren, these blokes are rats. And I have to get out of town for a while till Eddie tries to sort it all out. So while I'm away, you be careful in case they find out where I live and spray the place.'

'Don't worry. I'll move in with Clover.' Warren gave an audible sigh. 'Gee, it's good sharing a house with a gangster.'

'Get out, you little cunt. You thrive on all this drama.'

'Yeah. Like fuckin hell I do. So where are you going to go?'

'I dunno,' shrugged Les. 'I'd go down and stay with Grace. But she's in Melbourne. I can't go home, because it's flooded out all the way to Moree. I'm not sure what I'll do.'

'Listen,' Warren said seriously. 'Don't do anything till I get back. I might have something for you.'

'Yeah. Like what? A week hiding out in your advertising agency. I'd rather stay here and get shot.'

'No. I'm fair dinkum. This could be ideal.' Les heard Warren say something to someone off the phone. 'Hey. I have to go. I'll be home about lunchtime tomorrow. Don't make a move till I get back.'

'Righto, Woz. See you tomorrow.'

'See you then … Dudley Do Right.'

Les hung up the phone and took his empty coffee cup into the kitchen. My old mate Warren, he thought. I wonder what he's got in mind.

Norton's eyes suddenly lit up. Hey! He got me a free trip to Hawaii once. Shit, I'd be in that again. Les put his empty coffee cup in the sink and stared into space. Well, it looks like I've got the night off. So what to do? He had a look in the fridge. There wasn't a great deal in it. Les closed the door. Bugger cooking anyway. I'll order a pizza, have a shower then watch a video. I don't think ordering a pizza should be too life-threatening. Les started climbing out of his clothes as he picked up the phone again.

After a shower and a shave, Les changed into a clean T-shirt and shorts. His pizza marinara and garlic bread arrived. Les ate it in front of the TV with a bottle of orange juice then slipped on a DVD — *Million Dollar Baby* with Clint Eastwood — and watched it while he rubbed his knee with liniment. By the time the movie was over, tears were pouring down Norton's face and he felt worse than ever. God! What a movie, he sniffled, turning off the TV. And I think I've got troubles. Les blew his nose into a Kleenex tissue and tossed it into the kitchen tidy along with the pizza carton. That poor bloody sheila. After cleaning his teeth, Les turned off the lights and climbed into bed. He was that busy crying himself to sleep over the girl in the movie, he didn't even think about the risk of sleeping in the front room.

Despite the previous day's drama and his bedtime lachrymosity, Les slept like a baby and was up by eight the following morning. Outside it was another delightful summer's day. After getting cleaned up, he put on a pair of shorts and a blue T-shirt and strolled down to get the *Sunday Telegraph*. His knee had improved with a rub, even if it still wasn't a hundred per cent.

He hadn't made the front page. But the incident and a photo of the two cars was all over page three under a blazing header: VIOLENT BONDI BEACH ROAD RAGE. FOUR MEN IN HOSPITAL. Les waited till he was back home and had some coffee and toasted sandwiches together, then went through everything at the kitchen table.

Les Norton, waiter of Bondi, had been charged with assault and affray and been granted bail. Benjamin Rabinski of Bondi was in hospital with head injuries. Blah, blah, blah! Three unnamed males were also in hospital. After that was the usual beat up. But Les was pleased to see that Faheem Khazal of Wiley Park was helping police with their inquiries. Which in police jargon meant they hadn't charged the hoon who threatened Les with illegal possession of a firearm yet, and they were waiting for a statement from Benny. Ohh well.

I suppose it could be worse, thought Les, chewing on a toasted sandwich. At least the media hadn't arrived till after he'd been nicked and taken away, so there wasn't a photo of him trying to hide his face in the back of a police car. Nevertheless, rather than go down North Bondi and put up with stares and whispers behind his back or have various punters asking him what happened, Les decided to stay home and take it easy as Price suggested. He finished the papers and made another cup of coffee when the phone rang. It was Billy.

'Hello, Tiger. How's things?'

'Billy. How's it going?'

'All right. Hey, how come you never got your photo in the paper?'

'I don't know, Billy. I tried. Maybe they couldn't get a decent angle on me handcuffed in the back seat of a fuckin police car.'

Billy chuckled at the other end. 'So what happened? Price filled us in at work last night. But ...'

'Billy. It was a complete fuck up.'

Les told Billy the story much the same as he told Price. Adding it was the same detective who pinched him in the bomb case that did him a favour. Les could sense Billy shaking his head at the other end of the line.

'Fair dinkum. Jesus! There's some mugs out there.'

'Tell me about it,' said Les. 'And they all come to Bondi on the weekend.'

'You're not wrong.'

'So how was the pickle factory last night?'

'Busy. But Big Danny was on the door with me. And Eddie and some bloke called Ray were up on the roof with M-16s. Nothing happened, thank Christ! It would have been like El Alamein.'

'Can't say I know this Ray bloke.'

'Me either,' replied Billy. 'But you know Eddie, he pulls shooters out of his arse. So what are you going to do? Price said he told you to take a week off.'

'I'm not sure, Billy,' said Les. 'But Warren said he might have something for me.'

'Okay. Look, I gotta go. I have to take my wretched wife and horrible kids to soccer. Give me a ring through the week and let me know how you're going.'

'Okay. See you then, Billy.'

'See you, Les.'

Les hung up the receiver, looked at his watch then got another cup of coffee and settled back on the lounge to watch *Sunday* on Channel Nine.

The feature story was about Melbourne gangsters. And there was a great segment on big wave surfing, with an unbelievable shot of Ross Clarke-Jones coming down a wave in Hawaii that looked like the north face of K2. There was also another shot of Laird Hamilton getting towed into a wave in Tahiti that would have made Peter Garrett's hair stand on end. Count me salmon and trout there, shuddered Norton after he switched off the TV. Those blokes must have balls like coconuts. Next thing, the phone rang again. It was Eddie.

'Hello, Big Fellah. What's happening, son?'

'Eddie. How are you going, Shifty?'

'I'm all right,' replied Eddie. 'So you've managed to get yourself into some more strife.'

'Yes,' answered Les. 'And without any help from you at all this time. Thank you, Edward.'

Eddie laughed his deadly little laugh over the phone. 'Fair enough. Anyway. I've got some good news. And I've got some bad news.'

'Oh?'

'The good news is, I can do something.'

'You can,' Norton's eyes lit up.

'Yes. I can go and have a word with Big Arse.'

'Big Arse?'

'Yeah. Big Assad. He's the Lebanese Godfather. He's got a string of panel-beating shops around

Strathfield. We were in Vietnam together, and Big Arse owes me his arse. I saved it at a place called Duc Pho. I'll have a word with him and he'll sort these little mugs out in five minutes.'

Norton's eyes lit up again. 'Hey! Unreal, Eddie. So I don't have to piss off.'

'Yeah, well, that's the good news,' said Eddie. 'The bad news is, Assad's having a holiday with his family on some island off Fiji, and he won't be back till the end of the week. I tried to have a word with his brother, but Izhar just got pinched in Brisbane with some dud cheques and he's waiting to get bail. So you still better take your holiday.'

'Ohh.'

'But don't worry too much. It should all be sweet when you get back.'

'Shit! I don't know what to say. Good on you, Eddie.'

'No sweat … mate. So what are you going to do?'

'I'm not sure,' replied Les. 'I'm waiting for Warren to get home. He reckons he's got something lined up.'

'Okay.' Eddie paused for a second. 'Anyway. You know me. I don't like to stay too long on the blower.'

'Fair enough.'

'So give Price a ring when you get settled. And let us know what's going on.'

'Okay. And thanks again, Eddie.'

'No problemo.'

Well that's a bone, mused Les, feeling a little more relieved. Eddie can do something. And if I've got to piss off for a while, I just have to piss off. Les shook his head in admiration. Billy's right. The shifty little bastard knows everybody. Les glanced at his watch. Anyway. All I've got to do now is wait for the other Godfather to arrive home. Warren Edwards. The Godfather of garbage. Advertising.

Rather than get the shits stuck in the Sunday gridlock driving from Bondi to Clovelly and back, Les decided to leave his bike till he got back from wherever he got back from. He made his bed, did some washing and hung it on the line then pottered round the house sorting out bills and whatever. He was seated in the lounge room after giving his leg another rub when the front door opened and Warren walked into the kitchen carrying a white cardboard carton. He was wearing a denim shirt over a pair of jeans, his hair was scraggly and he looked like he hadn't shaved for days. After Warren placed the carton on the kitchen table, he stood in the doorway and stared at Les with a sardonic smile on his face.

'So what's doing, Boofhead? Is it safe to walk around the house? Or do I have to stand by the door with a sawn-off shotgun looking like an extra out of *GoodFellas*? You dopey fuckin big peanut.'

'It's okay, Woz. Eddie's got you a Kevlar vest. It's sitting on your bed next to your nightie.'

'I see you bought the *Telegraph*. You got a guernsey in the *Sun-Herald* too, you know.'

'Fuck the *Sun-Herald*.'

'My sentiments exactly,' said Warren. 'Fuck the *Sun-Herald*.'

Les looked serious. 'All jokes aside, Woz. Just be careful, mate. Eddie's sorted things out. But it'll still be a bit dicey till next week. Particularly at night.'

'Don't worry,' said Warren, unbuttoning his shirt 'As soon as I get cleaned up I'm packing a bag and splitting for Clover's.'

'I don't blame you,' said Les. 'Hey, what's in the carton?' he called out as Warren headed for the bathroom.

'Beautiful Bogenhuber Chardonnay,' Warren called out. 'The wine embraced by Australia. Help yourself.'

Les sat in the lounge room for a while moving his knee around, before getting up and going to the kitchen. He looked at the carton sitting on the kitchen table then got a knife, opened it and took out a bottle. The bottle had a white label edged with purple and printed in black, silver and gold; it looked impressive. Les read the label and suddenly screwed his face up.

'What the fuck . . .?'

Les left the bottle of wine on the table then went back to the lounge room and resumed exercising his knee. Warren walked back into the kitchen clean-shaven, and wearing the same jeans under a fresh white T-shirt. He got a Carlton longneck from the fridge and started drinking it, when Les came into the kitchen and picked up the bottle of wine.

'Warren,' he said. 'I just had a look at the label on this bottle of plonk.'

'And?' belched Warren.

'It says here, "Awarded both the silver and bronze medals at the Emu Springs Wine Festival".'

'That's right.'

Les nodded towards the TV set. 'Emu Springs is that shitpot little one-pub town on that ABC show *Something in the Air*. Frankie J. Holden, the singer out of OL'55, is the publican or something.'

'Right again,' said Warren, continuing to drink his beer.

'Well, how in the fuck could this stuff win a medal at a place that doesn't exist?'

'Easy,' said Warren. 'We were able to position some on the set. And while we were at it, we decided to award this fine Australian white a couple of gongs.' Warren looked at Les over his beer. 'Christ! What are you? Chairman of the Australian Society of Viticulture and Oenology or something?'

'That's bullshit!' protested Norton.

'Exactly,' replied Warren.

'I don't believe it,' Les put the bottle back on the table. 'So what's it taste like?'

'Shit,' replied Warren indifferently. 'No. More like baboon's piss. And from a very old baboon at that. But you *can* drink it.'

'You're absolutely fuckin unscrupulous,' stated Les.

'I don't know,' replied Warren. 'At least I'm not out on bail for bashing people in the street.'

'Ooohh. You know how to wound, don't you. You little dropkick.'

'With you, Igor, it's easy.' Warren took another swallow of beer and followed it with a gratifying belch.

'So what's this thing you've got lined up for me?' asked Les.

'This thing?' Warren smiled and patted Les on the shoulder. 'Mate. How would you like a week at a health resort?'

'A health resort?' said Les. 'Whereabouts?'

'Opal Springs Health Retreat. It's in the Opal Valley, near Cessnock. Where we shot the wine commercial.'

'Yeah? And how much is this gonna cost me?'

'Ohh — and how much is this gonna cost me,' aped Warren. 'You don't think I'd expect you to pay for it do you? You miserable big prick.'

'No,' agreed Les. 'So what's the catch?'

'There's no real catch,' said Warren. 'The director spat the dummy on the shoot and pissed off to LA. Part of his deal was five days at Opal Springs. You get there Monday morning and you leave on Saturday. Everything's paid for in advance. All you have to pay for are your phone calls and any extra treatments he's booked.'

Les looked at Warren for a moment. 'Okay,' he shrugged. 'Sounds good to me. Why not?'

'All you have to remember when you book in, is you're Leonard Gordon. And you're a film director.'

'I'm Leonard Gordon. And I'm a film director?'

'That's right,' said Warren, draining his beer then tossing the empty bottle in the kitchen tidy. 'If anybody should ask you, you work mainly with the South Australian Film Commission. But lately you've been shooting TV commercials.' Warren looked directly at Norton. 'Do you know how to act like an Australian film director, Les?'

'Like Max King? That prick who was going to shoot the Gull's movie?'

'That's it, Les. Always remember you're pharoah. You're absolutely precious, nobody can tell you anything and your shit doesn't stink. Walk around with your head completely up your arse and expect everybody to kiss it. But only if you'll let them.'

'Shit! This could be fun,' said Les. 'I often dream of acting out my fantasies.'

'Mate. You'll have a good time,' enthused Warren. 'There's plenty of fruity old sheilas get to these places. They get a bit of yogurt and fresh vegetables into them and they start to juice up. Even a bloke like you, with your robber's dog head'd be a chance.'

'And I'm a director,' said Les. 'Len Gordon. Les Norton. Hey, I like it.'

'There's four Australian authors up there at the moment too on a freebie, writing about the place.'

'Ohh that should be something to look forward to,' said Les. 'They're the most boring arses God ever put breath into. All they do is sit around with their index finger planted against one side of their face handing out words like gold watches. I can't wait to meet them.'

'I'll tell you who else is up there having a detox,' smiled Warren. 'Alexander Holden. The motivational speaker.'

'Alexander Holden? Not that little Pommy on TV used to be a Bible basher? The bloke with the buck teeth and the blond mullet? Hold on to your life.'

'That's him, Les.'

'And I've got to put up with that flip, too. Christ! I knew there was a catch.'

'Les. Les. How many times have I got to tell you,' insisted Warren. 'You don't have to put up with them. They have to put up with you. You're an Australian film director.'

'Yeah you're right. I forgot.' Les held up his chin. 'I'm a film director.'

'That's it,' said Warren. 'Now lift your voice a bit. Be a little more pronounced.'

'Aihm a film director,' modulated Les. 'Aihm a fill-um di-rehct-torrh.'

Warren clapped his hands together. 'That's it. Again.'

'Aihm a fill-um di-rehct-torrh.'

'Sensational. Hey. You're going places, baby.' Warren pointed to a long beige envelope sitting on the kitchen table as he moved towards the door. 'Everything you need is in that envelope. I got to piss off. Clover wants to feel my loving arms around her. And I want to feel her's. So I'll see you when you get back. Enjoy your five days at Opal Springs … Len.'

'I will. Thanks a lot, Woz.'

'No worries.'

'Hey before you go,' said Les, 'aren't you going to take some of this wine with you?'

'Not at the moment, Les,' replied Warren. 'Give some to those blokes that want to shoot you.'

The front door closed leaving Les alone in the kitchen. Bloody Warren, he smiled. He sure comes up with the goods at times. This is perfect. I can't see the place being anything special. But a week sleeping on a bunk eating bean sprouts and drinking herb tea might do me the world of good.

Les put the carton of wine out on the back verandah, then sat down in the kitchen and opened the opal-embossed envelope. It contained a letter confirming the booking, an opal-embossed card with the address and phone number of the resort, along with a detailed map of how to get there from the Cessnock turn-off on the F3. Les figured it to be a three-hour drive from Sydney, allowing for the traffic. He looked at the booking and thought he'd better make sure it was all kosher just in case Warren had screwed things up. Les took the card to the phone and rang the number.

'Hello. Opal Springs Health Retreat. This is Karla.'

'Yes. My name is Leonard Gordon. Aihm a fill-um di-recht-torrh. I believe you have a booking for me. For tomorrow. Is that right?'

'Just one moment, Mr Gordon. I'll check the computer.' Karla was back in seconds. 'That's right, Mr Gordon. Monday the fifth to Saturday the tenth.'

Les checked it with the booking sheet. 'Yes. That's it.'

'What time can we expect you tomorrow, Mr Gordon?'

'What time can you expect me?' Well when I fuckin get there. You dopey moll, thought Les, I'm a fuckin film director. 'Ohh. About nine. Would that be satisfactory?' he asked.

'That would be perfect, Mr Gordon,' said

Karla. 'We'll have your room ready for you. And we look forward to seeing you.'

'Same here. Thanks, Karla.'

'Thank you, Mr Gordon. Goodbye.'

Well, she sounded pleasant enough, thought Les. He replaced the receiver and was about to walk to the kitchen when the phone rang. It was Warren on his mobile.

'Hey, Igor. Are you there? Pick up the phone.'

'Yes, Warren, I'm here. What's up?'

'Have a look at your bedroom window.'

'What?'

'Go out on the front verandah and have a look at your window. See you.' Warren hung up, leaving Les holding the phone.

'What the …?'

Les replaced the receiver, walked down the hallway, then opened the front door and stepped trepidatiously round to his bedroom.

'Holy shit!'

Stitched erratically across the window was a row of ten bullet holes. Les went cold. Bloody hell! The bastards must have come last night and used a silencer. I didn't hear a bloody thing. Christ! I'm lucky I'm alive. He went over and poked his finger into one of the holes.

'What the …?'

Les had a closer look at the bullet holes. They were novelty shop transfers. Norton's eyes narrowed. What's the betting if I dusted around those bullet holes, I'd find fingerprints. And whose fingerprints would I find? Bloody Warren's. The stupid bastard. Les was laughing out loud when he went inside and got his digital camera. He was still laughing as he took a couple of photos and when he checked them out on the screen. Turning his camera off, Les went inside and rang Warren's mobile. It was switched off so Les left a message.

'It's Les. I'm on my way to see Eddie. The next bullet holes you see will be across your scrawny fuckin chest. In the meantime, the rent just went up. Double.'

After hanging up Les pottered around the house for a while then whipper-snipped the backyard. After a shower, he changed into a clean pair of shorts and a white reggae T-shirt he bought in Jamaica, then walked down to the Hakoah Club for a late lunch of veal schnitzel and vegetables smothered with creamed spinach all washed down with orange juice and two diabolical flat whites. After walking home, Les was pleased to see that his knee was a lot better. He wouldn't be able to run properly for a few days, but at least he could walk easily enough.

Les spent a lazy afternoon at home sitting in the backyard drinking beer, listening to music and reading his book, *MP* by Sean Doherty, the story of a drug-crazed Gold Coast waxhead. When the sun started to go down, he went inside and packed his bag for Opal Springs, figuring he wouldn't need much; shorts and T-shirts mainly, plus his training gear and a tracksuit. He also tossed in his ghetto blaster, some tapes, his book and a few other odds and ends. As he'd almost finished *MP* he tossed in another book he picked up at the Bondi markets for five dollars, *The World's Best Mystery Stories*.

It was an old hardback and Les figured at five bucks it was a bit of a rip-off, because it had three shillings and sixpence pencilled on the inside cover. The stories were by old writers such as Somerset Maugham, Guy de Maupassant, Sir A.T. Quiller-Couch. And the stories were leaden and not easy to read. But they had these quaint turns of phrase: 'he felt in an excellent humour', 'the colonel was a man of meticulous lucidity', 'Sir Auban's vocabulary possessed a forceful vigour of delivery'. Maybe when I'm up at this fat farm, I'll be able to impress those four authors with a few linguistic nuances, mused Les.

The Sunday night movie on SBS was an old Stanley Kubrick, *A Clockwork Orange*. Les half enjoyed it. But apart from the violence and weird camera angles, the other thing that stuck out was one of the young droog hoodlums was the sour-faced detective out of *Dalziel and Pascoe*, and he'd certainly piled on some beef since his droog days. Having to get up early for the drive to Cessnock, Les hit the sack straight after the movie. His last thoughts before he drifted off were, I'm a man of meticulous lucidity. I'm also a fill-um di-rehct-torrh.

The sun was barely peeping over a calm blue horizon the next morning and Les and the birds were up at the same time. Despite all the drama, Les slept well and after he'd cleaned his teeth he was in a good mood when he walked into the kitchen. There was hardly enough coffee left to make a decent brew, so he washed his toasted sandwiches down with Ovaltine. After changing into his Levi's shorts and a grey 4CA Cairns T-shirt, Les made sure the house was locked, bolted and barred securely, then threw his bag in the Berlina, hit the ignition and headed for Old South Head Road then Bondi Junction and the Harbour Bridge.

Traffic was light and mostly heading into the city. Les made good time and listened to the news and weather on AM before stopping at Turramurra to fill up, get the *Telegraph* and a carton of chocolate milk. By the time Les finished his milk, he was at the F3 turn-off near Hornsby. He slipped a tape into the cassette player, overtook a semi-trailer, and with the Chrome Daddies rocking the soul out of 'Lonesome Train', put the pedal a little more to the metal and sped towards the north coast.

Traffic was still light and it was turning into a peach of a day. Les switched off and bopped along to the music as he overtook the odd car and truck. His only real thoughts were his confidence Eddie would have everything sorted out by the time he got back and nothing could possibly happen to him at Opal Springs if he kept to himself and minded his own business. Though if he bumped into Alexander Holden, Les felt he might be tempted to tell him what he thought of his motivational waffle on TV.

Les cruised happily along listening to his music and before he knew it, he was at the Kurri Kurri–Cessnock turn-off 82. He turned left off the F3, then went left again at Freemans Drive. A little further on Bonnie Raitt was belting out 'I

Think I'm In Love With You' as Les passed a sign: CESSNOCK 29 KMS.

The road was still covered in morning shadows from the surrounding trees and wound steadily through hills and valleys with mountain ranges in the distance. Les noticed a farm here, a horse stable there, animals grazing in green fields, churches, houses and whatever as he motored through tiny hamlets with names like Mount Vincent, Brunkerville and Mulbring. I'll say one thing, Les smiled to himself as he slowed down at the Branxton–Cessnock turn-off, in the course of my criminal activities or whatever I certainly get to see some nice parts of Australia. Les passed through more little towns and traffic increased moderately as houses and small shops began to appear, then he saw a sign: CESSNOCK. POPULATION 22,000. ELEVATION 7000M. Next thing Les was taking a right at Vincent Street, the main road through Cessnock.

Vincent Street was a long, straight, narrow avenue, jammed with shops, small department stores and other buildings, and choked with traffic waiting at every corner for sets of traffic lights that seemed to take forever to change. Bloody hell! I don't believe this, scowled Les as he pulled up at another set of lights and waited behind an old black utility full of fertiliser while it spewed diesel fumes out of a rusty exhaust pipe. *At this rate, I'll get there next week.* He came to an amber light and put his foot down as it turned red. *Fuck it,* he swore silently. *If I've got to wait at another set of lights I'll go bonkers.* Finally, Les got to the end of Vincent Street, checked his map and before long he was out of the traffic and heading towards Opal Valley.

The hills and valleys now turned into long wide plains with mountain ranges in the distance. Les kept going till he found the Opal Valley turn-off and drove steadily on through valleys and vineyards past wineries with familiar names: Tyrells, Pepper Tree, Tamburlaine, etc. The narrow road rose and fell till eventually Les came to a crossroad and a sign on the right pointing towards Opal Springs Health Retreat. *Now we're in business,* smiled Les. *I can smell the bean sprouts and brown rice already.*

The road went past a golf course then quickly dipped down into a tree-flanked country lane barely wide enough for two cars. Les followed the narrow road till he came to another sign on the left pointing to the resort. Several magpies were whistling happily in the trees and it was all peace and tranquillity as Les turned and drove past two small lakes in front of a wide field leading to a vineyard and a farmhouse off to his right. It wasn't long before the road came to a security gate set between two solid concrete supports built into a cyclone-wire fence that skirted the surrounding trees. The gate was heavy black wrought-iron, two metres high, with spikes on top and three iron bars running across the front. A concrete lamp post with a security camera on it faced the approaching road, and five metres in front of it was a smaller concrete pillar with an intercom above a black metal plate that read OPAL SPRINGS HEALTH RETREAT. Behind the gate, the road wound its way up a steep hill thick with trees and through the trees, Les could just make out a huge modern building jutting out high over the valley. Les reached out and pressed the intercom button and a moment later a woman's voice crackled through the speaker.

'Hello. Reception. This is Karla. Can I help you?'

'Yes. My name's Gordon. Leonard Gordon,' answered Les. 'I believe you have a reservation for me?'

'Yes. That's right, Mr Gordon. Just one moment and I'll open the gate.'

'Thank you.'

Les watched the security gate rumble to the left then slowly drove through, not at all expecting what was waiting for him. On the other side of the gate, a man was sprawled face down on the road with his head angled to one side. It was a short man, wearing black bike shorts, gym boots and a blue T-shirt. Les couldn't see a helmet, but lying on the road to the man's right was a red mountain bike and a pair of wrap-around sunglasses. Les turned off the ignition and got out of his car to see if the man was all right.

When he got to him, the man's eyes were wide open and staring at the road and there was a wide bruise on his forehead weeping a little blood. Les was going to feel for a pulse, but didn't bother. One good look told him the man wasn't anywhere near all right. The man's neck was broken, and he was dead.

'Shit!' said Les. 'Welcome to Opal Springs Health Retreat.'

Les looked around as the security gate locked behind him and surmised the man must have come belting down the hill on his bike and smashed into the gate. If the force of the collision didn't break his neck, he must have broken it when he fell off his bike. Something about the man caught Norton's eye and he bent down to have a closer look at his face. When he did, Norton's jaw swung open like a trapdoor.

'It is him!' exclaimed Les. 'It's that prick on TV!'

The tubby little body belonged to Alexander Holden, the motivational speaker. There was no mistaking his buck teeth and beady eyes staring out from beneath the thick blond mullet. Well, if it isn't the little battler from a family of fifteen come good, smiled Les, silently mimicking the wind-up Holden used to give himself on TV. Going by the looks of things, Alex me old, I'd say your motivational days are through. Instead of holding onto your life, you should have held onto your handlebars. Despite the gravity of the situation, Les walked over to the car and got his digital camera.

Checking to see there was no one around, Les started firing off photos from all angles. I'll get all sorts of money for these when I get home, he schemed. A motza. I'll even get Warren to run them up on the internet. Come on, Alex, Les grinned, holding the camera right in front of the corpse's face. Give us a smile, mate.

Les stood back and took one last photo. 'Well, that's it, me old,' he said, turning off his camera. 'Thanks, Alexander. You've made my day.'

Then Norton's brow furrowed. Shit! Knowing my luck, they'll probably think I did it. No, he reassured himself. He's probably been lying there for a while. And my car pulling up would be on that security camera. Les walked back to the car and opened the door. Before he got in he had another look at Alexander Holden lying next to his mountain bike all alone in the middle of nowhere, and wondered if this might not have been an accident. After a moment or two Les shook his head. No. What else could it be? Les got in the car, started the engine and drove away.

After climbing five hundred metres up a steep, curving hill, Les stopped beneath a covered driveway in front of a huge polished wooden door with the retreat's opal motif across the front. Standing next to a desk on the right, was a girl in a brown Mao jacket and matching slacks. She was tall and lean with auburn hair and thoughtful grey eyes in a plain face dotted with freckles. Les got out of the car and as she got closer, he noticed two badges on the front of her jacket. A black oblong one had her name, 'Peta'. A round white one said, SOFA. Well, it's nice to know Peta's an environmentalist, thought Les. But I don't particularly feel like getting into a save our forests rave at the moment.

'Good morning,' said Les, officiously. 'I'm Leonard Gordon, the director. I have a booking here for five days.'

'Yes. Yes. That's right, Mr Gordon. How are you?' said Peta.

Being in the presence of greatness, Les noticed the girl's nervousness and decided to play on it.

'I'm in an excellent humour, thank you,' replied Les. 'And yourself?'

'Yes. I'm fine too, thank you, Mr Gordon.' The girl blinked at Les. 'And how was the drive up. I mean ... did you find the place all right, Mr Gordon?'

'No problem at all,' smiled Les. Something tells me I'd better not tell Peta there's a stiff lying at the front gate, he thought. She's likely to piss her pants. 'So are you here to park my vehicle, Peta?'

'Yes. That's right, Mr Gordon.'

'Excellent,' Les took his bag from the back seat. 'Well, if you can do that, I can manage my bag all right.'

'Are you sure, Mr Gordon?'

'Yes. Quite sure. Thank you, Peta.' Yeah. I shouldn't though. You should be carrying me and my bag inside, you slack moll. I'm a fuckin director.

The girl got behind the wheel of Norton's Berlina and drove off. As he turned for the door,

Les could sense her watching him in the rear-vision mirror. Hey. Warren was right. This being a film director's cool. Sheilas cough in their rompers as soon as they see you. Les pushed open the massive wooden door and stepped through.

Inside was a large bright area with a set of polished wooden stairs running straight up from the door. The entire wall at the end was a gentle waterfall and tucked in a corner beneath the stairs on the left was the door to an auditorium, opposite a lift on the right. Les gripped his bag and took the stairs straight up to the spacious interior of something that looked like the set from a James Bond movie. Les stopped for a moment to take everything in.

On his left was a long open room with a ceramic fireplace in the middle that faced a wide marble table. Lush furniture, statuettes and expensive bric-a-brac sat round the floors, and contemporary art, shelves of books, CDs and DVDs ran round the walls. Floor to ceiling windows divided the far wall which opened onto a long, wide verandah with magnificent views over the surrounding mountains and valleys. On Norton's right was the reception desk and foyer, next to a well-stocked gift shop. Away from the foyer, two change rooms were discreetly tucked behind a high frosted-glass screen, which led to a large dining room with more floor to ceiling windows opening onto another verandah. All the floors were polished wood and everything else was stainless steel, marble or imported slate, all set around beautifully designed ponds and fountains. Soft lighting made the surroundings pleasant to the eye and celestial music drifting down from the ceiling made the atmosphere soothing to the ear. Les couldn't help but give everything several tiny nods of approval. So this is where the rich and famous come to dry out. Nice one, Woz, you've done it again.

The only people Les could see were several women strolling round in casual designer clothing or gym gear, and one or two staff wearing crisp brown uniforms the same as Peta's. Les returned the perfect white smile of a woman walking past in an ivory and pink tracksuit and stepped over to the front desk. A dark-haired girl with a warm smile and an attractive face looked up. The name tag on her uniform read 'Karla'.

'Good morning,' she said pleasantly. 'You must be Mr Gordon.'

'That's right,' said Les. 'How did you know?' Don't tell me. Let me guess. I've got film director written all over me, haven't I?

'You're our only booking for today,' replied Karla. 'All our other new guests arrived on Sunday.'

'Ohh,' said Les.

Karla clicked at the computer. 'We've got you booked in for five days, Mr Gordon.' Les nodded and smiled. 'That's all been taken care of. And how will you be paying for your treatments?' she asked.

'Visa,' replied Les.

'No problem. Is this your first time here, Mr Gordon?'

Les nodded.

'Okay.' Karla finished clicking then handed Les a brochure, a white tag on a cord with 'Len' on it and two sheets of paper. 'That's a list of the activities for today, should you be interested. And this afternoon you're booked in for a hot stone massage. We'd also like you to wear your name tag at all times, if you could.' Les nodded and took everything he was handed. 'When you get settled in, you have an appointment to see the nurse and our dietician at the Wellness Centre.'

'Okey doke,' said Les.

'Well, that's about it, Mr Gordon,' smiled Karla. 'If you'd like to wait here for a moment, someone will be along to take you to your room.'

Les folded the two pieces of paper and put them in his backpack with everything else. 'Thank you, Karla,' he said. 'And may I say, your gracious sociability is matched only by a remarkable deep proficiency arising from your position.'

'Why, thank you, Mr Gordon,' beamed Karla.

Convinced he'd linguisted nuancely enough for the time being, Les drew a little closer to her over the desk. 'There is just one thing though, Karla,' he said quietly.

'Yes. What's that, Mr Gordon?'

'Did you know you have a dead body at the front gate?'

Karla gave Les a double, triple blink. 'A what?'

'There's a dead body at the front gate,' said Les. 'A corpse. A stiff. A terminally inconvenienced person.'

'Ohh my God!' Karla called out to someone behind Les, 'Mr Reid.'

Les turned as a well-built man with dark hair and smooth features, wearing a crisp white shirt and grey trousers came to the desk.

'Mr Reid. This is Mr Gordon. Mr Gordon, would you please tell Mr Reid what you just told me?'

The man offered his hand. 'I'm John Reid, the general manager. Is there a problem?'

Les shook the manager's hand. 'Leonard Gordon. The director. No. There's no problem,' said Les. 'It's just that there's a man's body lying inside the front gate. One couldn't help but notice it as one drove in. It could be Alexander Holden. I think I recognised the teeth.'

The manager closed his eyes for a moment. 'Ohh my God! I feared this would happen. Karla. You attend to Mr Gordon. I'll get the nurse. I'll have to ring the police too.' He turned to Les. 'I'm terribly sorry about this, Mr Gordon. I'll … I'll see you shortly.'

'No problem at all, John,' replied Les as the manager ran behind the desk and disappeared down a short hallway.

Pale faced, Karla stared at Les. 'Did you see the body as you came in, Mr Gordon?'

'I nearly ran over him,' said Les. 'And his pushbike.'

'And he was dead?'

'Extremely.'

'Ohh my God!'

A fair-haired girl, a little plumper than Karla, appeared behind the desk from the hallway where the manager had disappeared. Her name tag read 'Trish'.

'What's all the commotion?' she asked Karla.

'This gentleman just found Alexander Holden dead at the front gate.'

Trish turned to Les, wide-eyed. 'You did?'

'I did,' nodded Les.

Trish turned to Karla with a half smile on her face. 'Shit! Looks like Alex baby decided to check out early.'

A fit young bloke, shorter than Les, with corn-blond hair came up to the desk. He was wearing a brown T-shirt, shorts, trainers and a name tag with 'Michael' on it.

'Hey. What's going on?' he asked. 'I just saw John come flying out of the Wellness Centre with Judge Judy. He looked like he was going to fill his pants.'

'Alexander Holden is dead,' chorused Karla and Trish.

'What?' said Michael. 'We've lost our numero uno LOMBARD. When did this happen?'

Karla nodded to Les. 'This gentleman found him as he drove through the front gate.'

'And he was dead?' Michael asked Les.

'Stiff as a pool cue,' answered Les.

'Shit!'

'Michael,' said Karla. 'Why don't you show Mr Gordon to his room.'

'Yeah righto.' Michael picked up Norton's bag. 'This way please, Mr Gordon.'

Les followed Michael out through a thick glass door and over a bubbling pond then down a passageway landscaped with ferns and shrubs. They came out at a large open area, thick with lush green grass. Behind it, beautiful hills and valleys ran off into the distance. Les pointed to a white building on the right with darkened windows.

'What's in there?' he asked.

'That's the Wellness Centre,' answered Michael. 'That's where they book your treatments. And where you go to see the nurse or the dietician. At the back is an aerobics room and a stationary bike room. Down the stairs at the side is the badminton court and the gymnasium.'

'Right,' acknowledged Les.

Michael pointed to a fenced-off area to the left of the Wellness Centre. 'That's the tennis court. Underneath is the guests' car park and where we keep the mountain bikes. Over there's the staff car park. That green oval opposite the tennis court is where they throw boomerangs or frisbees.'

'Boomerangs?'

'Yeah. Mainly for any Japanese or American guests. They get off on it.'

'Cool,' said Les.

On the right a pathway led past a long row of oyster grey villas, one on top of the other. They were trimmed in white and green with their numbers out the front. Les surmised that's where he'd be staying and pointed to a large building sitting on top of a grassy hill to their left. A set of steps led up to the entrance in the middle and the right side of the building was encased in tinted glass.

'What's that?' he asked Michael.

'That's the indoor pool and the Healing Centre. There's a spa room and another outdoor pool at the back.'

'Healing Centre?'

'Yeah. Where you go for all your treatments. Like Swedish massage, trigger point therapy, private yoga, Pilates. Women can get mudwraps and facials or whatever. You should book in for a Cleopatra body wrap, Mr Gordon,' joked Michael.

'I might just do that,' said Les.

As they followed the path alongside the villas, Les indicated another, higher hill on the left, not as green but with an open dome at the top.

'What's up there, Michael?' he asked.

'That's Meditation Hill,' replied Michael. 'People go up there to do tai chi when the sun's coming up. The view's fantastic.'

'Sounds good,' nodded Les.

'Karla said you're a director,' enquired Michael.

'That's me,' said Les.

'Wow! That must be a great job.'

'Ohh, it has its moments,' Les replied breezily, thinking it might be a good idea to change the subject before he brought himself undone. 'Hey Michael, back at reception I heard you refer to Alexander Holden as a LOMBARD. What's that?'

Michael hesitated for a moment. 'If I tell you, you didn't hear it from me, okay?'

'Sure,' agreed Les.

'Well, we got a sort of code amongst the staff here. We use acronyms to describe different guests.'

'Ohh, yeah?'

'So if you hear someone refer to you as a LOMBARD, watch out,' smiled Michael. 'Because it means Lots Of Money But A Real Dropkick.'

Les laughed out loud. 'Good one,' he said, then he looked at Michael. 'So I gather Alex baby was a bit of a PITA?'

'A PITA?'

'Yeah. A Pain In The Arse.'

Michael laughed quietly. 'Yes. That's a good way of putting it.'

'So why was he a pain in the arse?'

'Ohh, he was always whingeing about something. You couldn't tell him anything. And he spoke to the staff and the other guests like they were shit.'

'Sounds like a nice bloke.'

'Terrific,' said Michael. 'So you found his body, Mr Gordon?'

'Yeah. Lying next to a mountain bike, with his Gregory Peck broken.'

Michael gave a derisive chuckle. 'That figures. Shit! Me and John. We warned him. Begged him. Not to go flat out down that hill after breakfast without a helmet. But not him.'

'Now he's gone to the big motivational seminar in the sky.'

'Yeah. It sure looks that way,' said Michael.

'So what do you do here, Michael?' asked Les.

'I'm a trainer. But I also help out wherever they want me to.'

'You look pretty fit.'

'So do you,' acknowledged Michael. 'I'd hate to get into a fight with you.'

'Not much chance of that, Michael.'

'Anyway, here we are, Mr Gordon. This one's yours.' Michael led Les down a side passage to the bottom villa. He swiped the door and waited for Les to step inside.

Norton's villa was as good as any modern one-bedroom home unit he'd seen. It had a tastefully furnished lounge room, separated by a sliding wooden door from a bedroom with a king-size bed facing a TV, a DVD and a stereo. The white walls were hung with colourful paintings and the floor was covered in wall to wall carpet. A desk sat next to a sparkling new kitchen with all mod cons, and a private balcony offered uninterrupted views over the surrounding valleys. Next to the bedroom, a marble bathroom dazzled with fixtures and luxuries. Les was particularly taken by the large white ceramic bowl instead of a sink that was sitting under a full-length mirror reflecting an array of exclusive toiletries.

'I think I can handle this all right,' said Les, casting an eye of approval over the surroundings.

'Yes. They're nice villas, aren't they,' agreed Michael, placing Norton's bag in the bedroom.

Les fished in his pocket and pulled out a ten-dollar bill. 'There you go, mate. Thanks.'

Michael shook his head. 'No. That's all right, Mr Gordon.'

'You sure?'

'Yeah. Put me in your next movie,' smiled Michael. 'Enjoy your stay at Opal Springs, Mr

Gordon.' Michael closed the door behind him and he was gone.

Les opened a sliding glass door and stepped out onto the balcony. Shit! How good's this, he thought, taking in the view while a gentle breeze drifted up from the lush green valley below. Apart from stumbling across the odd corpse here and there, it couldn't be creamier.

Les came inside and checked out the bar fridge. It was stacked with nothing but chilled Mount Franklin mineral water; the cupboards contained only jars of herb tea. Les picked up one that looked like it was full of toe nail clippings and without bothering to read the label put it back. Feeling a bit sticky from the drive, he opened his bag and changed into a clean blue T-shirt, his Speedos and a pair of grey training shorts. He looked at his watch and figured by the time the nurse got back from checking out Alexander Holden and had a cup of tea or whatever, he'd have plenty of time for a swim before his appointment. Taking a big, fluffy white towel from the bathroom, Les slipped into his thongs and headed for the pool area.

It was getting quite warm outside and although there were no people around, Les could hear disco music and voices coming from an aerobics session near the Wellness Centre. The only sign of life he saw on the way to the pool were two women cleaners in blue uniforms getting out of a white golf buggy at one of the villas down from his. The women smiled at Les, who waved and smiled back.

Les took the short flight of tiled stairs to the entrance, pushed open the door and stepped inside to the indoor pool. It was fifty metres long, deserted and crystal clear. It looked extremely inviting. But Les thought he'd have a look at the outdoor pool first. He walked down a marble corridor past the entrance to the spa room on the right and the high, frosted-glass door leading into the Healing Centre on the left. The entrance to the outdoor pool was opposite the Healing Centre. Les pushed open another door to find a large kidney-shaped pool sparkling blue in the sun, ringed with white banana lounges sitting beneath blue and white umbrellas. And no one around. This'll do me, smiled Les. He dumped his towel and everything else on a banana chair next to a shower and plunged straight in.

The water was crystal clear and gloriously invigorating. Les wallowed around diving up and down, swum a few laps then just floated around on his back taking it easy. He was half floating and half splashing at nothing when a sudden thought struck him. Seeing as I found Holden's body, when the wallopers get here, you can bet they'll want to see me. And me being here under a bodgie name and out on bail. I don't think I really need that. Shit! This could be a bit tricky. Norton quietly floated around for a while longer, then got out, towelled off and walked back to his villa.

Les didn't bother with a shower. He changed back into his Levi's shorts and T-shirt, combed his hair then sat down and read the *Telegraph*. After making sure Staria and Krull were all right, he put his name tag on, closed the door and headed for the Wellness Centre.

The counter was just inside the door as you walked in, where two women in gym gear were talking to a fair-haired girl in a brown uniform looking up at them from a computer. There was a waiting room on the right and a corridor with doors on either side ran off the waiting room. Several black and white photos hung in frames on the walls and a number of indoor plants were placed neatly in the corners. He stepped up to the counter as another staffer with her hair tied back in a tight ponytail appeared behind it from out of the corridor. For a moment there was a silence as everybody stopped what they were doing and turned to stare at Les. Christ! thought Les. Word certainly travels fast around here. After a moment or two, the girl with the ponytail spoke.

'Good morning, Mr Gordon,' she said pleasantly. 'How may I help you?'

'I've got an appointment to see the nurse and the dietician.'

'That's right. Please take a seat, Mr Gordon, and Judy will be with you shortly.'

'Thanks.'

Les took a seat and watched the others trying to make out they weren't watching him. It wasn't long before a happy-faced woman with short copper-coloured hair entered the waiting room and came up to him. She had a white coat over a yellow dress with a watch pinned next to her name tag.

'Hello, Mr Gordon,' she smiled. 'I'm Judy, the nurse. Would you please follow me.'

'Okay, Judy.'

Judy's office was just inside the corridor on the right. Les followed her inside, sat down opposite her desk and had quick look around. Her office was much the same as a doctor's surgery. Coloured charts for diabetes, heart and liver problems on the walls, a plastic skeleton in a corner, open closets full of bandages and bottles of pills and a desk strewn with the usual clutter of pens, scissors, desk calendars, medical books and paper.

'So how do you feel, Mr Gordon?' asked Judy.

From the expectant way Nurse Judy was looking at him, Les could read her mind. 'A lot better than Alexander Holden was, the last time I saw him,' he replied.

Judy's face lit up. 'Yes. I believe you found the body,' she said.

'Yep. Lying there flat out like a flounder having a … whatever.'

'That must have been awfully traumatic for you, Mr Gordon.'

'Nahh. I see dead bodies all the time,' answered Les.

'All the time?'

'Yeah. When I'm filming. Someone's always getting murdered in my movies.'

Judy tapped Les playfully on the leg. 'Ohh, you kidder, Mr Gordon.'

'I know,' smiled Les.

'So are you thinking of making a movie here, Mr Gordon?'

'I don't know. It'd be a good setting. I could call it *Death Takes A Detox*.'

'If you do, how about making me the murderer?'

'I don't know. Can you act?'

'Probably not.'

'Good. You'd be absolutely perfect for an Australian movie.'

'But I was in a couple of school plays,' Judy confessed.

'That could spoil things.' Les looked at Nurse Judy for a moment. 'When I told the manager about finding Holden at the gate, he said he was going to get you. What was the exact cause of death?'

Nurse Judy tapped the side of her neck. 'I won't go into medical details, but he broke his neck. He banged his head on the gate first, then broke his neck when he fell off his bike.' The nurse looked squarely at Les. 'Serves him right for not wearing a helmet.'

'My sentiments exactly,' agreed Les. He looked at the nurse for a moment. 'So, Nurse Judy,' he said. 'They tell me Alexander didn't make friends easily.'

'Make friends? Are you kidding. You had to get in line to hate him.'

'That's no way to talk about your resident LOMBARD,' smiled Les.

'LOMBARD? So you know already,' smiled Nurse Judy. 'Well, I like to think of him more as a WOLF.'

'A wolf?'

'Yes. A Whingeing Obnoxious Little Fart.'

Les clapped his hands. 'Hey, Judge Judy, I like it.'

Judy gestured. 'Anyway. That's enough,' she said. 'Let's get down to business, before you get me into trouble.'

Judy weighed Les, then clamped a black band around his left arm and took his blood pressure. She wrote something down, ran a stethoscope over him and took his pulse. She looked a little concerned, then wrote something else down.

'All good?' said Les.

'Your weight's not bad. But your blood pressure is one hundred and sixty-five over ninety and your pulse is over seventy. And it's defibrilating.'

Les screwed his face up. 'It's what?'

'It's out of rhythm,' said Judy. 'How long since you've seen a doctor, Mr Gordon?'

'I can't remember,' said Les.

'Do you drink much coffee?'

'No more than anybody else,' replied Les. Which was an out-and-out lie. He and Warren were always making plungers at home, and if he walked down to the beach Les would always find someone to have a couple of piccolos or a flat white with. While at work, Price had hired a young Maltese bloke called Elmo who'd won a barrista contest, and on a cold night Les and Billy would inhale enough mind-blowing cappuccinos to fill a steam engine. 'Though I do have a few on the set at times. Especially if we're behind with the shoot.'

'Fair enough. Well, if I were you, I'd ease up on the coffee. And see your GP when you get home.'

'Shit!'

'Don't worry, Mr Gordon. You're not going to join Alexander Holden just yet. But I do think it's a good thing you came here.'

'Yeah — right.'

The nurse looked at her watch. 'Anyway, Mr Gordon, I've got another patient waiting. And the dietician wants to see you.'

'Where's he?' said Les, getting to his feet.

'Down the hall to the left.'

'Okay. Well thanks, Judy.'

'My pleasure. Any problems, come back and see me. And don't forget, if you want a good murderer in your next film, I'm your girl.'

Les followed the corridor till he found a door half open with DIETICIAN on the front. He knocked lightly and stepped inside. Seated at a desk on the left was a solid man with short brown hair and a pleasant face, wearing rimless glasses. The office was much the same clutter as the nurse's, except the dietician's shelves were stacked with packets of food and the walls were hung with charts of herbs and vitamin groups.

'Hello,' said Les. 'I'm Mr Gordon.'

'Yes. I'm expecting you. Take a seat, Mr Gordon. I'm Dallas.'

'Nice to meet you, Dallas.' Les shook the dietician's hand and sat down on his right.

Dallas gave Les a quick once up and down. 'I believe you had quite a nasty experience this morning, Mr Gordon.'

'Not really,' said Les. 'I couldn't stand the prick when I'd see him on TV. He looked all right to me, lying there next to his bike. Staring into space.'

Dallas tried to hold back a laugh, but his eyes gave him away. 'Funny you should say that,' he smiled, 'but Mr Holden didn't make many friends while he was here either.'

'Yeah?' Hello, thought Les. Here we go again. 'So what was your beef with him? I mean, how could he cause you a problem?'

'I'm also one of the chefs here,' said Dallas. 'And believe me, the food at Opal Springs is first class. But nothing we cooked could please him. He'd complain just for the sake of complaining. And for the pleasure of making the staff jump through hoops.'

'Really?'

Dallas nodded tiredly. 'I felt like telling him to piss off over to Cessnock and get a bowl of chips and gravy. And a sausage sandwich.'

'Well, I guess there's just no pleasing some people, is there?' said Les.

'No,' answered Dallas quietly. 'There just isn't.'

'When was he supposd to check out?'

'Next Wednesday.'

Les smiled. 'Looks like he checked out early.'

The dietician's eyes lit up for a moment. 'Yes,' he said. 'I suppose you could say that, couldn't you.' He then became serious. 'But poor John, the manager. This sort of publicity is the last thing he needs. John's down the front talking to the police now.'

'Ohh well,' said Les. 'You know the old saying, any publicity's good publicity.'

'Yes. But you know what the papers are like. They'll probably say it was the food that killed him.'

'That's a thought,' agreed Les.

'It would make a good plot for a movie,' smiled Dallas.

'Yes. I could call it *Homicide and Hummus*.'

Dallas threw back a laugh. 'Anyway. Best we get down to business. You look quite fit, Mr Gordon. Do you eat good food?'

'I sure do,' said Les. 'All the time.' Which was true. Les did eat good food. But he ate lots of it. And he wasn't adverse to the odd pizza, KFC, ice cream and soft drink. If anybody else ate the amount of food Les did, they'd look like a sumo wrestler. But Les was lucky, he burnt it all off with exercise. 'Though I will admit, I do tend to nibble a few biscuits and that on the set,' he added.

'That's the worst thing you can do,' said Dallas.

The dietician stood up and began pointing to packets and tins of food on a shelf. Nuts, grains, legumes, wild rice, brown rice, wholemeal pasta. Les listened intently.

'All you really have to remember,' said Dallas, sitting back down again, 'is eat as much unprocessed food as you can.'

'Unprocessed?' said Les.

'That's right. It's simple.' Dallas looked at his watch. 'I have to go and help get lunch together. But see me before you leave the retreat. I'll write out a list of things you should add to your diet. And others you should lose from it.'

76

'I'll make a note.' Les rose to his feet. 'Thanks, Dallas.'

'Any time, Mr Gordon.'

Les left the Wellness Centre and strolled back to his villa. This time the disco music was coming from the indoor pool.

Back in his villa, Les opened a bottle of mineral water and took it out on the balcony. Well, there you go, he told himself. Looks like I learnt a few things today. My ticker's gone techno. I drink too much coffee. And I eat too much shit. Les took a long, thoughtful swig of mineral water. And the late Alexander Holden didn't win any popularity polls during his stay at Opal Springs. Norton was mulling this over when the phone rang.

'Hello, Mr Gordon? It's the front desk.'

'Yes.'

'The police would like to have a word with you, if that's all right?'

'If that's all right' meant they were going to have a word with him whether Norton liked it or not. 'Sure,' said Les. 'Send them round to my villa.'

'Thank you, Mr Gordon.'

Les hung up and swallowed the rest of his mineral water. Fuck! he cursed. Now how am I going to handle this? They'll know who I really am in about five minutes. Shit! I hope I don't get booted out, I only just got here. Les opened another bottle of mineral water and settled back on the lounge. Five minutes later there was a knock on the door, like an elephant was trying to smash it down with a teak log in its trunk. Hello, thought Les. Something tells me this could be the police now. He walked over and opened the door.

'Len Gordon,' boomed a voice. 'Yeah, pig's arse. What are you doing here, Norton? I knew it was you.'

'Ohh shit!' winced Les. 'Officer Bumbles. Do come in.'

Les stepped back and let the two detectives into his villa. The older of the two, wearing a grey suit and a blue tie, had a full face behind a bulbous nose and thin fair hair going grey. He was the one that spoke. The other detective, wearing a blue suit and a grey tie, had thick dark hair combed neatly above a lean, set face tinged with five o'clock shadow and looked at Les as if he was public enemy number one.

'Can I get you something, officers?' asked Les breezily, knowing the gig was up and he'd probably be out in the street before lunch, so why worry about it. 'Mineral water. Herb tea?'

'No thanks, Les,' said the older detective. 'Just

the look on your face when you answered the door will suffice. I'll be drinking that for the rest of the week.'

'Fair enough,' said Les, spreading himself back on the lounge. 'Anyway, grab a seat and let's have a nice friendly talk before you drag me out of here in handcuffs.'

'Yes, why don't we,' smiled the older detective, taking the chair from the kitchen. 'Bernie, why don't you get one of those chairs from the sundeck?'

Bernie slid open the door, got a chair and sat alongside his partner.

'Les Norton,' said the older detective. 'This is Detective Bernard Lennan. Bernie. Meet Les Norton.' Bernie nodded almost imperceptibly and continued to give Les the Charles Manson. 'And,' grinned the older detective, 'I think you know who I am, Les.'

'Yes, Neville,' nodded Les. 'Everybody knows who you are.'

The older man was Detective Neville Humble. Arguably the worst cop in New South Wales. He wasn't bad or corrupt. If anything, the opposite. He was just dumb. He'd make pinches, but he could never get them to stick. Lawyers loved him and it was through them he got nicknamed

'Officer Bumbles'. In one case, Bumbles had the defendant, a known forger, on toast, when the defendant's lawyer pointed out Detective Humbles' awful checked suit. The lawyer claimed it was immaterial. Bumbles got all flustered and the crook walked. Another time he got cross-examined over a confession, written and signed entirely in Bumbles' handwriting. Bumbles explained that was because the defendant wrote it with Bumbles' pen. And everybody knew Bumbles went with his wife and friends to a Marcel Marceau concert and Bumbles yelled out for Marcel Marceau to speak up.

Bumbles knew what was going on at the Kelly Club and had nicked Les on two occasions for assault. Les walked easily both times and Bumbles would have loved to have done something about Les and the club. But Price was looking after too many cops above Bumbles and he couldn't do a thing. Naturally, if he ever drove past the club, Les and Billy would smile and wave and invite him in for a coffee. And if either of them bumped into Bumbles somewhere they would patronise him ferociously. Yet despite his incompetence and everything else, Bumbles was a police hero.

A nutty university student had tried to shoot the police commissioner and Bumbles took the bullet in his arm. Everybody knew Bumbles had tripped over his own two feet. Everybody except the commissioner. After that, Bumbles got promoted and could do no wrong. Now here he was, parked on Norton's doorstep with the big red-headed Queenslander right in his sights.

'So what's going on, Les Norton AKA Len Gordon?' asked Detective Humble. 'What's a low-life like you doing in a respectable and exclusive establishment like this, mixing with people of quality and breeding? And under an assumed name. You're out on bail for assault and other related charges. If it wasn't for the slack justice system in this state, you'd still be in police custody.' Bumbles turned to his partner. 'I think we've got ourselves a nice little pinch here, Bernie.'

Norton took umbrage. 'If it comes to that, Bumbles, what are you doing up here? The last I heard, you were pushing papers in College Street. And you needed a wheelbarrow to do that.'

'My family comes from Kurri Kurri,' protested Bumbles. 'So I transferred to Cessnock. It's all right up here, too. Nice fresh air. Plenty of good golf courses. Newcastle's just up the road. I go fishing in Shoal Bay. It shits on living in Sydney.' Bumbles screwed up his face. 'Anyway, why am I telling you this? I'm the one asking the questions. Speak. How come you found the deceased's body?'

'Ohh, because I killed him,' said Les, tossing his hands in the air. 'I came howling through the front gate with the stereo on full blast playing Tupac, and I clobbered him coming down the hill. There. You happy?'

'We checked your car,' said Detective Lennan. 'It has got a slight dent in the front right mudguard.'

Les held his hands out in front of him and shook his head. 'Well, take me away and get it over with. Just give me one phone call before we go.'

'We'll get round to that,' nodded Bumbles. 'But come on, Les Norton AKA Len Gordon. Give us the guts. What are you up to?'

Les took a deep breath followed by a swig of mineral water. 'Okay,' he said. 'Here we go.'

Les told them everything, starting with the flat tyre on his bike. He didn't tell them about taking photos of Holden's body. But he did say Eddie was going to help him and he explained fully how he came to be staying at Opal Springs under another name.

'And that's it,' said Les. 'I'm just up here till things cool down with those hoons. Then it's back to the old steak and kidney. Or it was. Till you two put your heads in.'

'You say Jimmy Caccano gave you bail?' said Bumbles.

'That's right,' answered Les. 'Detective Caccano. At Waverley.'

'I know Jimmy Caccano. He married my niece. I was at the wedding. I also know Benny the Beak and his wife Lemuela. She and my missus used to play canasta.'

'Well there you go,' said Les. 'Why don't you ring up Detective Caccano, and see whether I'm telling the truth or not?' He pointed to his bedroom. 'The phone's next to the bed.'

Bumbles thought for a moment. 'All right. Why not?'

Bumbles took out a little black book then got up to use the phone, leaving Les and Detective Lennan in the lounge staring impassively at each other.

'So how's things?' asked Les. The detective didn't reply. 'Much crime up this neck of the woods?' Again the detective said nothing. Les half smiled. 'You making plenty of nice clean arrests and convictions with Bumbles?' The detective lowered his eyes to the floor. 'That's all right,' said Les. 'You don't have to say anything.'

Eventually Bumbles came back from the bedroom and stood looking down at Norton. 'I don't believe this. You're telling the truth. In fact Jimmy actually gave you a rap. He reckons you were stiff.'

'I told you,' said Les.

'And good on you for helping Benny. He's a nice old bloke.'

'Just doing what any other concerned citizen would do, Detective Humble.'

Bumbles turned to his partner. 'Well, it looks like we can leave this fine young gentleman in peace,' said Detective Humble wryly.

'That's me,' agreed Les. 'But what about the mysterious death of Alexander Holden?' he asked.

'Mysterious death?' said Detective Humble. 'You've been reading too many detective stories, homeboy. He came down the hill, hit his head on the gate and broke his neck. You don't have to be Sherlock Holmes to work that out.'

'And did the world a favour,' added Detective Lennan. 'I couldn't stand the prick on TV.'

'My sentiments exactly,' said Les.

'So we may as well get going,' said Detective Humble. 'Our friends in the media will be here shortly. And I'm playing golf this afternoon.' He pointed at Les. 'All I want you to do, is write out a statement and drop it off at Cessnock Police Station on your way home. Ohh, and do sign it with your right name. There's a good chap.'

'That's the least I can do,' smiled Les. 'Come on,' he said to both detectives. 'I'll walk out the front with you.'

The walk to the foyer didn't take long. But all the time Les couldn't help feeling Bumbles was still up to something and he'd be glad to see the arse end of him and his partner. They stepped through the glass door and across to the top of the stairs. Les could sense every eye in the place on them and secretly prayed Bumbles didn't bring him undone at the last moment.

'Well, Mr Gordon,' said Bumbles, offering his hand. 'Thank you for your cooperation. It was muchly appreciated.'

Les shook the detective's hand. 'It was my pleasure, Detective Humble. You too, Detective Lennan.'

'Ohh. And if by chance it had been a murder,' Bumbles said quietly, 'you were well in the clear.'

'I was?' answered Les.

'Yes.' Detective Humble handed Les a piece of paper. 'That is your car, is it not, sir?'

Les glanced at the description and registration number. 'Yeah. Why?'

'You tripped a red light camera in Vincent Street, Cessnock, this morning. So you couldn't have been here at the time of the incident.' Bumbles smiled. 'That shouldn't cost you much more than a three-hundred-dollar fine and a loss of two points.'

Detective Lennan smiled for the first time. 'Being in the film game yourself, Mr Gordon, we knew you'd appreciate that.'

The two detectives turned and Les watched them walk down the stairs. He looked at the piece of paper in his hand and cursed silently. Fuck it. I don't know which is worse. Getting a blister. Or seeing Bumbles get the last laugh. Whatever it is, it's much better than being nicked and getting tossed out of here on my arse. Les was ruminating on this when he felt someone at his shoulder. He turned and it was John Reid, the manager.

'Is everything all right, Mr Gordon?' he asked.

Les nodded and gave the manager a thin smile. 'Yes. Perfectly all right, thank you.'

'We're terribly sorry this had to happen, believe me. It's shaken up the staff and everybody else for that matter.'

'Yes. I heard Mr Holden cut quite a popular figure with everybody while he was here.'

'Ohh yes. He did indeed.' The manager shook his head sadly. 'Now I have to handle all the media kerfuffle.'

The sound of knives and forks clinking against plates drew Norton's attention to the dining room. 'And now I have to lunch. Dealing with the constabulary certainly does put a compelling edge on one's appetite.'

'Of course, Mr Gordon. Would you, ah . . . care to join us for mocktails in the library before dinner this evening?'

'I might just do that, John,' said Les. 'See you then.' Les walked over to the dining room as the manager hurried off down the stairs.

The dining room was half full and Les was the centre of attention the moment he walked in. Ignoring the stares from the other diners, he found a table to himself with a crisp white tablecloth and fabulous views over the surrounding hills and valleys. Placed on the table was a one-page menu saying what was available. Les couldn't find any pepper and salt or rolls and butter. Instead, a small bowl of chopped-up herbs and spices sat next to the menu and Sandra, an extremely pleasant waitress with neat ginger hair, placed a slice of soft rye bread and a small bowl of hummus on the table along with a fruit drink that tasted of mint.

She pointed out a salad bar at the end of the room and said she'd be back when Les was ready to order his main. Les thanked her, then strolled down to the salad bar and loaded up a plate with soyabeans and grilled eggplant, plus some mixed gourmet salad leaves, dousing the lot liberally with both tahini and roasted garlic dressing and adding some roasted beetroot and balsamic.

Les rather enjoyed the salads with their different dressings and backed up for another plate. When he'd finished his second one, the waitress asked him what he'd like for a main. Les chose the Sri Lankan vegetable curry with lentils, served with organic brown rice and raita.

For non-greasy, nutritious health food, lunch was delicious and Les soon figured out what was so good about it. Everything tasted fresh and alive and all the organic produce glowed with colour. While he was eating, Les also mulled a few things over.

Nobody had a good word to say about Alexander Holden, and the way he was lying on the road all alone, it still might not have been an accident. Besides that, if Bumbles said it was an accident, you could almost bet it was a homicide. Which meant there was a distinct possibility somewhere in Opal Springs Health Resort lurked a murderer. It was none of Norton's business and he really couldn't have given a rat's arse if Holden had been murdered or not. But while he was at the resort, Les knew he was going to get bored shitless with no booze and nowhere to go. Why not play Crime Scene Cessnock? Norton smiled to himself. I'm rapt in *CSI: Miami*. And me and Horatio Cain have both got red hair, haven't we?

Sandra brought Les a plunger of herb tea and Les looked up.

'Sandra?' he asked her. 'Besides the others in here, I've noticed groups of people at the end of the dining room all sitting at one table. Who are they?'

'They're on the program, Mr Gordon,' replied Sandra.

'On the program?'

'Yes, their stay at the retreat is more regimented. They have to be up at a certain time. Do certain activities and their diet is strictly controlled. You're an independent guest. You can do pretty much what you like.'

'Right.' Les indicated to a table of two men and two women who weren't dressed in gym gear. 'Who are those four people over there?'

'They're our writers in residence,' replied Sandra.

'I see.' Les smiled at Sandra. 'Was the late Mr Holden an independent guest?' he asked.

'Yes he was.'

'And how did you get on with him?'

Sandra paused for a moment. 'Mr Holden … could be a little demanding at times,' she replied quietly.

To Les, this was Sandra's diplomatic way of saying she would have liked to have dumped a plunger of hot tea over Holden's head. 'Okay,' smiled Les. 'Thanks, Sandra.'

Sandra took the plates away and Les poured himself a cup of herb tea. He took a sip and gagged. To a coffee drinker like Les, it tasted as if it had been strained through a wino's underpants. Yuk! grimmaced Les. They can stick that where the sun don't shine and the grass don't grow. Les poured himself a glass of water, and wishing it was a nice frothy cappuccino, washed away the taste of the herb tea while he casually checked out the punters.

Apart from a handful of men, they were mostly attractive, well-groomed, well-heeled women aged from thirty to fifty. One person stood out from the rest: an obese man with blond hair, pale skin and the pale eyes of an albino. He had a loud, giggling voice and was talking non-stop above the others at his table, who appeared to be listening to him with polite but tired amusement. Les gave him a quick once up and down. Under his baggy brown shorts and wrinkled grey T-shirt, the bloke was wearing black socks with his trainers. A definite no-no. Only three types of people wore black socks and trainers: backpackers, people with no dress sense, and garbos. And garbos at least had the dignity to wear football socks. Les switched his gaze to the writers in residence.

An older man with wiry greying hair and a younger one with untidy dark hair were seated next to a blonde in her forties and a younger, sallow-faced brunette. The older man had a set, boozy face and was wearing a brown jacket over a black skivvy, the younger man had a lean, bored face and was wearing a plain green T-shirt under a cheap denim shirt he'd ironed with a house brick. The blonde's hair was long, her eyes were tinted with blue eye shadow and she was wearing a loose blue floral dress under a chunky yellow necklace and earrings and could have been half a good sort in her day. The brunette's unevenly chopped hair was tinted with white making it look like a dead skunk lying on her head, and clinging to her scrawny flat chest was a black vest over a black T-shirt with a man's face on it that read, KAFKA DIDN'T HAVE MUCH FUN EITHER. A pair of black, oval-framed glasses sat halfway down her nose and Les tipped she'd relish eating the odd carpet. The writers weren't talking and gave off the impression they'd rather be somewhere else, and the only thing keeping them together was a mutual dislike for each other.

Earlier when he walked in, Les couldn't help noticing he was the centre of attention. He still was. But now as he sipped his water he spotted several aunties on the program giving him some surreptitious heavy once up and downs as well. The writers in residence had also been watching him intently. However, if he happened to glance in their direction, they too would quickly turn away. Les looked at his watch and thought, Well, yes, this is all very nice here, the views and everything else. But I think it's time Len Gordon, man of the moment and famous film director, made his departure.

Les picked up his serviette and dabbed pretentiously at the corners of his mouth for a moment before rising slowly and sublimely to his feet. Knowing all eyes were upon him, he paused to disdainfully brush some imaginary crumbs from the front of his T-shirt and punctiliously adjust his apparel. Then, his body rigid with composed decorum and his face a mask of supercilious indignation, strode magnificently from the dining room. If only Warren could see me now, Les smiled as he swanned past the library.

Back at his villa, Les read a story by N.A. Temple Ellis, and when he finished, felt he needed a good long swim to give his brain a rest. He changed into his training shorts and thongs, took another bottle of water from the fridge and strolled up to the indoor pool, stopping to exchange pleasantries with two women walking past.

The indoor pool was deserted. Les dipped a toe in the water while he took in the views and noticed several pairs of flippers lying against a wall next to a number of floats. Yeah, why bust my arse, thought Les. He found a pair of flippers that fitted, adjusted his swimming goggles, then dived in and proceeded to churn effortlessly up and down the pool.

After an hour or so of relaxed backstroking, breast-stroking and freestyle swimming, Les got out of the pool, dried off and walked back to his villa. He changed out of his Speedos but kept his training shorts and T-shirt on. Norton was going to relax and listen to some music when he looked at his watch. Shit! It's time for my hot rock massage. Where did the bloody day get to?

He left the villa and walked back to the Healing Centre.

Les pushed open the tall, frosted-glass doors and stepped into a large room with high ceilings that let in the light. The counter was in front of a display of women's cosmetics on the right and faced another display of imported shampoos and conditioners on the left. Placed around the polished wooden floors were roomy, comfortable lounges and coffee tables scattered with magazines. The waiting area was separated from the treatment room by a wooden partition running along the sides and several women in fluffy white bathrobes were seated on the lounges waiting for various treatments. Les returned the smile of a brunette having a big hair day and stepped up to the counter.

'Hello,' he said to a thin, dark-haired girl behind the counter. 'My name's Gordon. I'm here for a hot rock massage.'

'Hello, Mr Gordon.' The girl returned Norton's smile and checked a large diary. 'Yes. That's right. If you'd care to take a seat, Mr Gordon, Rita will be with you very shortly.'

'Thank you.'

Les found a nice comfortable lounge chair away from the others then settled back and listened to the celestial music drifting down from the ceiling. Before long a tall, lean woman wearing a black uniform walked up to him. She had shiny brown hair and a lean, pleasant face that matched her figure.

'Hello,' she said, offering her hand. 'I'm Rita. I'm your masseur.'

'Hello, Rita,' replied Les, rising to his feet and shaking her hand. 'Nice to meet you.'

'This way, please.'

Rita led Les back past the counter then around the other side of the partition to a room in the middle. She opened the door and Les stepped into a darkened room thick with the smell of sweet oil. Shelves of oils and towels ran along one wall, a towel-covered massage table stood in the middle and against another wall was a brazier full of river stones.

'Have you ever had hot rock therapy before, Mr Gordon?' asked Rita.

Les shook his head. 'No.'

'Ohh, it's lovely. You'll really like it,' she assured him. 'Now. If you'll just slip your T-shirt off and lie on the table.'

'Okay.' Les kicked off his thongs and placed his T-shirt on a chair and lay face down on the massage table with his face poking through a hole in the end. 'Are you comfortable, Mr Gordon?'

'Yes. I'm good,' said Les.

Rita dripped oil onto Norton's back and began giving it a gentle massage before placing four river stones along his lower spine.

'They're not too hot, are they, Mr Gordon?' she asked.

'No. They're nice,' crooned Les.

Rita took another river stone and began massaging Norton's neck and shoulders with it.

'Hey. That feels great,' smiled Les.

'I'm glad you like it,' said Rita, continuing to massage away. 'I believe you're a film director,' she said.

'Yeah. That's right,' lied Les.

'Have you made many films?'

'Fifteen.'

'Goodness. That's quite a lot,' said Rita, liberally dripping more oil on Les.

'Yeah, it's a few. But for the past year or so I've been directing TV commercials.'

'I imagine that would be a change,' said Rita.

'Yes, it is,' replied Les. And time to change the subject before I put my lying big foot in it, he thought. 'How about you, Rita? Are you into the arts at all?'

'Yes,' she replied excitedly. 'I like to write short stories. I intend to write a book.'

'Good for you, Rita,' said Les. 'You should have a talk to those authors that are staying here.'

'I tried,' said Rita. 'But they're very . . . reserved.'

'I see.'

'Except for the young one. He offered to look at my short stories. Back at his villa.'

'Ahh. The old come back and I'll look at your manuscript dodge,' said Les.

'Yes. I think it would have been, is that a thesaurus in your pocket, Mr Gritt, or are you just happy to see me?'

Les laughed through the hole in the massage table. 'What was his name?'

'Gritt. Benson Gritt.'

'Never heard of him.'

'He comes from Brisbane and he writes grunge. He certainly dresses and smells the part.' Rita stopped rubbing for a moment. 'Ohh dear. I really shouldn't be saying that about one of the guests.'

'That's okay,' Les assured Rita. 'Your secret's safe with me.'

'Thanks, Mr Gordon.'

'Call me Len. What about Mr Holden? How did you get on with him? I suppose you know I found his body.'

'Yes. That must have been awful.'

'Yeah. Well it wasn't quite what I was expecting as I drove in the gate.'

'No. You poor thing.'

'So did Mr Holden come to you for a treatment?' asked Les.

'Yes,' replied Rita shortly.

'And how was he? Bit of a LOMBARD?'

Rita shifted the stones on Norton's back. 'I thought of him more of a BERT.'

'A BERT?'

'Yes. A Boring Extremely Rude Turd.'

Les laughed out loud again. 'I've got to give it to you, Rita,' he said. 'You sure got a way with words. I reckon you'd be a killer as a writer.'

'You never know, do you, Mr Gordon,' replied Rita, suddenly pushing down hard on Norton's back.

Les waited a moment before he spoke. 'So what did Alexander Holden do to incur your wrath, Rita?'

'What did he do?' said Rita. 'Ohh, nothing was good enough. The stones were either too hot or too cold. The oil was rubbish. I didn't know what I was doing. He got up in the middle of his treatment, called me a stupid bitch, and walked out.'

'Really?'

'Yes. Then complained to the manager. Honestly, Mr Gordon. Len. I've been doing this for ten years. And no one's ever done that to me. I was in tears.'

'What a ... what a BERT.'

'You can say that again.'

'So I imagine, Rita, you won't be sending any flowers to Alexander Holden's funeral.'

'Only dead ones.'

Rita's gentle massaging along with the celestial music had Les feeling a little drowsy. He dropped off the conversation and closed his eyes. Rita finished his back then got Les to lie on it. She gave his chest and forehead a long soothing massage with the hot stones and he was finished.

'There you are, Len,' smiled Rita, as Les opened his eyes. 'How was that?'

'That was absolutely delightful, thanks, Rita,' answered Les. 'I feel great.'

'Thank you. I'll leave you to put your T-shirt on. There's a glass of cold water next to the chair.'

'Okey doke.'

Rita left, closing the door gently behind her, leaving Les covered in oil from head to toe. He got into his T-shirt and thongs, drank the water then stepped out into the light. Rita was standing by the counter with the girl from before.

'Well thank you for that, Rita,' said Les, shaking her hand again. 'I'd recommend it to anybody.'

'My pleasure, Mr Gordon. Enjoy your stay at Opal Springs.'

'I will. Goodbye? Rita. And good luck with your writing.'

Les pushed open the doors and walked past the two pools. Christ! I don't think I'd better go for a swim right now, he thought. If I do, they'll have to drop an oil boom in the water to control the slick. Les continued on to his villa.

Once inside, he got a towel and stood out on the balcony while he wiped oil from his face. Well there you go, mused Les. Another suspect. Bloody hell. The queue to hate Alexander Holden forms on the left. He closed the flyscreen door, came inside and took a look at the activities sheet. If he hurried, he had ten minutes to rally outside the Wellness Centre for the afternoon walk. That's just what I feel like, with my crook knee, Les told himself. A nice easy walk. He changed into his trainers, got a sweatband and headed for the Wellness Centre.

Grouped outside were a dozen women in an array of shorts and tops all holding bottles of water. Standing in front of them was Michael, looking at his watch. He looked up as Les approached.

'Hello, Mr Gordon,' he said.

'Hello, Michael,' said Les. 'Are you leading this merry bunch?'

'I sure am. And you're right on time. Okay, everybody. Let's go.'

Les exchanged smiles with some of the women then with Michael showing the way, they set off past the villas. Two hundred metres past Meditation Hill and the last villa, the path dipped down to a gate in the cyclone wire. Michael opened it and once they were all through, closed it behind them.

The road was quite hilly as it led past the villas belonging to the golf course next door, then levelled off through the trees surrounding the greens. The sun was going down taking the heat of the day with it, and it was quite pleasant marching along in the quiet countryside listening to the birds. The group sorted itself out into twos and threes and Les finished up with a stocky, no-nonsense sort of woman with short, brown hair whose name was Deliah. Deliah was forty, had three children and her husband was a meat wholesaler in Brisbane. Deliah didn't say a great deal, she was too busy walking, and she was good at it. Les had to drop back a gear on a couple of hills to keep up. He didn't come on with the film director jive. But eventually he managed to swing the conversation round his way.

'I suppose you know it was me who found Alexander Holden's body this morning?' Les asked Deliah.

'Yes,' she replied. 'It's the talk of the resort. I imagine it would have been quite a shock for you, Len.'

'Yes. My first impression of Opal Springs wasn't real good, I can tell you that, Deliah.'

'There was a great gaggle of reporters and TV cameras out the front earlier. But they're all gone now.'

'Yeah,' puffed Les as they motored up another hill. 'I don't think they were interested in me. But I had to give a statement to the police.'

'Ohh? And how were they?'

'All right. But can I let you onto a little secret, Deliah?'

'Sure.' Deliah's ears pricked up beneath her white sweatband.

'They think it might have been murder.'

'What?' Deliah's eyes widened. 'You're joking.'

Les shook his head. 'Of course they've only got

their suspicions. But you know what the police are like.'

'Goodness!' said Deliah. 'Murder.'

'Maybe. So how did you find Alexander Holden, Deliah?' asked Les. 'Did you have much to do with him?'

Deliah shook her head. 'No. I avoided him. He used to keep to himself most of the time anyway.'

'How come you avoided him?'

'He was a very rude man. Very obnoxious. He used to go out of his way to get people off side. Then seemed to gloat about it.'

'Fair dinkum?'

'Yes. He brought poor Lionel to tears.'

'Lionel?' said Les.

'The fair-haired man at our table.'

'Ohh, the albino.'

'That's him,' said Deliah. 'He's French.'

'What did he do to upset him? Tell him to get out of those black socks?'

'That,' smiled Deliah. 'He also called him a punishing great bore who ought to keep quiet and listen for a change. And the only reason people put up with him was out of politeness. Otherwise they'd tell him to shut the fuck up and piss off. If you'll pardon my French.'

'That's not a bad blast,' said Les.

'That wasn't all, either. One night in the library, Lionel said he auditioned for a part in a play, but missed out because the producers were biased. Holden told him to audition as a stand-in for Phyllis Diller, if he could afford a dress. If he couldn't, Holden said he had an old bleached blonde aunty who was almost as fat and ugly as Lionel, and he could borrow one of hers.'

'Shit!' smiled Les. 'He certainly gave it to him.'

'Mind you,' said Deliah. 'Part of what Holden said was true. But there was no need to say it in front of everybody. It wasn't in the best of taste.'

'No,' agreed Les. 'So what did Lionel do?'

'Nothing. He got up and left. But I'll tell you, Len. If looks could kill, Alexander Holden would have been dead long before you found him at the front gate.'

'Really?'

'Yes. Really.'

Les turned around to find they were fifteen lengths in front of the field just as Deliah found another gear.

'Come on,' she said. 'Let's have a go on these hills.'

Deliah's arms started swinging and her bum started wiggling and with his sore knee, Les had the pedal to the metal keeping up. The road levelled and rose and at the end of the walk, a steep hill climbed two hundred metres up to the gate. Deliah beat Les up the hill by a good five lengths.

'Well, that was fun,' puffed Deliah as they waited for the others.

'Yeah. Real fun,' said Les. 'Christ, Deliah. You're a little pocket rocket.'

Deliah smiled and swung her arms up and down. 'It's all in the arms, Mr Gordon. All in the arms.'

Michael let everyone back through the gate and Les said goodbye to Deliah. I wonder how long before my secret will do the rounds? Les smiled to himself as he opened the door to his villa. The manager's going to have a heart attack when it gets to him. Two bottles of mineral water later, Les got under the shower.

When he got out and started to shave, Les unexpectedly found himself getting an unbelievably bad headache and he felt sweaty. Shit! I don't feel so good, he winced. It must have been the lunch. Or was it Rita banging those rocks on my head? Surely it wasn't the walk. Anyway, I'll have dinner. But fuck it. They can stick the mocktail hour in their arse. I'm not in the mood.

Les changed into a clean pair of shorts and a George Thorogood T-shirt. He switched the TV on and massaged his throbbing temples while he watched the ABC news. Sure enough, there was the retreat and the manager being interviewed at the front gate, along with footage of Alexander Holden in full cry. He was found by a guest entering the retreat. Blah, blah, blah! It was a tragic accident. Mr Holden was a good bloke and popular at the retreat. Blah, blah, blah! It was a shock to both the staff and the other guests. Blah, blah, blah. Ohh, what a load of bullshit. Les switched the TV off and sulked moodily at the floor for a while, then got up and left for the dining room.

The dining room was full and again Les could feel he was the centre of attention as he walked in with his headache getting worse by the minute. Deliah was with a group of others on the program and Lionel. Lionel appeared to be in a good mood after the death of Alexander Holden and was prattling away non-stop letting everybody know it. Les forced a smile and gave Deliah a wave then found a table to himself. He noticed the authors were at the same table as before, wearing the same clothes and the same blank expressions; the only difference was the blonde had swapped her chunky yellow jewellery for red. Les was also able to pick out John Reid seated at a long table near the salad bar, having a serious discussion with several guests. He didn't appear to see Les arrive. If he did, he didn't acknowledge him, which suited Norton down to the ground.

Les ordered vialone nano risotto with mushroom and saffron threads for an entrée, and wasabi-crusted barramundi on wok-tossed green noodles for a main. He finished this with a green, pineapple-tasting drink and baked banana with pineapple and yogurt sorbet for dessert. The food was delicious and despite his headache, Les was hungry at first. But in the end he found himself having to force the food down. As soon as he finished eating, he left abruptly and went back to his room.

Someone had lit an oil lamp in the bathroom and sitting on the bed were two sheets of paper. One was a list of the following day's activities. The other said he'd been booked in for a lymphatic massage in the afternoon. Les irritably tossed the two sheets of paper on the floor, blew out the oil lamp then climbed miserably out of his clothes and flopped into bed.

There wasn't a great deal on TV and what there was Les wasn't at all interested in. His headache now felt like the worst hangover he'd ever had, and he would have killed for some Berocca and a handful of Warren's Panadeine Forte. Convinced he'd be tired from the early morning start, the events of the day and the exercise, Les switched off the TV, turned out the lights, and pushed his aching head into the big fluffy pillows.

Les managed to go to sleep. But he kept waking up with his head feeling like it was going to explode. He'd get up, have a drink of water, then climb back into bed and doze off. Only to have a bad dream then wake up tossing and turning with his head throbbing worse than ever. Bloody hell! What the fuck's wrong with me? Les cursed to himself. I've never had a headache like this in my life. Les bashed at the pillows to try and get comfortable and managed to doze off before waking up again from another bad dream.

After an abysmal night's sleep, Norton woke up the next morning feeling dreadful. His head ached, his eyes were puffy, his brain felt like mush and, to top it off, he was in a rotten mood. He splashed some water on his face, cleaned his teeth and stared blankly at the miserable figure looking back at him in the mirror. God! I don't ever remember being this sick. I must be getting some sort of Asian flu or something. Some bloody health retreat they're running here. He dragged his arse into the kitchen, put the kettle on and found a jar of Opal Springs Special Herb Tea. He made a plunger, took a sip and grimaced.

'Ohh, yuk!' he spat. 'That's all I fuckin need.'

Les forced some more down. But all it did was send him racing to the toilet. After a painful dump, he came out, wiped some sweat from his face and picked up the sheet of paper with the day's activities on it. He'd missed the morning walk and he didn't feel like breakfast. I could go for a swim, thought Les. But what I need is something to make me sweat whatever it is out of me. The gym under the Wellness Centre. There's got to be a rowing machine or a bike in there. And I can see the nurse on the way. Les climbed gingerly into his training gear, wrapped a sweatband up in a towel and left.

Although a thick bank of clouds had gathered over the distant hills, it was another warm sunny day outside and Les could hear music coming from the Wellness Centre as he walked over. There was no one around and when he put his head in the door of the Wellness Centre, there was no one in there either. A message written on a whiteboard said the nurse would be in at eleven. Bugger it, Les cursed silently as his head kept throbbing away. He closed the door and walked around the side.

A group of women, led by a dark-haired instructor with a sensational body, were prancing around a room in front of a mirrored wall. In the bike room adjacent, a circle of people were pedalling like fury, urged on by a brown-haired young bloke in a black T-shirt and shorts, while down in the badminton court, Peta was putting a group of women lying on mats with thick rubber bands through a stretching session. Yeah, wouldn't that go well right now, thought Les. Me exercising in a room full of other people. He ripped off a hot, rancid fart and took the stairs down to the gymnasium.

The gym was large, bright and modern with views over the valley. Banks of weight stations stood on the left as you walked in and there was a change room on the right. The back wall was floor to ceiling mirrors reflecting rows of cardiovascular machines facing a bank of TV sets suspended from the ceiling. Except for a pumped-up body-builder in a red muscle shirt and black tracksuit pants working out on a triceps lift, the gymnasium was empty. This'll do me, thought Les, as the door closed behind him. I'll grunt out an hour on one of those walking machines, have a swim, then see if I can force down whatever they give you for breakfast. Les caught the body-builder's eye as he walked in. The body-builder ran a hand through his tinted blond hair and looked at Les as if Les had no right to be in the gymnasium while he was using it, then ignored him. Les ignored the body-builder straight back. After placing his towel on a speaker box near a rack of weights against one wall, Les walked over to the first walking machine he saw and studied the panel of buttons and lights. He set the machine for six kilometres an hour and started stepping out.

Les wasn't breaking any records as he marched along. But in his condition it felt like he was running a marathon through Death Valley. He puffed, grunted and farted away while toxic-smelling sweat seeped into his sweatband and T-shirt. All that was on the four TV sets was a morning show and a boring advertorial full of orthodontically perfect Californian women gushing about some face cleanser guaranteed to make an eighty-year-old Eskimo look like Paris Hilton. Shit a brick. There's got to be something better to watch than this, frowned Les. The TV remote was sitting on a padded bench; Les stepped over, picked it up then got back on the walking machine. It was hard to tell what button on the remote worked which TV, but eventually Les was able to find a movie in progress: Leslie Nielsen in *Wrongfully Accused*. This'll do me, smiled Les. I've seen it before, but Leslie Nielsen's always good for a laugh. Les placed the remote on the walking machine and proceeded on his gruelling way to nowhere.

Leslie Nielsen had just walked into the hospital wearing a white coverall with Hemak Meat Co. on the back, posing as a doctor, when a deep rasping voice boomed out from amongst the weight stations at the far end of the gymnasium.

'Hey. What the fuck are you doing? I was watching that.'

At first Les thought he was hearing things. 'What?' he called out.

'I said, I was watching that.' It was the body-builder in the red muscle shirt.

'Watching it?' replied Les. 'How can you be watching it from down there?'

'I was watching it in the fuckin mirror.'

'In the mirror. Ohh, don't give me ...'

Les pondered for a moment then, rather than start an argument, reluctantly agreed. Though from Norton's point of view, the bloke was being a bit of a mug and he didn't like the way he spoke to him either.

'Yeah, righto,' replied Les dully.

Les picked up the remote and started pushing the buttons, but he couldn't change the channels properly. Two TV sets would show the advertorial and the morning show, while the others kept showing Leslie Nielsen. Finally they all showed nothing but Leslie Nielsen.

'Hey. I told you to change it back,' bellowed the bloke.

'I am,' said Les. 'But I can't figure out the remote.'

'Ohh, what are you? Some kind of moron?'

'Keep it up, Shithead,' muttered Les, as he stabbed at the buttons on the remote.

Flexing his muscles, the bloke got up and stood next to a biceps lift. 'Hey!' he yelled. 'I said change the fuckin thing back. I won't tell you again.'

Les looked helplessly at the remote then glared angrily at the bloke in the red muscle shirt. 'Here. You want it changed back?' he yelled. 'Change it your fuckin self.' Les flung the remote at the bloke who was still staring heatedly at Les from the other end of the room. It hit the big man in the chest then dropped on the floor and the batteries fell out.

Muscles looked at his chest then looked at the remote lying on the floor and glared at Les. 'What the fuck do you …?'

'You heard,' Les shouted back at him. 'Stick it in your arse.'

Les stared at the bloke for a moment then ignored him and put his aching head down to pound out another kilometre. Another jolt of pain made Les close his eyes momentarily and he never noticed Muscles come charging across the gymnasium. Next thing Les knew, Muscles had yanked him off the walking machine by the neck of his T-shirt, spun him around and had him pinned against the mirror wall with a massive right arm.

'How would you like me to break your fuckin neck,' hissed Muscles.

Les eyeballed Muscles viciously. 'This morning,' he snarled, 'I'd fuckin love it.'

Les brought his right knee up and collected Muscles in the balls. It hurt. But Muscles was wearing a groin protector, so it didn't hurt enough. Muscles grunted then grabbed Les in a headlock with his right arm and started punching Les on the top of his head with his left fist. For his size, the big man's punches weren't all that hard. But the way Norton's head was throbbing already, it felt like he was being hit with a ball-peen hammer. He tucked his head in, bent down and grabbed Muscles by the bottoms of his tracksuit pants. Making sure he had a tight grip, Les stood up, lifting Muscles off his feet at the same time, and ran the big body-builder face first into the rack of weights. Muscles yelped as his nose got smashed against one of the barbells and he slid down the weight rack onto his backside. Blood started running down his face and his jaw dropped as he blinked up into the wild eyes of an extremely put out, red-headed Queenslander. Les shook his aching head then stepped back and sunk his right foot into Muscles' solar plexus. Muscles' eyeballs bulged with pain as he tried to suck some air into his ruptured lungs when Les belted him in the face with two solid left hooks. Les pulled his fist back to cream Muscles with a short right, when he heard a voice behind him.

'I think he's had enough, Mr Gordon.'

His face a darkened mask of rage, Les spun around to find a very nervous Michael the trainer holding the remote while he kept well out of punching range. Les glared at Michael for a moment then lowered his right arm.

'You think so?' said Les.

'I'm sure so,' replied Michael.

Les turned and looked at the semi-conscious Muscles. 'You could be right,' he said. He grabbed Muscles by the front of his muscle shirt and hoisted him to his feet. 'Come on. Get up, you fuckin big sheila,' said Les. 'You're not hurt that much.'

The big man's red shirt hid a lot of the blood. But he still looked an ashen-faced wreck. Nevertheless, he wasn't getting any sympathy from Norton. Les turned Muscles towards the door, gave him a push then booted him up the backside.

'Now fuck off,' said Les. 'And don't annoy me again.'

Muscles winced at the pain, picked up a towel and dragged his sorry arse out of the gymnasium. Les turned to Michael and gave him an indifferent shrug.

'Shit! I wasn't wrong when I said I'd hate to pick a fight with you,' said Michael.

'Ahh. He just caught me in a bad mood,' answered Les.

'Why? What's up?' asked Michael.

'I've got a rotten fuckin headache, Michael,' winced Les. 'Fair dinkum. It feels like there's an Irish dance company inside my head.'

'You've got caffeine withdrawals,' smiled Michael.

'I've got what?'

'Do you drink much coffee, Mr Gordon?'

Les looked at Michael for a moment. 'Yeah. Gallons,' he replied honestly.

'That's what it is.'

'But it's only been a day or so since I had a cup of coffee,' said Les.

'That's all it takes, Mr Gordon. Now your body's getting rid of all the toxins. I hate to tell you this, but it'll get worse before it gets better.'

'Shit!'

Michael handed Les the remote then followed him back to the walking machine. Les placed the remote on the panel before he got back on and started striding out the kilometres again.

'The nurse won't be in till eleven,' said Michael. 'But you can get some Nurofen at the store in the lobby.'

'I can?' said Les. 'Thank Christ for that.'

'I've never had caffeine withdrawals because I don't drink coffee,' said Michael. 'But I know it can be pretty bad.'

'You better bloody believe it,' said Les, his head throbbing with every step. 'Hey, Michael. Do you know who that big goose in the red top was?'

'Yeah, Kendrick. He only comes here to use the gym. But because he's a friend of the manager, he likes to push his weight around. Between you and me, Mr Gordon, he's a PUMA.'

'A Puma?'

'Yeah. A Pumped Up Musclebound Arsehole.'

'I like it,' chuckled Les. 'Hey, Michael,' he asked, seriously. 'Did you see what happened?'

'Yeah. I just came out of the change room when I saw him run down and drag you off the machine then shove you up against the mirrors.'

'You want to be in my next movie, Michael?'

'You bet I do.'

'Okay,' said Les. 'Well just in case Steve Steroid tries to charge me with assault, I'm going to front the boss and tell him what happened. Will you back me up, if I need a witness?'

'Sure. Not a problem.'

'Thanks.'

Michael looked down as a pager bipped on his waist. 'I have to go, Mr Gordon. They want me in the pool.'

'Righto, Michael. See you later.'

Les watched Michael hurry out the door then turned back to the TV sets just as Leslie Nielsen got flattened with a bedpan.

Les finished his walk under the hour and didn't bother with any more exercise; the thought of doing even one sit-up made him feel his head would burst open like a dropped rockmelon. He gulped down some water, got his towel and walked up to the outdoor pool. There was no one there again and this suited Les because after kicking his trainers off, he fell straight in, clothes and all.

The water was just as refreshing as before, but did nothing for Norton's headache. He flopped around for a while then got out, wrung the water from his training gear and with a towel wrapped round him, trudged back to his villa.

After hanging his wet gear out on the balcony, Les changed into a pair of denim shorts and a black *Two Fat Ladies* T-shirt. I don't know about food, he thought, as he slipped into his thongs, but I can't wait to get some Nurofen into me. And I'll have to sort out that drama in the gymnasium with the manager too. But first I need one or two words. Les opened his book of mystery stories to 'The Knights of the Silver Dagger' by Ashton Wolfe. Here they are, he smiled. I think I can remember all that. Les closed his book and walked up to the foyer.

There was no one in the gift shop and Les had no trouble finding the Nurofen. He took them over to the front desk where Karla gave him a warm smile.

'Good morning, Mr Gordon,' she said. 'How are you today?'

'Yeah, great,' winced Les, trying his best to return Karla's smile. 'Could you charge these to my room, please?'

'Certainly, Mr Gordon,' replied Karla, her smile turning into a knowing one.

'And I'd like to see the manager, Mr Reid, too, if I could?'

Just as Les said that, the manager appeared from the corridor and came up to the desk wearing another crisp white shirt.

'Mr Gordon,' he said seriously. 'I was hoping to see you.'

'And I you, sir,' replied Les, giving what he could see of the manager a haughty once up and down. 'Earlier this morning, Mr Reid, I was assaulted in the gymnasium by a footpad.'

'A footpad?'

'Yes. A ruffian. A curmudgeon of the most bedizened asperity. And the person in question was not even a guest here.'

The manager blinked at Les. 'If the person you're referring to is who I think it is, Mr Gordon, he left the nurse's office earlier with a broken nose, two black eyes, a badly bruised sternum and a limp.'

'Indeed, sir,' replied Les. 'Only because when the blackguard had me by the throat, I managed to slip beneath the scoundrel's grasp and, using my body as a pivot, was able to fling the villian against a stack of weights. Whereupon I was able to catch my breath until the timely arrival of Michael. I daresay if it had not been for him, my assailant would still be throttling me. Michael, I might add, is an extremely viligant young lad who saw the whole unseemly incident.' Les took a deep breath and paused for effect. 'I might also add,' he said solemnly, 'the violent assault upon my person was all over a remote control. Which was not even in my possession at the time of the attack.'

The manager blinked at Les. 'I don't quite ...'

'Mr Reid,' interjected Les. 'I don't know what kind of establishment you're running here, but since my arrival, I have been confronted by a dead body. Questioned obdurately by the local constabulary. And assaulted by ne'er-do-wells of intemperate volition. At this stage I do not wish to take the matter further. But in the future, may I suggest you lift your game.' Les gave the manager another withering once up and down. 'And now if you will excuse me, sir, I wish to breakfast.' Les turned on his heel and strode over to the dining room. Jesus, I'm good, he told himself. Bloody good. And why wouldn't I be? I'm a di-recht-orrh.

The dining room was emptying out; Les found a nice table and sat down. The first thing he did was tear open the packet of Nurofen, pour himself a glass of water and take six. I'll see how they go first, thought Les, then I'll take another six. He looked up as Sandra placed a glass of fruit cocktail on the table.

'Good morning, Mr Gordon,' she smiled, noticing the painkillers sitting on the table. 'How are you this morning?'

'Sandra,' said Les, beckoning her a little closer. 'I'll give you five hundred dollars to drive into Cessnock and bring me back a flat white. You can take my car.'

Sandra shook her head. 'I'm sorry, Mr Gordon. I can't do that.'

'I'll make it a thousand dollars,' pleaded Les. 'It doesn't even have to be from a coffee shop. Go into a motel and just get me a sachet of Nescafé. Even a cheap, generic brand will do. I don't care.'

'Drink plenty of water, Mr Gordon. And eat some bananas. I'll be back when you're ready to order.'

'Thanks,' said Les.

The salad bar was open again, only this time it was full of beautiful fresh fruit, cereals, Bircher Muesli and jugs of low-fat milk. Les filled a bowl with Bircher Muesli, slices of fruit and a dollop of fruit compote, then drowned the lot with soya milk. While he was organising his cereal, he noticed a dark-haired girl next to him wearing a white T-shirt and black shorts. She had soft brown eyes set in an attractive face, but looked as if she'd been out all night drinking cheap wine.

'You look how I feel,' said Les.

'Then you must feel like shit,' replied the girl.

'What would you do for a cappuccino right now?' Les asked her.

'For a cappuccino. Bun a first-grade rugby league team.'

'What about a double-shot latte and some almond biscotti?'

'Two first-grade rugby league teams. And I'd give Frankenstein a blow job.'

'I've got a packet of Nurofen back at my table.'

The girl grabbed Les by the front of his T-shirt. 'Did you say Nurofen?'

Les nodded her a smile. 'Care to join me for breakfast?"

'You got me, handsome. Where's your table?'

The girl followed Les back to his table and they both sat down. Les slid the packet of Nurofen across to her then watched as she ripped four out and gobbled them down faster than he did.

'They're good, these caffeine withdrawals, aren't they?' said Les. 'I got about an hour's sleep last night.'

'I don't think I even got that,' the girl replied.

'You drink much coffee?'

'Drink much coffee? I live in Leichhardt. There's a bloody coffee shop on every corner.'

'I live in Bondi,' said Les. 'It's even worse.'

'I never knew before,' mumbled the girl through a mouthful of Bircher Muesli.

'No. Me either,' said Les, through a sad smile. 'So what's your name? If you don't mind me asking?'

'Estelle. What's yours?'

Estelle was a graphic designer and shared a house she was paying off with a schoolteacher named Ray, who had a girlfriend in the police force. Estelle's family lived at Nambucca Heads where she had two brothers, both carpenters. Estelle had always promised herself a week at Opal Springs. And when she got an unexpected bonus at work, she booked herself in. She jokingly now wished she hadn't. But knew it would all work out for the best at the end. Les told her he was a country boy from Queensland, owned a house at Bondi, then gave her a line of bullshit about being a film director. Thankfully Estelle wasn't all that impressed and changed the subject.

'Is that right you found Alexander Holden's body?' she said.

'Yeah,' nodded Les. 'Sprawled out on the road like a dead cane toad.'

'That must have been awful.'

'I dunno,' shrugged Les. 'He just looked the same as he did on TV. Except his mouth was open and nothing was coming out.'

'That'd be a change,' laughed Estelle.

Les finished a mouthful of Bircher Muesli. 'Did you see much of him while you were here, Estelle?' asked Les.

Estelle shook her head. 'No. I haven't been here that long. But would you like a bit of gossip, Len?'

'I'd love a bit of gossip, Estelle,' answered Les.

'You see the woman at the table over there wearing an apple green tracksuit?'

Les discreetly moved his gaze to where Estelle indicated. Sitting opposite two others was a toothy, buxom brunette with her hair held in place by a red Alice band. She was enjoying a cup of herb tea and laughing away as if she didn't have a care in the world.

'Yeah,' nodded Les.

'Holden was bonking her something ferocious.'

'Fair dinkum? The brazen hussy,' said Les.

'I know. Disgraceful, isn't it,' smiled Estelle. 'Then she gave him his marching orders.'

'She give him the arse?' said Les.

'Yes. And evidently it didn't go over too well, either,' Estelle said quietly. 'She didn't just prick his ego. She stuck a bayonet in it.'

'Go on,' said Les. 'What's her name?'

'Nerine Lushnikof. Her huband's a cardiologist on the North Shore.'

'A man after my own heart,' said Les, taking another look at the woman in the green tracksuit.

Estelle finished her cereal and looked at her watch. 'Shit! I have to make a move, Len. I've got yoga in ten minutes.'

'Go for your life,' said Les. 'If I stood on my head right now, it'd explode.'

Estelle stood up. 'Thanks for the Nurofen. You may have just saved my life.'

'Anytime.'

Estelle looked at Les for a moment. 'What are you doing tonight?'

'I don't know,' shrugged Les. 'They got a karaoke bar in here? Or a rave? I'm always up for a disco biscuit and non-stop techno.'

'Give me a ring. I'm in room sixty. We might get together and watch a DVD or something.'

'Okay,' said Les. 'Sounds good.'

'See you then.' Estelle ran a serviette across her mouth and left the dining room.

Well there you go, Les Norton the evil drug pusher. Taking advantage of another poor young woman's craving. Les finished his cereal and was looking at the menu when Sandra hovered at the edge of the table.

'I'll have free-range poached eggs on organic rye toast, please,' said Les.

'Thank you, Mr Gordon.'

The Nurofen cut in just after Les finished his poached eggs and was trying to force down a cup of herb tea that looked like a racehorse's urine sample. The pills didn't blot out the pain completely. But compared to how Les felt before, it was bliss. What I might do now, Les told himself, is go back to my room and put my head down for an hour. Les took one last sip of herb tea and left the dining room.

Walking past the study, Les noticed the morning papers on the marble table. He went in to find only the *Financial Review* and the *Sydney Morning Herald*. Shit, frowned Les. How am I going to find out what's happening to Staria? This is bad. He looked at the front page of the *Herald* and on one side was a photo of Alexander Holden next to the headline: MOTIVATIONAL GURU KILLED IN TRAGIC ACCIDENT AT HEALTH RETREAT. Les perused the front page then picked up the paper to keep as a souvenir. He was walking away when he noticed the writers in residence seated in front of the bookshelves. They were dressed much the same as before and scribbling into large notebooks. They saw Les and quickly made out they didn't. Les looked at them, then stopped and did a superbly executed double-take before turning to the young writer with the dark hair.

'Excuse me,' said Les. 'You're not Benson Gritt the author, are you?'

The man looked up at Les. 'Yeah, that's right,' he said.

'A friend just bought me your latest book for my birthday.' Les looked quizzically at Benson and clicked his fingers.

'*Rat Sandwich*,' said Benson.

Les nodded emphatically. 'Yes. That's it.'

'Had your friend read it?'

'Of course,' replied Les. 'She said it was very confronting, yet still managed to maintain its existential complexity. I'm looking forward to reading it.'

Benson stared at Les a little admonished while the other writers stared daggers at Benson for getting recognition instead of them. 'Thanks,' said Benson.

Les looked at his watch. 'I have to go. But we must catch up.'

'Yeah. Okay.'

Les pushed open the glass door alongside the pond then ambled casually along the passageway past the Wellness Centre. As he followed the path to his villa, Les glanced up at the clear blue sky. I know, boss. I know. Someday all my lies are going to catch up with me. But it is fun.

Back at his villa, Les picked up his copy of *MP* and made himself comfortable on the bed to have a read then catch up on some glorious, relatively pain-free sleep. He'd just got to the part where Michael Petersen and Nat Young were getting into a fat spliff in the Narrabeen car park when this awful racket started up from directly beneath his balcony.

'What the fuck?'

Les walked over and found two plumbers had pulled up in an old white ute, with the radio on some FM station blaring a totally inane morning show featuring three idiots all yelling over the top of each other trying to be funny. With this in the background, the two plumbers were now hammering and sawing air-conditioning ducts for the villa next door. Les stared down at them and fumed. Well I can forget fuckin sleep, he cursed silently. So I may as well do something. He threw down his book, looked at his watch and picked up the day's activities sheet. There's a deep water running class in five minutes. If I get my finger out I should make it in time. Still cursing the two plumbers, Les changed into his Speedos and headed for the indoor pool.

When he got there, Les was surprised to find the only other person in the pool was Michael wearing a remote microphone on his head.

'Michael,' said Les. 'I'm here for the underwater running. Where is everybody? I'm not too late, am I?'

'No. You're it, Mr Gordon,' said Michael.

'Ohh.' Les smiled. 'Well, it looks like I've got my own personal trainer.'

'You sure have.'

Les dropped his towel on a seat and got down to his Speedos. 'Hey. I saw the boss.'

'Yeah. He told me. You spun him out.'

'I had to drop your name. I hope you don't mind?'

'No. That's okay. I just told him what I saw. But I didn't tell him you kicked Kendrick in the stomach. Or up the backside.'

Les gave Michael a pat on the shoulder. 'You're a good man, Michael. We'll make a movie star out of you yet.'

'Thanks.' Michael clapped his hands. 'Okay, Mr Gordon. You want to get in the pool and we'll get started.'

'Righto. And Michael. You can call me Len.'

'All right, Len.'

Les flopped into the shallow end of the pool and got good and wet. When he surfaced, Michael had the remote switched on and some disco music pumping. Michael said something into the mike, but between the remote mike and the music, it was just a blurry echo bouncing off the glass walls.

'Hey, Michael,' said Les. 'There's only the two of us in here. You're not going to need the microphone. And you want to piss that music off too?'

'Suits me, Len,' said Michael. 'I've heard it a million times.'

Michael stopped the music, then put Les through a routine of underwater walking, running, star jumps, shadow boxing and other aerobic exercises. He then threw Les a noodle — a long, thin float — and got him to do the same things with the noodle wrapped around him. Les was fit. But he was surprised how much underwater swimming got you pumped. After forty-five minutes, Michael got Les going flat out for two minutes non-stop and when they finished, oily sweat was running down Norton's face forming a thin slick on the water.

'Okay, Len,' said Michael, checking his watch. 'That'll do you.'

'Shit,' puffed Les. 'This is the first time I've tried this. It's harder than you think.'

'You got it easy,' said Michael. 'You should be here when there's a dozen or more people in the pool, all bumping into each other.'

'Yeah. I can imagine.' Les floated around for a moment then dragged himself out of the water and got his towel.

'How's your head feel now?' asked Michael.

'Still aching a bit. But it's a lot better, thanks,' Les smiled. 'I think the half a packet of Nurofen with my breakfast helped.'

'Keep drinking plenty of water, Len.' The beeper on Michael's shorts went off. 'Shit! I have to go again, Mr Gordon. They want me at reception.'

'Righto, Michael. See you later. And thanks.'

'No problem.'

Les watched Michael disappear out of the pool, had three paper cups of water while he towelled off, then walked back to his villa.

When he got inside, Les was delighted to find the plumbers had gone. He got a bottle of Mount Franklin from the fridge, drank some then lay back down on the bed. Ohh yes, he smiled. Peace and quiet. Beautiful. Les closed his eyes and started to relax when the phone rang next to the bed.

'Ohh, shit!' Les picked up the phone. 'Hello,' he said, flatly.

'What the fuck's going on? Fair dinkum. I can't send you anywhere.'

'Warren?'

'Who else?'

'Shit!'

'So what's going on up there, Ugly? Holden's death was all over the news last night and the papers this morning. What have you done this time, you big goose?'

'Warren,' said Les. 'You are not going to believe this.'

Les told Warren everything. Everything except the fight in the gymnasium and spreading a rumour there'd been a murder.

'Fuck me!' said Warren. 'That's unbelievable.'

'Yeah,' agreed Les. 'It could only happen to me. But how lucky was I? Bumbles was a mate of the cop who pinched me for belting those hoons. Otherwise I'd've been out of here on my arse. And probably bunged up in the local nick trying to get bail.'

'I still can't believe it,' said Warren. 'You found Holden's body. Wait till I tell Clover. She'll faint.'

'Yeah. I can just imagine,' said Les.

'So how's the Len Gordon film director thing going?' asked Warren.

'Ohh, mate. Like a charm. They're giving me a-la-carte treatment. I got sheilas hanging off me like chokos. I can't go wrong.'

'God. I've created a monster,' sighed Warren.

'No,' said Les. 'You've created a fill-um di-recht-orrh.'

'You couldn't direct dodgem cars, you dill.'

'Thanks, cunt.' Les sat up on the edge of the bed and got his water. 'Hey. I'll tell you something,

Warren. You reckon they didn't hate Alexander Holden up here.'

'They did?'

'Yeah. He went over like rabies in a guide dogs' home.' Les told Warren the things he'd found out about Alexander Holden. 'And that's only since yesterday. I reckon there'll be heaps more.'

'Yeah, well, why wouldn't they hate him?' said Warren. 'He was a dropkick.'

'How do you know?' said Les. 'You never said anything to me. I just couldn't cop him on TV.'

'Ohh, he ripped people off. Sent people broke with his motivational bullshit. I know two people who were in business and paid a bomb for his advice. Now one's working on the council. The other's serving coffee.'

'Don't mention coffee.'

'You've watched his show. You know the bloke comes on, says he's the lead singer in a band called Painted Rainbow. And they owe all their success to Alexander Holden.'

'Yeah. I think so,' said Les.

'He's an Australian. The band broke up years ago and ended up half a million dollars in debt. The bloke hung himself in Chicago.'

'Fair dinkum?'

'That Kiwi racing driver who disappeared owing two million dollars? He was another one took Holden's advice.'

'How come Holden kept getting away with it?' asked Les.

'You know the old saying, dude. There's a mug born every minute. And Holden found plenty in America. You know what Seppos are like. They'll believe anything if they think it'll improve their lives or their mind. Look at all those weird Yank Bible bashers on TV.'

'And Alex baby was their Jesus and Gandhi rolled into one. Their guru.'

'That,' agreed Warren. 'Plus some people did actually kick a goal after listening to his waffle. But from their own ability. They just didn't know it and they think it was him.'

'Yeah,' said Les. 'I wonder why he went out of his way to get so many people offside while he was up here?'

'That was his real nature. That smiling little Pom on TV was just part of the image he conjured up.'

'Like advertising, Woz,' smiled Les.

'Exactly. You don't think half the crap you see advertised on TV is the same when you go to buy it, do you?'

'No,' said Les. 'You left a shining example on the table at home. You shit of a thing. I shoved it out the back.'

'Good on you. Give it a few hours to age.'

'I just hope it doesn't blow up and burn the house down.'

'Me too,' said Warren. 'There's two bags of pot in my wardrobe. So apart from the drama with Holden, everything's all right up there?'

'Mate, I'm drying out at the moment. But the place is unreal. I can't thank you enough for the gig, Woz.'

'No worries. Okay. Well, I got to go. I'll see you when you get back, Ugly. Try not to bash anybody.'

'No chance of that,' said Les. 'See you when I get home.'

Les hung up and lay back on the bed. There's some more suspects in the mysterious death of Alexander Holden, he mused. Maybe someone here is one of Holden's old customers and done their arse. But if someone here did kill him, how did they do it? They couldn't pick the gate up and hit him on the head with it. Or pick the fat little turd up off his bike. Les shook his head. The plot gets thicker and thinner at the same time. Maybe tomorrow I'll go down and check out the alleged crime scene. Les got his copy of *MP* from where he left it and had another read.

Les got to the part where MP sent his surfboard factory broke when he dozed off. Time passed. Les blinked his eyes open and looked at his watch.

'Shit! I'd better make a move or I'll miss lunch.'

Les splashed some water on his face, dropped another two Nurofen, then changed into his Levi's shorts and T-shirt and headed for the dining room.

The writers in residence were ensconced in the library as Les walked past. This time Benson Gritt caught his eye, and Les nodded back. The dining room was emptying out. Les found a table, had a quick look at the menu, then went to the salad bar and loaded a plate with shaved fennel and tomato and wholemeal pasta and pinenuts, then sloshed everything with roasted capsicum and dijon dressing. This went down easy. So easy, Les backed up for more. Sandra placed a pineapple drink on the table and asked how his headache was. Les said it was much better and ordered ginger and chilli stir-fried snapper with Asian vegetables and brown rice for a main. This too was delicious and Les mopped his plate with a small slice of rye bread covered in hummus. He managed to get a cup of herb tea down. But would have sold his soul for a piccolo. Contented and feeling much better than earlier in the day, Les looked at his watch. He had plenty of time before his lymphatic massage. Why not call in on the writers in residence?

They were still seated in the library, earnestly scribbling down notes, when Les approached them. Benson Gritt looked up as Les smiled and offered his hand.

'Benson,' said Les. 'I just thought I'd have a quick word. I've always wanted to meet you. I'm Leonard Gordon. The fill-um di-recht-torrh.'

'Hey. How are you doin?' Benson shook Norton's hand.

The other writers stopped scribbling and showed interest. Les turned to the older man.

'I know your face,' said Les.

'Tobias Monk.'

'Of course.' Les shook his hand. 'You had the book ...?'

'*Chained to Destiny.*'

'That's the one,' nodded Les.

'It should have won a literary award,' Tobias Monk said sourly. 'But the judges were against talent that year.'

'They always are,' sympathised Les. 'And you're ...?'

'Danica Bloomfield.'

'Of course,' said Les, shaking the blonde's hand. 'I saw you on *A Current Affair*.'

'It was the *Midday Show*,' said Danica.

'Same horse. Different jockey,' smiled Les. 'And you're ...?'

'Harriet Sutton.'

'The Adelaide Writers' Festival,' said Les, shaking the brunette's hand. 'Two years ago. I heard you speak.'

'It was the Melbourne Writers' Festival, actually,' Harriet Sutton said impassively. 'Last year.'

Les shook his head. 'You'll have to forgive me. I've been so busy lately. I simply lose track. And ... what was the book again?'

'*The Fruits of My Labia*.'

'That's the one,' beamed Les. 'It got marvellous reviews. A dark sojourn with many issues, one critic described it.'

'I don't remember that one,' said Harriet.

'You'd get so many reviews, I imagine you'd lose track,' beamed Les. 'If you don't mind me asking, what's so much talent doing under one roof?' Les nodded to a big white lounge chair. 'Do you mind if I sit down?'

'Not at all,' said Danica.

Les made himself comfortable and smiled at the writers as if he was flattered to be in their company. 'So …?'

Tobias Monk spoke. 'We've been engaged by a leading magazine, in conjunction with the resort, to present our views on Opal Springs.'

'From four different perspectives,' said Harriet.

'That should be interesting,' said Les. 'Enjoyable, too, I would imagine.'

'Are you kidding?' said Danica. 'There's no booze. No coffee.'

'If they catch you with a cigarette, they throw you out,' hissed Harriet.

'The food, if you can call it that, is abominable,' moaned Tobias. 'You'd think they could at least barbecue a few sausages or something for invited guests.'

'All I want is a can of VB,' said Benson.

'Why don't you just drive down to Cessnock?' asked Les.

'We've got no cars,' said Tobias Monk.

'We were driven here in a van,' muttered Danica. 'Like bloody prisoners.'

Les nodded sagely. 'I feel your pain,' he said. 'So how long have you been here?'

'Since last Saturday,' said Tobias. 'We leave next weekend.'

'And it can't come quick enough,' added Danica.

'Fair enough,' said Les easily. Christ! Imagine the review these four lemons'll give the place. They'll make it sound like a cross between Dachau and the pub with no beer.

'And what brings you here, Leonard?' asked Benson.

'Ohh, I'm having a detox,' replied Les breezily. 'I'm also scouting out a location for a movie.'

'You're thinking of shooting a movie at Opal Springs?' said Benson.

'Possibly,' nodded Les.

'What are the names of some of your films?' asked Danica.

Les paused and gazed across the verandah. 'Ohh, *Beyond The Valley. A Window to the Soul. The Copper Curtain.*'

'I don't remember seeing any of those,' Harriet said, over her glasses.

'No. We had them dubbed and sold them on the European market,' replied Les. 'Mainly in France. There's a big market for quality Australian drama over there.'

'Right,' Harriet said slowly.

'But who wants to talk about my films,' said Les. 'And, to be honest, I've been shooting TV commercials for the last eighteen months.'

'I believe that's very lucrative,' said Tobias.

'It helps to pay the bills,' said Les. He ran his eyes over the four writers. 'I imagine you people would know I was the one that found Alexander Holden's body.'

The mention of Holden's name swept over the writers in residence like a blast of cold air coming in from Antarctica.

'Yes. So I believe,' said Danica impassively.

'Lucky you,' muttered Benson.

'Well, I'll let you in on a little secret,' said Les. 'When I was questioned by the police, they gave me the impression that they think he was murdered.'

'Murdered?' the writers chorused.

'So they seem to think,' nodded Les.

'Huh. That wouldn't bloody . . .' Tobias stopped short.

'Dear me,' said Harriet Sutton, her voice dripping with sarcasm. 'The tragedy of Holden's untimely demise gets sadder all the time.'

'Which means it's possible,' continued Les, 'there's a murderer on the loose at Opal Springs. Which also means, not a bad idea for a book and a movie.'

Danica batted her eyelids. 'What an interesting concept. I could call it *The Murdered Motivator*.'

'What about *Motivational Murder*?' said Harriet.

'Hey. Not bad,' said Les.

'How about *Bed Bugs and Bircher Muesli*?' suggested Benson.

'Good. Good,' said Les.

'I'd have to think on it for a while,' pontificated Tobias.

'Do that,' said Les. 'Anyway,' he continued. 'Why don't you kick it around between you? I'm always open to ideas.' Les dropped his voice. 'And keep an eye out. See if you can spot a potential murderer.'

'I might just do that,' Benson said thoughtfully.

Les looked at his watch. 'I have to go,' he said, rising to his feet. 'I'm having a Cleopatra body wrap in fifteen minutes.'

'I'd love one of those,' sighed Danica.

'Ladies. Gentlemen. It's been an absolute pleasure,' said Les. 'Possibly we can continue our conversation this evening after dinner.'

'Yeah. I'd dig that,' said Benson.

'That would be lovely,' agreed Danica.

'Until then.' Les gave a tiny bow and a scrape and exited the library.

Christ! What a bunch of whingers, thought Les as he strode across the grass back to his villa.

Everything's on the house. They're getting paid for the gig. This'd be a beautiful quiet place if you were a writer. And they're still complaining. The blonde didn't seem too bad. But I read something about that Monk bloke. They reckon he's a bit up himself and he couldn't write a shopping list. I did notice one thing though, concluded Les, as soon as I mentioned Alexander Holden, they all spewed.

Back in his villa, Les got a bottle of mineral water from the fridge and took it out on the balcony. He had plenty of time before his massage and he didn't feel like reading. He went back inside and picked up the activities sheet. There was a fitness ball class in fifteen minutes. Why don't I give that a lash? Les finished his bottle of Mount Franklin and dropped the empty in the kitchen-tidy. What's the betting I find someone else who hates Alexander Holden? The gym gear he wore earlier in the morning was still wet, so Les changed into a spare set and headed for the Wellness Centre.

There were six women on the badminton court when Les got there, all standing in front of a young brunette instructor sitting on a fitness ball. The women were all shapes and sizes, wearing different types of gym gear and trainers.

The instructor had a perfect figure under a white midriff top, with a heartbreak arse tucked into a tiny pair of skin-tight black lycra shorts, and the way she was sitting on the fitness ball with her legs apart gave Les more heart fibrillations.

'Hello,' said the girl. 'I'm Antoinette. If you would all like to get a fitness ball and a mat from the corner, we'll get started.'

Being the only bloke, Les felt a little self-conscious. But he did as he was told and joined the semi-circle of women seated on their fitness balls facing Antoinette.

'All right. The fitness ball is for your core muscles,' she said, patting her perfect little six-pack stomach. 'And all movements should be slow and controlled. We'll start with an abdominal crunch. Now lower your back onto the ball with your hands behind your head, your feet firmly on the floor and your knees at ninety degrees.'

Along with the others, Les did as he was instructed, trying his best not to wobble all over the place. Les had seen fitness balls before but never bothered with them. If he wanted to keep his abdominal muscles hard he'd do hundreds of sit-ups and crunches, then he and Billy would slam medicine balls into each other's stomachs. But as Antoinette ran them through double arm raises, oblique crunches and diamond hip lifts, Les could feel the tension on his torso and realised fitness balls weren't just for women.

'You going all right over there, Len?' asked Antoinette, noticing the sweat and strain on Norton's face.

'Yeah, not bad,' grunted Les.

Actually, Les was having a horrible time. He kept wobbling all over the place, because instead of concentrating on the exercises he couldn't keep his eyes off Antoinette's unbelievable arse. Also, the chilli and ginger fish he had for lunch kept coming through and Les knew if he didn't get rid of the gigantic hot fart building up inside him before much longer, he'd end up with a double hernia. They finished with a double arm raise with leg extension and Les thanked the almighty, because if the session had gone much longer he would have either attacked Antoinette or exploded.

'Thank you, everybody,' said Antoinette. 'You went well. Now would you mind placing the fitness balls and mats back where you got them.'

Les didn't mind one bit. Trying his best to stand straight, he strode across the badminton court, dumped the ball and mat in a corner then double-timed it through the gymnasium door straight into the change room, where Michael was stacking towels on a bench.

'Hello, Len,' he said pleasantly.

'G'day,' Les replied bluntly and let rip a fart that went for at least five seconds and almost brought the walls down.

'Holy shit!' exclaimed Michael.

'Almost, Michael,' replied Les, his face spread with relief. 'But sometimes a man's just gotta do what a man's just gotta do. And better you copped it than the women in the fitness ball class.' He squeezed out another small one then winked at Michael. 'See you, mate.'

Michael sniffed the air. 'Yeah. See you.'

Les left Michael to it and headed for the gymnasium door. The last thing he heard above the sound coming from the TV sets was Michael coughing and gagging his way out of the change room.

All the straining had brought Norton's headache on again, and back at his villa he opened a bottle of mineral water and dropped another two Nurofen. After they went down, Les looked at his watch and found it was time for his lymphatic massage. He finished the bottle and without bothering to change, headed for the Healing Centre.

The same girl was behind the desk. Les told her why he was there and was asked to take a seat and 'Harold' would be with him shortly. There was only one other woman in there, a blonde in a white robe. Les smiled at her as best he could then sat down and massaged his temples while he listened to the celestial music drifting down from the ceiling. Before long a tall man in black with dark curly hair and smiling eyes came up to him.

'Hello,' he said, offering his hand. 'I'm Harold. I'm your masseur.'

'Hello, Harold,' said Les, shaking the man's hand.

'Would you follow me, please?'

'Righto.'

Les followed Harold to another room at the side that was brighter than before and had little in it except for some towels, a couple of acupressure charts on the wall, a chair and a massage table.

'You can leave your clothes on, Mr Gordon,' said Harold. 'Just lie on your back on the massage table.'

'Okay,' said Les, lying down and making himself comfortable.

'Have you ever had a lymphatic massage before?'

'No.'

'It's just a light massage that stimulates the lymphatic vessels in your body and eliminates any excess toxins.'

'Right.'

Harold started running his hands along Norton's arms, gently squeezing and prodding at the same time, and Les felt like a tube of toothpaste getting the last bits squeezed out of it. While he was massaging away, Harold gave Les a talk on the benefits of the treatment. Les closed his eyes and let it go in one ear and out the other as the Nurofen slowly started to kick in.

'And how has your stay been so far at Opal Springs, Mr Gordon?' asked Harold.

'Apart from finding Alexander Holden stone cold dead at de gate when I arrived, not bad, mon,' replied Les.

'Yes. I heard about that,' said Harold.

Aha, thought Les. I'll bet I've got another one here. 'And how did you get on with the late Alexander Holden, Harold?' asked Les. 'Did he give you any trouble?'

Harold shook his head. 'No. I didn't have much to do with him.'

'Ohh?' Les was a little surprised.

'But I can tell you a funny story, Mr Gordon, if you're interested.'

'I'm interested, Harold. Tell me.'

'Well,' said Harold. 'You know we've got four writers staying here?'

'Yeah,' answered Les. 'I've met them.'

'I worked back one night, and I went to the library to get a book. I walked in just as Alexander Holden was giving them one of the worst serves I've ever heard.'

'Fair dinkum?' said Les.

'Yes,' nodded Harold. 'They were ropeable. Especially the woman in glasses. She said she'd like to break his neck. He was lucky he left when he did.'

'It was that bad?'

Harold nodded. 'The writers were all a bit up themselves when they first arrived. But this took the wind right out of their sails.'

'So what did he say?' asked Les.

Les listened intently as Harold started on his legs and told him what was said in the library. Les could hardly believe what he was hearing.

'Shit! What a bagging,' said Les, when Harold finished.

'Yes. It was a good one all right,' said Harold. 'Evidently he had a cousin who writes a literary column for one of the weekend papers. So he had plenty of ammunition.'

Les shook his head. 'I wonder what made him rip into them like that?'

'From what I can gather, that was just his nature,' shrugged Harold.

'Nice bloke,' muttered Les.

Harold gave Norton's left leg one more rub then stopped. 'Okay, Mr Gordon, I'm finished. It might be an idea to take it easy for a while. But you should sleep well tonight. And you'll feel a lot better tomorrow.'

'I couldn't feel any worse,' said Les, resting on his elbows. 'I was up all night with bloody caffeine withdrawals.'

'I know exactly what you mean, Mr Gordon,' sympathised Harold. He exited the room leaving Les a glass of cold water on the chair.

There was no one at the desk when Les left the Healing Centre, and outside it had clouded over ominously, with the sound of distant thunder rolling in from the mountains.

Back in his villa, Les took a large notepad provided by the retreat and wrote down what Holden had said to the writers. He checked through what he'd scribbled down, then put it to one side and while he was at it, wrote out a quick statement to leave with the police on the way home, then spread himself on the lounge with a bottle of mineral water. I don't know whether I feel better or worse after that, Les pondered as he sipped some water and massaged his temples. I do know one thing. I've found another four suspects: the writers in residence.

I'm told writers can be very precious at times. Especially the carpet-eating variety in sensible shoes. And Harriet baby said she'd like to break Holden's neck. Les finished his mineral water and looked at the activities sheet. If he hurried he still had time for the evening walk. Les brought his gym gear in off the balcony, left what he had on, then wrapped another sweatband round his head and walked up to the Wellness Centre.

Michael was standing out the front with two men and a group of women that included Deliah. Michael saw Les and smiled.

'Hello, Len,' he said.

'Michael,' replied Les. 'Ready to take us all for a brisk walk in the bracing Opal Valley air?'

'I sure am,' answered Michael.

'The air up here is absolutely beautiful,' said a blonde woman wearing blue knee-length shorts and a matching top.

'It certainly is,' agreed Les. 'Michael and I were only talking about the air earlier. Weren't we, Michael?'

'We certainly were, Len,' said Michael. He looked up at the sky then checked his watch. 'Okay, everybody. Let's go. With a bit of luck we should beat the rain.'

'Do you mind if I join you again, Deliah?' Les asked her as they moved off.

'If you can keep up, Mr Gordon,' she answered, 'by all means.'

'I'll try to keep up,' said Les. 'But I'm going through caffeine withdrawals.'

'Ohh, won't you be a lot of fun.'

'Probably not,' said Les. 'And call me Len, if you like.'

The group followed Michael past the villas and through the gate, then along the path round the golf links. The wind had picked up and the temperature had dropped while directly above them thunder cracked loudly across the now leaden sky. Les had a whinge to Deliah about his headache, which was why he was a little abrupt in the dining room the night before, and told her about his massages. Deliah had tried the hot stones and agreed it was lovely. She'd had trigger point therapy the day before, which she recommended, and she'd been kept busy on the program with body pump, badminton and walking. The kids had rung her from Brisbane telling her to get home soon because Dad was a lousy cook and they were sick of eating KFC and pizzas.

'So what did you think of my little secret, Deliah?' asked Les, as a blast of thunder rattled across the sky. 'About the police thinking Holden's death might have been murder?'

'I told one woman,' said Deliah. 'And do you think she could keep her mouth shut? Now half the blessed resort knows about it.'

'Well,' Les said easily, 'you know what some women are like.' As he said that, a horrendous blast of thunder exploded above them followed by dots of rain. 'Shit, Deliah. I'm glad we've got a good weight allowance. Because I think the track's going to get a bit heavy.'

'I think you're right, Len,' said Deliah, dropping back a gear. 'Come on. Let's get cracking before it starts to pour.'

Fifty metres further on, Les was motoring to keep up with Deliah when the dots of rain turned into huge drops. Then it got heavier till finally the rain was coming down in cold, biting sheets. Next thing everybody was getting peppered with hail. A concerned Michael ran to the front then started jogging backwards as he faced everyone.

'Look. This could get dangerous out here,' he shouted above the rain and thunder. 'The clubhouse is just a bit further round the bend. If you want to wait there, I'll go and get the bus.'

'Bus,' scoffed Les. 'Deliah and I are both Queenslanders. We live for danger. Am I right, Deliah?'

'You heard the man,' said Deliah, her hair a straggled mess as she splashed on without losing a beat. 'Let's keep going.'

'Are you sure?' shouted Michael.

'Of course we're sure,' said Les. 'What do you think we are? A bunch of poofters?'

'Okay,' said Michael. 'If you say so.'

Except for a few mild curses, the conversation was very limited after that. Everybody was going flat out to get back to the resort before they either got drowned or struck by lightning. Deliah took to the wet track like Tobin Bronze so Les didn't bother trying to keep up and she was waiting at the gate when the rest of them arrived just as the rain began to clear.

'You've done it again, Deliah,' said Les. 'You're a legend.'

'I keep telling you, Len,' she smiled. 'It's all in the arms. All in the arms.'

The rain stopped as suddenly as it began and the sun appeared through a break in the clouds, shining down on the soaking wet walkers.

'Look at that,' said Michael. 'As soon as we get back it stops.'

'Yeah, there's no justice,' said Les. 'I just spent two hundred dollars on a tint and facial.'

Getting caught in the storm together formed a common bond and everybody was laughing as they walked into the resort. Les said goodbye to Deliah, and, soaked from head to toe, sloshed off to the pool, straight through the rivulets of brown water that had run down from Meditation Hill and spilled across the pathway.

The pool was empty when he got there, so Les jumped straight in, trainers and all. He splashed around for a while, treading water and duck diving, then got out and sloshed back to his villa.

After a bottle of mineral water and two more Nurofen, Les hung his wet gear on the balcony then had a shower and a shave. He changed into his Levi's jeans and a white T-shirt he bought at Torquay, then after looking at the phone thoughtfully for a few moments, picked it up, pressed zero and rang room sixty.

'Hello,' came a woman's voice.

'Estelle. It's Len. How are you?'

'Better than I was,' she replied. 'What about yourself?'

'About the same,' said Les. 'Only I just got back from the afternoon walk and we all got caught in the storm.'

'That would have been fun,' said Estelle.

'Actually, it was in a way,' said Les. 'So what's doing tonight? You still want to watch a DVD?'

'Sure. Why not?'

'Your place or mine?' asked Les.

'Your place,' suggested Estelle. 'About eight o'clock. Is that all right?'

'Okay. What do you fancy watching?'

'Get something with Robert de Niro in it. I like him.'

'Me too. You want some more drugs?' asked Les.

'Are you trying to get me hooked?'

'Yeah.'

'Okay,' said Estelle. 'More drugs it is.'

'I might need some myself,' said Les. 'I had a lymphatic massage earlier.'

'So did I,' said Estelle. 'What did you think?'

'I'm not sure. But Harold's a nice bloke.'

'Yes, isn't he.'

'Okay,' said Les, winding up the small talk. 'I'll meet my pusher at the front desk and I'll see you back here at eight.'

'See you then.'

Les hung up and looked at the phone. I might be having myself on a bit here, he thought. But I hope Estelle only wants to watch TV and have a talk. Because even though she's not a bad little sort and I was keen during the fitness ball class, for some reason I don't feel like a root right now. I feel a bit off, actually. I know what I should do. Ring Eddie and let everybody know what's going on. Les went to pick up the phone again and changed his mind. No, bugger it. I'll ring him tomorrow. Let's go and see what the bait layers are slopping up in the mess tent. Les splashed some water over his face, towelled it off and proceeded to the dining room.

He walked in to find the dining room three-quarters full. The writers in residence were at the same table; Les gave them a friendly nod and they all nodded back. Estelle and Deliah were seated amongst the others on the program. Les gave them a smile each and found a table near the verandah. As he sat down he noticed John Reid at one end of a group of diners at his table, talking to two middle-aged couples, two of whom were wearing matching shorts and shirts in garish yellow checks. The manager looked at Les briefly, Les smiled, got a nod back, then the manager resumed his conversation. Les picked up the menu and studied it for a moment before Sandra arrived with the hummus, his piece of bread and a plunger of herb tea.

'Hello, Mr Gordon,' she said pleasantly as always. 'How are you tonight?'

'Not too bad, thanks,' said Les. 'Okay, Sandra. I'll have the Thai organic beef salad with glass noodles for an entrée. The lemon myrtle free-range chicken breast with sweet potato, spinach and ricotta tart for a main. And the strawberry compote with malted hazelnut soy ice cream for dessert.'

'Thank you, Mr Gordon.' Sandra took the menu and left for the kitchen.

Les poured himself a cup of herb tea and after forcing a couple of mouthfuls down, put it aside for a glass of water. As he sipped it he picked up on a strange vibe in the dining room, especially amongst the guests on the program. Les suddenly looked up to find the manager standing at his table, wearing a crisp blue button-down shirt and matching trousers.

'Do you mind if I join you for a moment, Mr Gordon?' he asked evenly.

'Not at all, John,' replied Les.

'Thank you.' The manager pulled out a chair and sat down.

'So what can I do for you, John?' asked Les.

'Mr Gordon,' the manager said awkwardly, 'there's a rumour going round the retreat that Alexander Holden was murdered.'

Les raised his eyebrows. 'Murdered?'

'Yes,' said the manager. 'Did the police say anything to you?'

'Nothing of that nature,' replied Les. 'They seemed convinced it was an accident.'

The manager shook his head. 'Damned if I know. But I can certainly do without this. If the media get wind of it there'll be hell to pay.'

Les nodded sagely. 'I understand fully.' He drew the manager a little closer. 'But I've got a fair idea where the rumour may have originated.'

'Where? Amongst the staff?'

'No.' Les indicated with a slight nod. 'From over there. The writers in residence.'

'Them?' said the manager.

Les nodded. 'I was talking to them earlier and happened to mention the retreat would make a perfect location for a movie. A murder mystery. Starring Russell Crowe and Nicole Kidman. I'd like to fly Jack Nicholson in to play one of the chefs.'

The manager gave Les a double blink. 'You said that?'

'Yes. But only as an aside,' replied Les. 'Being writers they've undoubtedly got a little carried away. Particularly Harriet Sutton.'

'Mmmm,' mused the manager. 'I think I should have a word with them. Publicity like that would be poison.'

'I could just imagine,' agreed Les. 'But if you do say something to them, would you be so kind as to leave me out of it?'

'Of course.' The manager looked up as Sandra arrived with Norton's entrée. 'Anyway. I'll leave you to enjoy your dinner. Thanks for your help, Mr Gordon.'

'Any time at all,' smiled Les. He watched the manager return to his table and started on the entrée.

Even though Les wasn't all that keen on eating, he found the entrée delicious. He finished it and had another drink of water when Sandra arrived with his main.

'Sandra,' said Les, as she placed it on the table.

'Yes, Mr Gordon.'

'That long table where the manager's seated. Is that some special kind of table?'

'Yes,' she replied. 'That's the captain's table.'

'I see,' nodded Les. 'And those two couples

sitting there tonight. Would they happen to be Americans?'

'Yes. They arrived today,' smiled Sandra. 'How did you guess? Can you hear them from over here?'

'No. The clothes.'

'They're nice, aren't they?'

'Yeah,' said Les. 'If you want to look like a table in a Mexican restaurant.'

'I'll be back with your dessert,' said Sandra.

The main was as tasty as the entrée. Les ate it, but couldn't finish his dessert. He wiped his mouth, looked at his watch then poured himself another glass of water and strolled over to the writers' table.

'Hello,' he said. 'And how's everyone tonight?'

'Not bad I suppose,' replied Tobias Monk.

'Ohh, fair to middling,' said Danica Bloomfield.

'Yeah, all right,' nodded Benson Gritt.

'I'd kill for a cigarette,' said Harriet Sutton.

Les smiled benignly at them. 'Have you thought any more on what I said earlier?' he asked.

'Yes,' said Danica. 'This would be a great place to set a murder mystery. I've actually scribbled down a brief synopsis.'

'You'll have to show me,' said Les. 'It might make a good script.'

'I've ... ahh, come up with a few ideas myself,' said Tobias.

'What wonderful minds you must have,' smiled Les. 'And have you anyone in mind you think could be the murderer?'

As one they all turned to Lionel's table.

'Him,' said Danica.

'Yes. Him for sure,' said Harriet.

'The albino? Ohh, of course,' smiled Les. 'You've obviously all read *The Da Vinci Code*.'

There was an odd silence at the table for a moment before Tobias spoke.

'I can't believe that load of rubbish sold twenty million copies.'

'No. Me either,' agreed Benson.

'Twenty-two million I heard,' said Les.

Harriet shook her head that hard her glasses almost came off. 'It's wrong. Plain wrong.'

Les finished his glass of water and placed the glass on their table. 'Anyway. I have to go. I'll probably see you at breakfast.' He gave a tiny bow and scrape. 'Ladies. Gentlemen.' There was a muffled chorus of goodbyes as Les turned and walked over to the library.

There was a good selection of DVDs alongside

the books. Everything from *The Godfather* to *Chopper*. Les found what he was looking for that also happened to be one he hadn't seen, Robert de Niro in *City by the Sea*. Les took the cover to the desk, got the DVD, charged another packet of Nurofen to his account and walked back to the villa.

The oil lamp had been lit again when Les walked inside and a sheet of paper listing Wednesday's activities was sitting on his pillow with another saying he'd been booked in for trigger point therapy in the afternoon. Les folded them and placed them on the table in the lounge room. After setting the lights, Les used the toilet and found his mouth felt dry and bitter. He cleaned his teeth, gargled with warm water, then kicked off his trainers, switched the TV on and lay back on the bed. Ten minutes later there was a soft knock on the door. Les went over and opened it and Estelle was standing on the doorstep wearing a blue T-shirt and tight, blue, knee-length shorts.

'Did anybody follow you?' Les asked tightly, looking over her shoulder.

'No. I kept in the shadows,' replied Estelle.

'Okay. Come in. The gear's on the table.'

'Cool.'

Les closed the door and stood with his back to it for a moment as Estelle went over to the table and opened the fresh packet of Nurofen.

'Those Nuro's are really good, man,' said Les, stepping away from the door. 'But, Jesus, they make you paranoid.'

'Tell me about it,' said Estelle, washing four down with a glass of water. 'I've been freaked out all day. I'd hate to get busted in here.'

'Yeah. Especially with your flatmate taking out a cop,' said Les. 'You'd never live down the shame.'

'I'd probably lose my job too.'

Les watched Estelle put the glass in the sink. 'So how are you anyway?' he asked.

'All right, sort of. I just feel a bit … I don't know?'

'Yeah. I'm the same. But I managed to find a Robert de Niro movie.'

'You did? Which one?'

'*City by the Sea*. I haven't seen it. Have you?'

'No. But I heard it's good.'

Les pointed to the bedroom. 'Well it's in the DVD player ready to go.' He smiled at Estelle. 'I'd offer you a drink, Estelle. But it's pretty austere in here. Unless you're a Trappist monk.'

Estelle shook her head. 'That's okay. I've drunk enough mineral water today to flood Lake Eyre.

And I'd rather slash my wrists with a broken light bulb than have another cup of herb tea.'

'Then let's watch the movie.'

Les fiddled around with the remote. After a bit of hoo-hah the movie started then he fluffed the pillows and lay back on the bed next to Estelle.

The movie was deep and dark and totally devoid of laughs. But the acting was first rate and the New York settings were good. Les and Estelle were exchanging comments as they watched it when unexpectedly the phone rang.

Les turned to Estelle. 'Who the bloody hell's this?' He reached over and picked up the phone. 'Hello?'

'Mr Gordon?'

'Yeah.'

'This is the front desk. We've had a complaint from one of the other villas. Would you mind turning your TV set down?'

'Turn it down? I can hardly hear the thing myself.'

'I'm sorry, Mr Gordon. But there has been a complaint.'

'Yeah righto,' said Les reluctantly. He hung up and turned to Estelle. 'Some dill wants me to turn the TV down.'

'Christ!' said Estelle. 'They must have a bionic ear. If that's loud, I need a hearing aid.'

Les shook his head. 'Buggered if I know.'

He turned the TV down and they settled back and watched the rest of the movie. The ending was sort of all right and Les gave the movie a mental six out of ten.

'What did you think?' he asked Estelle.

'Yeah, not bad,' she replied. 'I wouldn't have liked to pay fifteen dollars to see it though.'

'No. Me either.'

Estelle wasn't wearing make-up and her hair could have done with a detail. But she still looked very inviting lying back against the pillows. Les smiled at her, she smiled back at Les, so Les bent his head down to kiss her. The instant their lips met they both recoiled, choking and gagging, then sat on the bed staring at each other in disgust.

'Ohh, Les,' said Estelle. 'I don't know how to say this but ...'

'Yuk! I think I know what you're going to say,' said Les.

'Your breath. It smells like ... like you've been using Dynamic Lifter for toothpaste.'

'Shit!'

'Exactly.' Estelle looked at Les. 'What about mine?'

Les looked back at Estelle. 'Like a vulture that's just eaten a rotten hyena.'

'Ohh my God!'

Les smiled at Estelle. 'Between the caffeine withdrawals and all the toxins coming out from our lymphatic massage, we've certainly turned out to be a couple of romantics, haven't we?'

'I think we can forget the foreplay,' said Estelle.

'I think we'd better forget the whole thing,' said Les.

'I think you're right,' agreed Estelle. 'Maybe we'll feel better tomorrow.'

'Maybe we will.' Les stopped and grinned at Estelle. 'Come here, good looking,' he said. 'Even if you do stink, I'm still going to give you a cuddle.'

'Why thank you,' said Estelle with a tiny bat of her eyelids. 'You're not bad looking yourself. You big stinker.'

With their faces turned well away from each other, they both gave each other a hug then Les helped Estelle up off the bed.

'Do you want me to walk you back to your villa?' Les asked.

'No. That's all right,' said Estelle. 'Think what the neighbours would say.'

'Yeah. We're both high on drugs too. Hey, talking about drugs. Here. Take some of these.'

Les handed Estelle six Nurofen. 'You can pay me tomorrow.'

Estelle looked at the six white pills in her hand. 'Shit. What if I haven't got the money by then?'

'That's okay. Just work the corner of Wellness and Healing till you get it.'

'Gee, thanks, Big Lennie.'

Les walked Estelle to the door and opened it. 'I want to kiss you goodnight too,' he said. 'Close your mouth. Tight. Tighter.'

Les closed his mouth tight as well and gave Estelle a quick peck on the lips. She pecked Les back then batted her eyes again and placed one hand over her chest. 'Ohh dear. Be still, my beating heart,' she breathed.

'I know,' said Les. 'I'll probably be up all night pulling myself. See you tomorrow, Estelle,' he smiled.

'See you then.' Estelle returned Norton's smile. 'And, Len, thanks. I still had a fun night.'

'Me too.' Les blew her a kiss then closed the door and Estelle disappeared along the pathway.

Well, what about that, thought Les as he got out of his clothes. I knew something was wrong with me. Estelle was the same. But what a nice girl. And there's always tomorrow. Les blew the oil lamp out then switched off the lights and climbed into bed. His last thoughts as he pushed his head into the pillows and closed his eyes were, how dare some arsehole tell me to turn my TV set down. Don't they know I'm a bloody fill-um di-rehct-torrh?

Les still had a twinge of a headache when he woke up the next morning, there were a few mild bruises on his head from the fight with Kendrick and his knee was a little sore from trying to keep up with Deliah in the thunderstorm. But compared to the day before, he felt like he'd been born again. He cleaned his teeth then put the kettle on and made a pot of herb tea. He managed to get a cup down before he was sent running to the toilet again. When he got out, he poured himself another cup and took it out on the balcony to find the clouds had gone, leaving a blue sky behind them. Les was wondering what he should do first when the phone rang. He left his tea and went to the phone.

'Hello?'

'Len. It's Estelle.' Her voice was tight and strained.

'Estelle. How are you? Is something ...?'

'Len. I won't be able to see you today. I have to leave. My parents have been in a car accident.'

'Ohh no! What happened?'

'They were coming back from Macksville, and another driver forced them off the road.'

'Shit! Are they all right? I mean ...'

'I'm not sure. They're both in Coffs Harbour Hospital.'

'Gee, Estelle. I'm really sorry. That's awful.'

'I'm just about to leave now and catch a plane in Newcastle. But I wanted to let you know. And maybe we can catch up in Sydney some time.'

'Yeah all right. Give me your phone number.' Les got a biro and they exchanged phone numbers. 'Honestly, Estelle. I don't know what to say. I just hope it's not too serious. Are they in intensive care?'

'No. I don't think so.'

'Well, at least that's something. Look, you get going,' said Les. 'And I'll be in touch.'

'Okay.'

'Goodbye, Estelle. And good luck, mate.'

'Thanks, Len.'

Les hung up the phone and stared into space. The poor little bugger. What a bastard of a thing to happen. She was nice, too. Les picked up the activities sheet, took it out on the verandah and went over it while he finished his cup of herb tea.

He'd missed the morning walk and the tai chi class on Meditation Hill. There was a boxercise class on in fifteen minutes. But knowing his luck, Les figured being in a confined space, he'd miscue and end up knocking some poor woman out. Apart from the fight, the stint on the walking machine the day before wasn't too bad. Yes, that followed by a swim and breakfast would do admirably. Les tossed the remainder of his herb tea over the balcony, got into his gym gear and headed for the Wellness Centre.

There were two women in the gym already going for it on the walking machines when Les walked in; a bottle blonde and a brunette both wearing black leotards and white headbands. Les placed his towel on the speaker box and gave the women a smile each then climbed aboard the same machine as yesterday for another six-kilometre hike along the road to nowhere. The women were watching a movie on all four TV screens, *Be Cool* with John Travolta. The ladies will get no argument from me over this one, smiled Les as he strode along. Chili Palmer is one cool dude.

Les was marching along sweating it out and quite enjoying himself when Peta walked in with two women all dressed in gym gear, much like the two other women. Les caught her eye and gave her his best film director's smile. Peta smiled back. But she wasn't as nervous as when she first saw him. She took her tracksuit top off and started putting the two women through a light workout on the weight stations. As Peta adjusted the weights and showed the two women how to work the machines, Les was surprised at how fit she looked in her white T-shirt.

Les was watching the movie absolutely fascinated at the size of the four black heavies who worked for the record company boss. One had no neck at all, another had a neck as thick as Norton's waist, and one had arms that big, it was a wonder he could bend his elbows. I doubt if I'd throw a remote control at any of these boys, thought Les. He was marching steadily on when Michael appeared out of nowhere with a vacuum cleaner strapped to his back and started vacuuming the gym. Eventually he worked his way over to Les.

'G'day, Michael,' said Les. 'How's things, mate?'

'Pretty good thanks, Len,' replied Michael.

'Shit! They get their money's worth out of you,' commented Les, nodding to the vacuum cleaner on Michael's back.

'You can say that again,' said Michael. He

switched off the vacuum cleaner to have a breather.

'So what's the story?' asked Les. 'Do they get you to do other jobs besides train people?' He nodded to the front door. 'I notice Peta's up there putting two women through their paces. But when I first arrived she was working out the front.'

'Yeah. We do pretty much what the management wants,' said Michael. 'Everything from the fitness classes to helping out in the kitchen to gardening.'

'How many trainers are there?'

'About six, on and off.'

'Right,' nodded Les as he marched along.

'So how are you feeling today, Len?' Michael asked.

'Compared to yesterday, Michael, like a two year old. These two women are lucky they're watching a movie I like, or I'd flatten both of them.'

'That's good,' smiled Michael.

'Talking about yesterday,' said Les. He gave Michael an ironic smile and told him about going back to his villa full of Nurofen to get some sleep and as soon as he settled down the two plumbers arrived on the scene. Which was how he indirectly ended up doing the underwater running class.

'Fair dinkum. All the bloody villas here. And they have to lob outside mine.'

'It would have been after ten o'clock,' said Michael.

'Why's that?'

'Because the management won't take deliveries or let tradesmen call before ten in the morning. It disturbs the guests.'

'How considerate,' said Les.

'Yep. You're like little silkworms to us,' said Michael.

'And why wouldn't we be?' winked Les.

'Exactly.' Michael started up the vacuum cleaner. 'I'd better keep going,' he said. 'I've got a bike class in fifteen minutes.'

'Okay. See you, Michael.'

Michael went back to his vacuuming. A while later the two women finished their walking and before long Peta ended the other two women's workout on the weight stations, leaving Les alone in the gym. Les kept plodding along till the movie ended and when he looked up at the clock he was surprised to find he'd been walking for an hour and a half. Pleased with his effort, Les switched off the machine then picked up his towel and wiped his face. After drinking two cups of cold water he headed for the outdoor pool.

There was no one in the pool when Les got there, so he kicked off his trainers and, still wearing his sweaty gym gear, jumped straight in the water. It felt sensational and Les flopped around till he cooled off, then got out. After a quick shower, he wrung the water from his gym gear, wrapped a towel round himself, and walked back to the villa.

By now Les was famished. He hung his wet gear on the balcony, tossed his *Two Fat Ladies* T-shirt over his Levi's shorts and left for the dining room. Outside, there was no one around except for the two same girls doing the cleaning. Les gave them a smile and a wave and continued on his happy, shiny way.

The writers in residence were ensconced in the library in much the same clothes doing much the same thing and Les gave them a cheerful smile also as he went past. The dining room was emptying out when he walked in and Les soon found a table that suited him. He then walked straight over to the salad bar and filled a bowl with Bircher Muesli, fresh fruit and anything else that took his fancy and took it back to his table. This time he had a different waitress: Valerie. A bigger girl than Sandra, with dark hair. She was just as pleasant, however, when she put Norton's fruit drink and plunger of herb tea on his table and took his order for poached eggs. While he was waiting, Les backed up for some more muesli and fruit before ripping into the two perfectly poached eggs. As an added bonus, the herb tea didn't taste like dog's piss this time and Les was able to down another half a cup before he left. On the way out he thought he might call in and say hello to the writers in residence.

'And how's everybody this morning?' he said pleasantly as he walked up to where they were seated in the library. 'Another lovely day outside. It's a wonder you're not out there getting into some of the activities.'

'No thanks,' said Danica. 'I can think of better things to do with myself than prance around in a room full of stupid women dressed up like Olivia Newton-John singing "Let's Get Physical".'

'As Duc François de La Rochefoucauld said in 1613,' intoned Tobias Monk, 'to preserve one's health by too strict a regime is in itself a tedious malady.'

'Yeah,' agreed Benson Gritt. 'Whenever I feel like exercise I lie down until the feeling passes.'

'Fair enough,' smiled Les. 'What about you, Harriet?'

'Exercise is crap,' she answered sourly. 'If you

are healthy, you don't need it. If you are sick, you shouldn't take it.'

'Well, I'm glad we cleared that up,' said Les. 'So apart from health issues, how's everything else?'

Harriet looked directly at Les. 'The manager came up to us yesterday,' she said. 'And virtually accused us of spreading a rumour that Alexander Holden was murdered.'

'Did he?' said Les. 'That's funny. He accused me of much the same thing.'

'He did?' said Danica. 'And what did you say?'

'I told him where to get off,' replied Les. He drew in closer to the others. 'I'll tell you something,' Les said quietly. 'I don't like him. All he thinks about is himself and his precious bloody resort.'

'I couldn't agree more,' said Tobias. 'Otherwise they wouldn't serve up that abysmal feculence they call food.'

'Yes. Surely a small cocktail bar wouldn't be the end of the world,' lamented Danica. 'I mean, really.'

'Well, you know what it's like,' shrugged Les. 'Some people have just got no consideration for others. My advice is to take no notice of him. He's beneath your dignity. Anyway. I have to go. I'm having an aromatic salt glow in ten minutes.'

Tobias produced a small folder of notes and offered them to Les like they were the Dead Sea Scrolls. 'I have here some notes I've put together,' he said. 'You might like to study them.'

'I'd love to look at them,' said Les. 'But after lunch when I'm more relaxed. Until then ...' Les gave everyone an oily Liberace smile and left. I dig those writers, thought Les as he went past the Wellness Centre. In fact, I'm getting to like them more and more every day.

Back in his villa, Les sprawled out on the lounge and pondered what he should do. He didn't need any more exercise for the moment so he was about to pick up a book and kick back, when he snapped his fingers. I know what I have to do. I have to ring Eddie. Les went to the bedroom, picked up the phone and dialled.

'Hello?'

'Hello, Eddie. It's Les. How's things?'

'Les. Where the fuck are you? We've been wondering what's going on.'

'Eddie,' said Les. 'You're not going to believe this.'

Les told Eddie everything that had happened since he'd left Sydney. Eddie was gobsmacked.

'Wait till I tell Price and the others,' said Eddie when Les had finished. 'They'll piss themselves.'

'It could only happen to me,' said Les.

'But what about Caccano being a prick relation of Bumbles?'

'I know,' said Les. 'It's totally bizzare.'

'And Holden was lying there when you drove in.'

'Yep. Dead as a dodo. I'm lucky I didn't drive over him.'

'Christ!'

'But you reckon they didn't hate him up here,' said Les. 'Everybody was crooked on him.'

'What's not to hate?' said Eddie. 'He was a complete dropkick.'

'Yeah? What do you know about him?'

'Only what people tell me,' said Eddie. 'But I met a bloke once had a real good restaurant in Balmain done his arse because of him.'

'He did?'

'Yeah. The last time I heard, the bloke was working in a pub somewhere in the bush or something.'

'What was his name?' asked Les.

'Ohh, Dennis, David. Something like that,' said Eddie.

'Dallas?' said Les.

'Yeah. It might have been. I can't remember.'

'All right.'

They talked a short while longer then Eddie had to go.

'So you'll be back on Saturday,' said Eddie.

'Yep. Bursting with new vim and vigour.'

'Good on you,' chuckled Eddie. 'Okay. I'll see you then.'

'See you, Eddie. Say hello to everyone for me.'

Les hung up the phone and stared across the villa. Maybe I've found another supect? Dallas the dietician. He's also a chef. And this is like working in the bush, sort of thing. Les went back to the lounge and picked up *The World's Best Mystery Stories*, turning to 'The Familiar' by J.S. Le Fanu.

After what felt like a thousand pages of drama between Captain Barton and General Montague, standing in the triumphant presence of infernal power and malignity, Les felt as if he'd been bashing himself over the head with a sand-filled doorstop.

'Holy shit!' he gasped. 'I've got to get out of here. Some of these sentences go for half a page.'

Les put the book down and picked up the activities sheet. There was another deep water running class in ten minutes. That'll do me. I could handle a swim right now. He changed into his Speedos and walked up to the indoor pool.

Michael was poolside with his portable mike on when Les arrived and this time there were ten other guests in swimming costumes and robes getting ready to jump into the water; one out of shape, balding man and nine women. Everybody recognised Les when he walked in. Les returned a few smiles as he put his things on a chair and went up to Michael.

'Looks like I've lost my personal trainer this time,' said Les.

'Looks like you have,' said Michael. 'But you'll be okay. Just watch out you don't cop a kick in the Niagras. Remember I told you it gets a bit congested when there's a mob in the pool.'

'I'll certainly be on my guard,' said Les, running his eye over the other guests.

Michael clapped his hands. 'Okay. Everybody. Let's go.' He switched on his mike then the stereo system and everyone jumped into the shallow end of the pool.

Michael was right about the congestion. Les had half an idea what to do, but some of the others didn't have a clue. They were all bumping into each other and churning up the water as Michael called out instructions over a background of disco music echoing around the pool. Les managed to keep out of harm's way, then Michael threw everyone a float. They all started doing the same routine with the floats and Les was getting a sweat up when Michael told them to wrap the floats around their necks, turn and move forward. Les turned round and found himself behind a woman with her back to him, wearing a black one piece and a white bathing cap. Les moved back to give her room, when suddenly she kicked out and her right heel slammed into his groin. Les winced and swallowed a curse along with a litre of water as the pain shot up through his stomach. He left the others and drifted motionlessly to the edge of the pool, where he slowly bobbed up and down, holding his balls with one hand and the side of the pool with the other. The woman who kicked Les saw him floating there and kept going. Michael saw the pain on Norton's face, but there wasn't much he could do. So he kept yelling instructions while Les floated around like a crippled aircraft carrier.

The session ended not long after and Michael switched off the music. 'Okay, everybody,' he said. 'That was great. You went really well. Please put your floats back against the wall.' He walked over to Les as the others got out of the pool and knelt down. 'Are you all right, Len?' he asked.

'Yeah, terrific,' grunted Les, sweat-faced with pain. 'I'll be singing falsetto for the next few days. But at least you did warn me.'

'Do you want to see the nurse?'

'What's she going to do?' Les left his float in the water and dragged himself painfully out of the pool. Then, mustering as much dignity as possible, collected his things and without saying a word, left the indoor pool wishing he could crawl back to his villa.

Inside, Les spread himself back on the lounge, put his feet up and waited for the pain to subside. That fuckin moll, he cursed silently. I wish I could remember what she looked like. I'd go and kick her fair in the snatch. Jesus, that hurt. Les closed his eyes till finally the pain began to ease. When he looked at his watch it was time for lunch. He rose from the lounge, put on his Levi's shorts and a clean white T-shirt, got his name tag then walked up to the dining room.

The dining room was full and the writers in residence were at their usual table. Les gave them a brief smile and found a table close to the verandah. He checked the menu, then went down to the salad bar and filled a plate with spiced lima beans, roasted mushrooms, grilled zucchini and flaked almonds and doused it liberally with tahini and herbed tomato dressing. Valerie brought him his bread and hummus and a plunger of herb tea and Les ordered pumpkin, spinach and tofu lasagne with tomato and fresh basil sauce for a main. He backed up at the salad bar for some mixed leaf salad with wasabi lime dressing and got that down just as his main arrived.

The lasagne was delicious and Les wiped every last smear from his plate with his piece of rye bread. He was sitting sipping a cup of herb tea when a woman came up to his table. She had dark hair swept up on her head in a loose bun, a thin nose, full lips and deep green eyes that bored into you like two power drills. A tight sleeveless blue lycra midriff top covered the top half of her full body and her neat bum was squeezed into a pair of blue knee-length shorts. There was no name tag around her smooth, elegant neck and despite a lack of make-up, she was still extremely attractive.

'Mind if I sit down?' the woman asked.

Les shook his head. 'No. Go for your life,' he answered.

The woman sat down, looked at Les and smiled. 'Look. I'm really sorry about what happened in the pool today,' she said.

Les stared at her for a moment. 'Ohh. Was that you?'

The woman nodded. 'I wanted to come over and apologise,' she said. 'But you left in a bit of a hurry.'

'Yeah. Well, I wanted to get out of there before I started telling Jesus Christ and the rest of the pool all about it.'

The woman gently shook her head. 'God! That must have hurt. I kicked out really hard.'

'Well you know what they say,' said Les. 'Only when you laugh.'

'I didn't see you laughing.' The woman smiled and offered Les a perfectly manicured hand overflowing with diamond and sapphire rings. 'I'm Vanita Raquelme.'

Les took her hand. 'Len Gordon. Nice to meet you, Vanita.'

Vanita's green eyes swept across Norton's face. 'So what brings you to Opal Springs, Len?'

'Ohh, have a bit of detox. Iron out a few lumps and bumps. What about you, Vanita?'

'Much the same. Have the treatments. Relax. Take in the music.'

'Yes. It's relaxing all right,' said Les.

'They tell me you're the person that found Alexander Holden's body.'

'That's right,' said Les.

'He wasn't a very nice man.'

'So I hear. Did you have much to do with him?'

Vanita shook her head. 'No. I just used to sit back and watch the way he spoke to people and carried on. Actually, I would have liked to have done to him what I did to you.'

Les tossed back a laugh. 'So are you on a program, Vanita?'

'No. I'm an independent guest.'

'Same here.' Les offered Vanita a cup of his herb tea and they fell into a bit of chitchat.

Vanita came from Melbourne and lived in Middle Brighton. She used to be a dancer and was married to a merchant banker. They couldn't have children. But they adopted two. Her husband drank more than he should and their marriage looked like ending in divorce. Les told her he was single, came from Queensland, lived in Bondi and gave her the usual bullshit about being a film director before changing the subject.

'How long are you here for?' Les asked Vanita.

'Till Friday,' she replied. 'What about yourself?'

'Saturday.'

'Good,' said Vanita. 'Well, why don't you meet me in the library before dinner tonight? And let me shout you a mocktail for giving you that South Melbourne uppercut earlier. They're free, but I'd still like to buy you one.'

'Okay, Vanita,' smiled Les. 'That would be nice. Thanks.'

Vanita looked at the solid gold, diamond encrusted Patek Philippe watch shining on her wrist. 'I have to go. I'm having private Pilates in ten minutes.'

'Okay. Enjoy yourself. I'll see you this evening.'

'Bye.' Vanita rose elegantly from the table and left.

Les watched as Vanita carried herself from the dining room with just the right amount of wiggle in her bum and movement in her shoulders to show she was a woman that had style and could afford to look after herself. Married or not, thought Les, I'd certainly like to play chasings with the lovely Vanita back at my villa. But I very much doubt if a toad like me would appear on Mrs Raquelme's radar. But what a lovely person to talk to. And how considerate of her, to come up and apologise for kicking me in the nuts.

Les looked at the Timex watch sitting on his wrist, that he'd bought off a wharfie for fifty bucks, and pondered what he should do. He had plenty of time before his trigger point therapy. Why not go back to the villa, take it easy, and have a read? But not J.S. Le Fanu. Les rose from the table and left. He couldn't see the writers in residence as he went past the library, which suited him for the time being.

Back in his villa, Les picked up *MP*. He got to where Sean Doherty described Michael Petersen as looking like an albino Ethiopian distance runner, when a thought occurred to him. His camera. He'd forgotten about the photos he'd taken of Alexander Holden lying at the front gate. Les put *MP* down, got the camera from his bag then turned it on and started flicking through the photos on the screen.

Looking at them, Les had no doubt the editor of some sleazy magazine would snap them up. Especially the close-up of Holden with the bruise on his forehead. But what was it that aroused his suspicions when he last looked at Holden's body before he got back in the car? Suspicions that had been compounded by all the hatred for Holden. Les twisted the camera around and looked at the photos from all angles till he felt he was imagining things. But there was one way to satisfy his mind. Take a walk down to the scene of the accident. Les put his cap and sunglasses on and with his camera in his hand, left for the stairs in the foyer.

There was no one in the driveway when Les stepped outside the front door; he turned right and followed the road as it wound its way down through the trees to the gate. Although the road was short, it was quite steep and Les figured Holden must have been some sort of weird thrill-seeker if he liked to pedal down it flat out on a mountain bike. When Les got to the bottom, there was no one around. He could glimpse the resort rising above the trees, but they were thick enough to block anyone's view from above. He stepped across to the gate expecting to see a chalk outline of Holden's body. But there was nothing. Either the rain had washed it away or cars driving out had erased it. More than likely Bumbles didn't bother and had Holden's body out straight into an ambulance. Les switched his camera on and started playing Horatio Cain.

After half an hour of comparing photos and looking around at all angles, Les was convinced he had been imagining things. There were a few scratches and a chip in the road back from a short concrete pole with a remote button on it to let yourself out. But nothing even remotely suspicious. Bumbles was right. It was an accident. Holden had simply come belting down the hill, and either his brakes had failed or he wasn't watching what he was doing, and he slammed his obnoxious little head into the gate, killing himself. If he hadn't been such a mug and worn a helmet it might have been a different story. Les clicked his camera shut and started walking back up the hill. He was halfway to the front door when another thought occurred to him. Why the fuck was he doing this? There was nothing in it for him. And if by some strange coincidence it did turn out to be murder and he knew who it was, it was highly unlikely he'd puff out his chest and make a citizen's arrest. Holden was such a turd, he'd probably shake the killer's hand. Les trudged on up to the driveway.

Back in the villa, Les put his camera away and went out on the balcony to enjoy the view and work out what to do. If he timed it right, he could have a nice relaxing swim then go straight in for his trigger point therapy. And afterwards join the others for the evening walk. Then by the time he had a scrub it would be time for mocktails in the library with the banker's wife. Followed by dinner and a quiet night at home with a DVD. Les took in his training gear, put that on over his Speedos and thongs and headed for the pool.

When he got there, Antoinette was teaching a young Asian girl how to swim. But apart from them Les had the pool to himself. The good-looking trainer remembered Les from his clumsy efforts on the fitness ball and gave him a big smile. Les sheepishly returned her smile and placed his things on a chair then found a pair of flippers that fitted. He put them on and dived into the beautiful clear water. After adjusting his goggles, Les put his face down and started cruising effortlessly up and down the pool. While he was swimming, he mulled a few things over.

Despite finding nothing at the gate, Les still thought there was half a chance Alexander Holden had been murdered. How the killer did it was another thing, but there was no shortage of people with enough motive. Tomorrow he'd get a mountain bike and ride down the hill. It would probably turn out to be another waste of time. But he'd still get some exercise and it would give him something to do. The Asian girl got out of the pool and left with Antoinette. Les backstroked two more laps then it was time for him to get out also. He towelled off, put his gear back on and followed the hallway down to the Healing Centre.

Several women wearing white robes were seated on lounge chairs when Les walked in, and the same girl in black was behind the counter. She smiled, asked Les to take a seat and said Stanley would be with him soon. Les thanked her, found a vacant lounge and settled back listening to the gentle celestial music drifting through the Wellness Centre. Before long an older man wearing a black uniform came up to him. The man had thick dark hair, a set face, carried no fat and had a handshake like a steel band tightening.

'You Len? The bloke for the massage?' he asked.

'Yeah. That's me,' replied Les.

'Follow me, mate. My name's Stan.'

'Righto, Stan.'

Les followed Stan round to a room spread with muscle charts and shelves of towels on the walls. It was thick with the smell of liniment and in the middle was a massage table. Stan pointed to the massage table.

'Drop your daks and plonk your arse on there,' he said.

'Okay.' Les did as he was told and sat on the edge of the table. Stan stood behind him.

'You got any pain there?' Stan shoved a finger like a metal rod into Norton's shoulder blades.

'Ohh, yeah,' groaned Les.

'What about here?' He clamped his hands across Norton's shoulders and dug his thumbs in.

Les nearly cried. 'Yeah,' he whimpered.

'What about your legs?'

'I got a crook right knee.'

Stan came around, lifted Norton's leg up and rotated his knee. 'Yeah,' he said. 'You got a bit of a tear in the cartilage. And you got crook tendons in your shoulders.'

'I thought I might have,' said Les.

'Righto. On your guts,' said Stan. 'And I'll see if I can sort you out.'

'Okay.' Les lay face down on the massage table and felt Stan start to rub oil into his back. 'You been working here long, Stan?' asked Les.

'Nah. I'm only fillin' in for a couple of weeks. I work out at Kurri Kurri.'

'For yourself?'

'Yeah. I used to be a miner. But I give it up to do this. The money's not as steady. But it's ten times better than being stuck down some coal mine covered in dirt and shit all week.'

'I imagine it would be.' I also imagine Stan doesn't give a stuff much about the management's silkworm policy towards the guests either, thought Les. Shit! This is going to be nice.

Stan stopped rubbing oil into Norton's back and started massaging. Stan's manner might have been a little gruff, but his strong miner's hands felt great as he pushed and probed and moved the muscles and blood around.

'You're the bloke that found Holden's body out the front, aren't you?' said Stan.

'Yeah, that's me,' said Les.

'How did you handle that?' chuckled Stan. 'I'll bet your eyes were sticking out like dogs' knackers.'

'It did come as a bit of a surprise,' agreed Les.

'Did you have a camera with you?'

'No,' lied Les.

'Ohh, bad luck. I reckon you would have got some grouse pictures.'

'Yeah. I probably would.' Les winced as Stan dug his fingers in and found a tender spot. 'Did you have much to do with Alexander Holden, Stan?' Les asked.

'No. But I give him a rub,' replied Stan.

'Yeah? How did you find him?'

'All right. He even slung me fifty bucks when I'd finished.'

'Shit! Nothing wrong with that, Stan.'

'No. He used to get bagged a lot, though. Mainly by the sheilas working here.'

'Fair dinkum.'

'Yeah. But you know what sheilas are like,' said Stan. 'Especially the ones working here.'

'They seem all right to me,' said Les.

'Nahh! They're all up themselves. If you ask me, half of them need a good root.'

Les grunted as Stan worked a finger under his shoulder blade. 'And you're not talking about ginseng either, are you, Stan?'

'No, mate. The old pork sword's the go. That and a good cock whipping. Pulls the little girlies into gear every time.'

'I must remember that, Stan,' said Les.

'Take it from me, mate,' Stan assured Les.

Les closed his eyes and half dozed off under the firm, pleasant pressure of Stan's strong hands. He told Les to lie on his back then started working on the front of his shoulders, his arms and his legs, giving his right knee extra treatment. Les lay back with his eyes closed saying nothing and trying not to yell when Stan dug his thumbs into his forearms. Finally Stan gave Les a light slap on the shoulder and stopped.

'Righto, rollicks. You're done,' he said.

Les opened his eyes. 'Ohh thanks.'

'I think I've broken up a few knots in your shoulders. And your knee should be a lot better. Just hit it with a bit of WD-40. And don't run on it for a while.'

'All right.'

'Okay, Len. If I don't see you out the front, I'll see you next time I'm looking at you.'

'See you, Stan. And thanks again.'

Stan left, closing the door behind him. Les got up and put his clothes on, and as he stood on one leg to get into his shorts, noticed his knee was almost back to normal and his shoulders were the best they'd felt in years. Well, I'll be buggered, thought Les. Young Stanley's a bloody good masseur. He's also the only bloke apart from the manager to have a good word for Alexander Holden. Les opened the door and stepped outside.

Back in his villa, Les felt pumped up and ready to go. He would have liked a run, but he decided to take Stan's advice and just go for a walk as planned. Les drank two bottles of mineral water on the balcony then went to join the others outside the Wellness Centre.

This time they were being led by a tall lean girl with frizzy brown hair poking out in a lumpy ponytail from under a baseball cap; her name tag read 'Amanda'. There were the same walkers from the thunderstorm. Les saw Deliah and walked over to her.

'Okay if I join you again, Deliah?' he asked with a smile.

'By all means Len,' she smiled back. 'Just as long as you can keep up. And for a big, fit Queenslander, you're not real good on a wet track.'

'Yeah. Well, watch out today, Deliah. I just had trigger point therapy. And I'm ready to rumble.'

'Did you get Stanley?' asked Deliah.

'Yes, it was.'

'Isn't he great?' said Deliah. 'He's just the best masseur. And hasn't he got a lovely nature?'

'Yes. You could almost say Stan's nature's gentleman,' agreed Les.

Amanda looked at her watch. 'Okay, everybody,' she said. 'Let's go.'

'Come on, Len,' said Deliah. 'It's a lovely afternoon. And today my little boots are made for walking.'

They moved off slowly. But once they were through the gate and started winding their way up and down the hills alongside the golf links, Deliah put the pace on. However, with his knee almost back to normal and his caffeine withdrawals behind him, Les felt he had a new lease of life and strode along while Deliah's stocky little arms swung up and down in perfect timing with her stocky little backside swinging from side to side. After a while Les began to see why Deliah was such a good walker. She was efficiency plus. Everything about her moved in perfect unison and she didn't waste one kilojoule of energy. Les had to admire her.

Although the pace was on, Les and Deliah still managed a bit of chitchat. What activities they'd been doing, the food at the resort. Deliah's kids were still whingeing about the food at home. All Dad fed them now was steak and eggs out of a frypan with chips from the local fish shop, covered in tomato sauce. Deliah also said that since the death of Alexander Holden, Lionel was becoming a complete pain in the arse. His surname was Bouris. And the other guests on the program were starting to call him Lionel Don't Bore Us. It also turned out he was a closet queen. And he wasn't French, he was a New Zealander. Before Les knew it they were at the end of the walk with the final hill looming up in front of them. As usual, Deliah was full of confidence.

'Come on, Len. Let's see what you're made of,' she said and dropped back a gear.

'Righto,' answered Les. 'I'll do my best.'

Les was tempted to break into a run then wait for Deliah at the gate, shining his nails on his T-shirt. Instead he fell back and let Deliah beat him by several lengths.

'You went well today, Len,' said Deliah. 'Just remember to get those arms going.'

'Yes, I know,' said Les, overdoing his puffing. 'I walk like a gorilla.'

'Not quite,' laughed Deliah. 'But close.'

The others filed through the gate then they all went their separate ways. Les had a good sweat up and went straight to the pool. This time he took his sneakers off before he jumped in.

Back in his villa, Les showered and shaved then rubbed some hemp body lotion into his face before dabbing it with Lomani Pour Homme. He ironed his Levi's shorts and tucked in a white Margaritaville T-shirt he'd bought in Florida then watched the start of the ABC news while he had another bottle of mineral water. Well, he thought, looking at his watch. I think it's time I joined Mrs Raquelme for pre-dinner mocktails in the library. And what day is it? Wednesday. I also think it's time I started putting a bit of shit on the writers in residence. Whistling cheerfully, Les dropped his empty bottle in the kitchen tidy and locked the villa.

People were eating in the dining room and there was a small crowd in the library when Les arrived at the entrance. John Reid, the manager, was in there wearing a crisp white shirt and dark trousers talking to some people and the writers in residence were standing around looking their usual literary selves. Except this evening Benson Gritt was wearing a wrinkled brown shirt that hadn't seen a washing machine or an iron since Thomas Edison discovered electricity. The marble table was covered with champagne glasses full of a white, frothy drink and Vanita was standing over the other side, dressed in a burgundy Dolce & Gabbana leisure suit. Her make-up was perfect and her beautifully groomed hair was parted in the middle, allowing it to fall around her shoulders in a swirl of shining onyx. She'd tastefully sprinkled herself with expensive bling-bling, and standing there in her leisure suit, Vanita made Missy Elliott look like Condoleezza Rice. She was talking to a balding, wizened little man with a paunch who was wearing a plain black tracksuit. Vanita caught Norton's eye and smiled an invitation to join her. The writers looked at Les, hoping he might join them; Les gave the writers a smile and walked straight up to Vanita. If Vanita looked beautiful from across the room, up close she was stunning.

'Len,' she said, letting her deep green eyes do all the talking. 'How are you?'

'Real good thanks, Vanita,' replied Les. 'How's yourself?'

'I'm absolutely tip top, thank you. Ohh, Len, this is Max.'

'Hello, Max,' smiled Les.

'Len. How are you? You look great.' Max's hand slid into Norton's like a dead goldfish.

'I'm good thanks, Max,' said Les.

'Max is here with his wife,' said Vanita. 'That's her over there in the blue tracksuit.'

Les turned around. A female version of Max with awful make-up and a thinning jet-black rinse was talking to some people near the fireplace. 'She looks quite nice,' said Les.

'The looks you can forget,' said Max. 'If it wasn't for pickpockets I'd have no sex life at all.'

'Yeah?' said Les. 'I thought marriage was a wonderful institution, Max.'

'So who wants to live in an institution?' said Max. 'Believe me, Len, the most remarkable thing about my marriage is for thirty years my wife has served me nothing but leftovers. The original meal has never been found.'

'Now come on, Max,' said Vanita. 'You know you're one of God's chosen people.'

Max gestured. 'So why couldn't he have chosen someone else to marry Hannah?' Max looked over Norton's shoulder. 'I have to go. Dracula can't get the coffin open. Hey. Wonderful talking to you, Len. You too, Vanita.'

Les watched Max scurry off with his drink and turned to Vanita. 'He was a funny little bloke.'

'Yes. Him and his pickpockets,' chuckled Vanita. Her deep green eyes bored into Norton's brown ones. 'I'll bet you don't have that problem.'

'Vanita. It's that long since I've had sex, I've forgotten who gets tied up.' Les rubbed his hands together. 'Well I suppose I'd better grab myself a drink.'

'Les. It's my shout, remember.' Vanita picked up a full champagne glass from a coffee table next to them and handed it to Les. 'There you are. I've been saving one for you.'

'Ohh. Thanks very much,' said Les. He clinked his glass against Vanita's. 'Cheers, Vanita.'

'Yes. Cheers, Len.'

Les took a sip, then another and licked his lips. 'Hey, these are beautiful,' he said. 'What are they?'

'I think they're the pina coladas you have when you're not having a pina colada,' said Vanita.

Les had another sip then drained the glass and licked his lips. 'I hope you don't think I'm a pig,' he said to Vanita, 'but that was delicious. I'm going to get another one. Can I get you one?'

'It's still my shout,' said Vanita.

'Hey. Don't worry about it,' winked Les. 'When big Lennie's in town, money's no object.'

Les eased his way over to the table just as a fair-haired girl in brown placed a fresh tray of drinks on it. He was politely waiting for her to take them off the tray when the manager came up to him.

'Mr Gordon,' said John.

Les turned slightly around. 'Ohh, good evening, John. How are you?'

'Excellent, thank you,' smiled the manager. 'Mr Gordon I was wondering if you might like to join the other guests and myself for dinner at the captain's table?'

'Why I'd be only too delighted,' said Les. He nodded to Vanita. 'Is it all right if I bring a friend?'

John ogled the cleavage in Vanita's leisure suit. 'Absolutely.'

'Okay,' said Les. 'I'll see you over there.' Les took the two mocktails back and handed one to Vanita. 'Hey, guess what. We've been invited to dine at the captain's table.'

Vanita batted her eyelids at Les. 'And why wouldn't we?' she said.

They got into a bit of chitchat about their day. Vanita told Les the delights of her Pilates session and a facial afterwards. Les told her about the delights of pressure point therapy with an ex-miner and trying to keep up with Deliah the flying housewife from Brisbane. They were on their third mocktail when the girl who brought the drinks came over.

'Excuse me, Mr Gordon,' she said. 'Would you care to join us for dinner now?'

'Okay,' said Les. 'Thank you.'

Les and Vanita finished their drinks and began to move off. On the way out of the library they walked right past the writers in residence. Tobias Monk caught Norton's eye.

'Good evening, Len,' he said, trying not to be pompous.

'G'day, mate,' said Les. He turned to Vanita. 'Vanita. Have you met the writers in residence?'

'No,' she replied.

'Well, this is Toby, Danny, Benny and Harry. Team literature. This is Vanita.'

'Hello,' Vanita said pleasantly. 'Nice to meet you.'

The writers took to Norton abbreviating their names like a circus tent had collapsed over them.

'Yes. Likewise,' seethed Harriet Sutton.

'We'd love to stop and chat,' said Les. 'But we have to join the manager at the captain's table.' He gave the writers in residence an expectant look. 'Some other time perhaps?'

'Of course ... Lennie,' said Tobias Monk deliberately.

'That's me,' grinned Les. 'Big Lennie. As in McPherson. Delightful chap. Bad luck he's not with us any more.'

Les escorted Vanita over to the captain's table and Sandra pulled their chairs out for them. The table was half full with formal but friendly country women and a couple of older men all dressed very neat and casual. Seated directly opposite them were the four Americans in their ghastly matching outfits. One couple wore yellow and blue Hawaiian prints. The other two wore black, green and red checks. There were introductions all round then the Americans immediately started braying about what a fine time they were having in Australia. They'd actually seen some kangaroos in the hills next to the resort. One of the country women had seen them too and politely informed the Americans they were wallabies. It turned out the buzz-cutted American men's names were Chuck and Orville. And their frumpy overweight wives were Lori and Beckie-Jean. They all came from Jefferson City, Missouri, where the two men were damn proud to be executive directors at Wal-Mart.

Les picked up the menu and ordered assiette of scallop, oyster and salmon, with a citrus dressing and avocado and cherry tomato salad for an entrée. And organic beef and wild mushroom barley risotto for a main. The strawberry and poppyseed pancakes with coconut meringue sorbet sounded okay for dessert.

Les sipped a glass of water as he waited for his food to arrive while across the table the Americans started honking about life in Missouri. Les sipped his water and turned quietly to Vanita.

'Vanita,' he said, 'I don't wish to sound rude, but if any of those Seppos from Wal-Mart start going Give me a W, give me an A, give me an L, give me a hoo hoo and a squiggle, I'm going to go over and give them what you gave me in the pool. Only a lot harder and with the toe of my trainers.'

Vanita looked down at the table for a moment. 'Len, I think there's something you should know about me,' she said, slowly.

'Ohh?' said Les, feeling he'd just put his foot in it.

'I'm a very sophisticated woman. I'm married to a very rich man and I have a wide range of very wealthy friends in Victoria. I attend social events and host parties in Melbourne people would kill to attend if they could get an invitation. I'm also on a first-name basis with the Premier,' Vanita continued, 'and my husband has contacts high up in the government and the police force. But I'm telling you, if those Yanks even look like they're about to do what you just said, I'm going to start a food fight.'

The entrées arrived and everybody began eating. As usual, the food was delicious and Les ripped in. Sandra brought his main and Les couldn't believe beef could be so tender. He could have eaten the steak with a spoon. After dessert Les was brimming with contentment. He had a cup of herb tea and turned to Vanita.

'I hope you don't mind, Vanita,' he said. 'But I might leave. This is all very nice. But ... And I think it might be best if we weren't seen leaving together.'

'I'm glad you suggested that, Len,' said Vanita. 'You go. And I'll call round to your villa in ...' Vanita looked at her watch. 'Fifteen minutes.'

'You'll call round to my room?'

'Yes. And I'll bring a bottle.'

'Okay,' said Les. 'I'll see you then.'

Les excused himself and rose from the table. He said goodnight to everyone, including Vanita, and left the dining room. As he went past the library, he didn't nod to the writers in residence and didn't notice the filthy looks they were giving him.

Back in his villa, Les used the toilet then looked at himself in the mirror as he washed his hands. Is this really happening? he asked himself. That woman absolutely oozes class. Why would she want to be seen with a toad like me? Of course. She used to be a dancer. And she thinks I'm a film director. She probably wants to talk about show business. Fair enough. I don't know about the bottle though. I wouldn't have minded a week off the piss.

Les blew the oil lamp out and picked up the activities sheet from his pillow. There was plenty to do and he had a pranic healing session in the afternoon. He kicked off his trainers and slipped a cassette into the ghetto blaster and with Dave Tyce and the Headhunters growling a filthy back beat into 'Moan and Shuffle' went out onto the balcony to take in the evening.

Les was watching the moonlight over the valleys and thinking about how good Vanita's cleavage looked under her leisure suit, when he suddenly began to get an erection. Within seconds his erection turned into a rock hard, humping boner and the next thing, Mr Wobbly started going insane. He'd thrown off his chains and was banging on the cell door with his little enamel mug, screaming to see the warden. Fuckin hell! What's going on? pondered Les. I'm likely to attack Vanita as soon as she walks in the door. I'm out on bail and she's a married woman for Christ's sake. They'll hang me. Les tucked a furious Mr Wobbly up under the band of his shorts, got a cold bottle of mineral water from the fridge and drank half as he tried to compose himself. It wasn't long before there was a gentle knock on the door. Les opened it, and Vanita was standing in the shadows with the front of her leisure suit unzipped a few extra centimetres. In her hand was a white plastic bag.

'May I come in?' she purred.

'Sure, Vanita,' said Les, a tiny trickle of perspiration running down his forehead. 'I'll turn the music off,' Les switched the ghetto blaster off, turned to Vanita and nodded to the plastic bag. 'What have you got in there?'

'This.' Vanita opened the bag and took out a blue bottle of mineral water.

'Wow!' said Les. 'Santa Vittoria. Now you're talking lady.'

'I know,' whispered Vanita. 'Quick. Get two glasses.'

'Coming right up.'

Les took two glasses from a cupboard, opened the bottle of Santa Vittoria and poured two drinks. He handed one to Vanita and she clinked Norton's glass.

'Good health, Len,' she said softly.

'Yeah. Good health, Vanita.' Les swallowed half his glass and burped quietly into his hand. 'Ohh, yeah,' he said. 'Taste those bubbles.'

'I know,' said Vanita, licking her lips. 'You can really feel them sliding down your throat.'

The way Vanita licked her lips sent a shiver down Norton's spine and had Mr Wobbly ready to attack Vanita, chop her head and limbs off then bury them along with her torso somewhere out in the bush.

'Yes,' said Les slowly. 'You can certainly feel those bubbles all right.'

Vanita finished her glass of Santa Vittoria and put the glass on the kitchen table. She then moved up against Les and put her hand on his throbbing boner.

'Ooohh, Mr Gordon,' she smiled. 'Is that a telephoto lens in your pocket, or are you just glad to see me?'

'Jesus, Vanita,' croaked Les. 'You'd better take it easy.'

Vanita put a finger over her lips. 'Shhh. My mother always told me never to speak with my mouth full,' she smiled.

Vanita pulled the front of Norton's shorts down, took Mr Wobbly out of Norton's jox then bent down, put his knob in her mouth and started giving Les an unbelievable polish. Les looked down at her and broke into a sweat.

'Jesus Christ, woman,' he gasped. 'What are you doing to me?'

Vanita kept polishing away before she stood up and smiled right into Norton's face. Les looked at her for a moment then grabbed Vanita and started kissing her passionately. She slipped her tongue into Norton's mouth and Les thought his brain was going to explode. He started kissing Vanita's neck then pushed his tongue into her ear and Vanita sighed like a zephyr of wind passing through tall trees. That was all Les could take. He unzipped the front of Vanita's leisure suit and slipped the top off along with her pink up-lift bra. He helped her kick her pants and trainers off then slid her matching pink knickers off and eased Vanita back onto the bed. Les then pushed her knees apart and buried his face in her ted. Vanita had powdered it and it smelled, felt and tasted like the best ted Les ever had his face in. Vanita kicked and squealed and pushed on the back of Norton's head as he got stuck into it. Les wolfed away as long as he could, then got up, tore his clothes off and with semen dripping all over the place, got between Vanita's legs and sunk Mr Wobbly in down to the bone. Vanita gave a little scream, then held onto Les and started riding with him.

Les had barely been pumping for five minutes when, feeding off Vanita's threshing and screaming, Mr Wobbly swelled up like a cane toad forcing Les to arch his back, thrust like mad and blow his brains out. He rolled off to get his breath. But someone forgot to tell Mr Wobbly the round was over. The little swine refused to go to a neutral corner. If anything he was rampaging up and down determined to keep going. Les gave Vanita and himself a quick wipe with a fluffy white towel and sunk Mr Wobbly in again.

After that it was nothing more than a perverted, noisy, filthy sex fest between two more than consenting adults and a rock hard Mr Wobbly. They sucked and fucked, pushed and probed and licked and kissed all over the bed. They did it sideways, lengthways, upside down, any way in which Vanita could contort her Pilates-trained body. Les tied Vanita's hands behind her back with a sweatband and gave her a doggie while he slapped her arse. They had a great game of chasings from the bathroom to the kitchen which finished on the balcony with Les giving it to Vanita on the outdoor table with a cushion under her wonderfully sculptured derrière. How many times Les blew and Vanita orgasmed, Les lost count. The only time they stopped was for Les to rub some hemp oil lotion into Mr Wobbly and when the phone rang while they were in the middle of an excrutiatingly sensational sixty-niner.

'Yeah, hello, what,' Les panted into the receiver, his face barely centimetres from Vanita's ted, as she resumed polishing away at the other end of the bed.

'Mr Gordon. It's the desk again. I'm terribly sorry. But we've had another complaint from one of the villas. Would you mind turning your TV down?'

'Turn the TV down?' said Les. 'I haven't even got the bloody thing on. I've got a friend around and we're talking, that's all. Listen.' Les held the phone out for a moment. 'There. Can you hear a TV set?' he demanded.

'No.'

'Good. Well, tell whoever it is to piss off and mind their own business.' Les slammed the phone down and sunk his face back into Vanita's ted.

The clock radio was creeping towards midnight when they finally finished having their filthy way with each other. Vanita was snuggled up against Les, Les was laying back against the pillows wondering what hit him, while Mr Wobbly was sitting there with his eye on both of them.

'I have to go, Len,' said Vanita. 'It's getting late.'

'Yeah, righto,' said Les.

'Len,' Vanita said seriously. 'I really like you. So I don't wish to come across as being impolite or pretentious, but tomorrow, if we see each other, let's show a little discretion. Is that all right?'

'I understand perfectly, Vanita,' said Les. 'Naturally I'll smile and say hello when I see you. Then leave it at that.'

'And then we'll meet again for mocktails in the evening.'

'Sounds good to me.' Les drew Vanita to him and kissed her. 'Hey, Vanita,' he said. 'Before you go …'

'Yes,' cooed Vanita.

'You reckon we got time for just a little quicky?'

Vanita smiled and gave Les a friendly slap on the chest. 'Ohh, Mr Gordon. You are awful.'

They had a quicky for ten minutes then Vanita got into her clothes, took a bottle of Mount Franklin with her and left, giving Les a kiss goodnight and saying she'd see him tomorrow. By this time Les was shattered, in the nicest possible way. Even Mr Wobbly had decided to take the rest of the night off. Les had a quick shower then dried off and rubbed some more hemp body lotion into Mr Wobbly.

'Well, haven't you made an nice pig of yourself tonight, you little devil,' said Les, as he rubbed the lotion into where Mr Wobbly had a few pieces of bark missing. He slipped on a plain white T-shirt and a clean pair of jox and tucked Mr Wobbly away then looked at himself in the mirror. 'As for you, Big Lennie. You're nothing but a sex-crazed animal. Grhhh! Rrrhh!'

Les switched off the lights, got into bed and was asleep almost as soon as his head hit the pillow. The big Queenslander's last thoughts before he blacked out were, if this is what health food and lymphatic massage and all the rest of it does to you, bring it on, baby.

After a fabulous deep sleep, Les bounded out of bed early the next morning. His headache was gone and apart from his knee still giving him a slight twinge, he didn't have an ache or a pain in his body. He put the kettle on then cleaned his teeth and splashed water on his face.

'Hello, super screw,' Les smiled to himself in the mirror. 'Mirror mirror on the wall, who's the greatest lover of them all? Why, you are.' Norton walked into the bedroom and started laughing as he climbed into his Speedos and gym gear. 'Give me an L, give me an E, give me an S. What's that spell? Les. I can't hear you. What's that spell? Les. I still can't hear you. LES!!!' Yeah, that's more like it.

Les made a cup of herb tea and took it out onto the balcony to find another beautiful day dawning. He checked the activities sheet and looked at his watch. He still had plenty of time to catch the tai chi class on Meditation Hill and photograph the sunrise. After doing the herb tea tango, Les got his camera and walked out the door.

Outside he wasn't sure where the path was that led up the hill. There was a path behind the pool area; maybe it ran up from there? However, all Les could find when he got there was a workman's area littered with rolls of aqua duct, iron bars, wire, pieces of wood and whatever scattered around the resort's generator. But no separate path. Then he noticed a small group of people climbing up the far side of the hill. Les double-timed it round to where a wooden stairway ran up in front of the villas further along from his. Les climbed the path and came to an area that had been scooped from the top of the hill and paved with slate tiles. There was a stone bench seat on either side and a small fountain stepped into the tiles trickled softly towards one of the seats. Six women and one man were lined up facing the sun on a rim above the tiled area, and below them Peta was standing in front of the fountain in her gym gear. She saw Les and smiled. Les smiled back then put his camera down on the closest seat, climbed up to the rim and joined the end of the line.

'All right,' said Peta. 'We'll begin. I'll tell the story and all you have to do is follow my movements. Start by bending your knees slightly and holding your arms out in front of you.' Peta waited till everyone was ready then began.

'In the beginning there was heaven and earth. Along came man and opened up his heart to heaven and earth. He painted a rainbow across the sky and reached through the clouds. As the clouds parted the rain fell and the man drank. Two swallows travelled, the male swallow dived towards the female swallow and the female swallow dived to greet the male and they formed a union. The man embraced the universe and brought all the energy towards the earth and into himself. He raised the ball of energy to the male side and then to the female side. He turned to gaze at the moon and deflected any negative energy away from himself. He followed the clouds and gathered fish from the sea, watching the waves playing on the shore.'

It was the first time Les had ever done tai chi, but he managed to follow Peta's instructions easily enough and it was beautiful doing the gently flowing movements in the still, crisp morning air as the sun rose and tinted the clouds over the valley with pink, orange, grey and amethyst. Also beautiful was the way Peta told the story. Her voice was soft and melodic and she put so much feeling and hidden emotion into the words Les went all warm inside and a tiny tear trickled from the corner of his eye. The session ended all too soon and Les went up to Peta as the others began walking back down the hill.

'Hey, Peta,' said Les. 'I've never done tai chi before. That was unreal.'

'I'm glad you liked it,' Peta smiled.

'Have you been doing it long?'

'Yes. I used to do it every morning with my brother. It's a beautiful way to start the day, don't you think?'

'It sure is,' agreed Les. He took his camera out of its cover and clicked it on. 'Peta,' he asked. 'Could you do me a favour? Would you mind taking a photo of me standing on the rim with the sun behind me?'

'Sure. No problem,' said Peta.

Les handed Peta his camera, then stepped up to the rim. Peta climbed to the opposite rim facing the sun, took two photos then came down and handed Les back his camera.

'Thanks for that, Peta,' he said.

'A pleasure,' said Peta. 'I have to join the others.'

'Okay. I'm going to take some more photos.'

Peta trotted off down the hill and Les climbed back onto the rim with his camera just as two brightly coloured hot-air balloons began rising slowly from a distant valley. As they drifted against the painted sky, Les began clicking away. If any of these photos turn out as good as I think they will, he smiled, zooming in and out with the telephoto lens, I'm going to get one blown up and hang it on the wall at Chez Norton. Les came down from the rim and checked the photos on the screen. Ohh, yeah. Consider that one on the wall. I haven't brushed up too bad, either. Les put his camera back in its case and returned to the villa. He left the camera in his bag then strolled down to the Wellness Centre to catch the others for the morning walk. There were the usual dozen people gathered on the grass. Michael was in charge, but there was no sign of Deliah.

'G'day, Michael,' said Les.

'Hello, Len,' answered Michael. 'How are you today?'

Les closed his fists and shook his arms in front of him. 'Michael. You've got no idea.'

'It's good to be alive, isn't it?' winked Michael.

'Mate. You wouldn't be dead for quids,' Les winked back.

Michael looked at his watch. 'Okay, everybody. Let's go,' he said.

Les fell in and they walked up to the gate. When they got outside, Les didn't have Deliah setting her usual gruelling pace so he just tagged along with the others doing it easy. Everybody else had a walking partner or whatever to talk to. So rather than be a butt-inski or annoy Michael, Les plugged along on his own, thinking about this and that while he enjoyed the sunshine and the morning air. One thought did stick in his mind. If he felt and performed this well after four days of living a healthy lifestyle, how good would you be after four weeks? It was definitely health food for thought. They got to the end of the walk and again Les felt like sprinting up the hill. But rather than be a mug, he fell back and finished somewhere in the middle of the field. Les still had a good sweat up, however, when they got inside the gate and went their separate ways. So he continued on straight to the pool, kicked his trainers and shorts off and jumped in wearing his T-shirt. After a quick shower, he took a towel from one of the cabana chairs and walked back to the villa. He hung his T-shirt on the balcony then guzzled down two bottles of mineral water before he changed into a pair of shorts and his Margaritaville T-shirt from the night before and headed for the dining room.

The writers in residence were at their usual table when Les walked in and Vanita was seated with Max and his wife. Tobias Monk looked up from a bowl of muesli he'd been sourly staring into as if it had been poisoned and gave Les a thin smile. Les gave Tobias a cheerful grin then stopped at Vanita's table.

'Hello, Vanita,' said Les politely. 'How are you this morning?'

'I'm good thanks, Len,' she smiled. 'How are you?'

'Unreal. I did tai chi on Meditation Hill, then went for a power walk. I feel great.'

'I just had a swim. That's all,' said Vanita.

Les turned to Max. 'Max. What about you in your tracksuit. You look like you could run a marathon.'

'Marathon, shmarathon,' shrugged Max. 'All this healthy living is making me violently ill.'

223

'Max. Better to be ten times ill than one time dead,' said his wife.

Les turned to Max's wife and noticed she had a wall eye that was right up against her nose. 'You must be Hannah,' said Les. 'Nice to meet you, Hannah. I'm Len.'

'Len. Those shoulders,' said Hannah. 'How are you?'

'Real good thanks.' Les turned to Vanita. 'Okay. I'll leave you and your friends to enjoy your breakfast. I might bump into you in the library this evening.'

'That would be nice,' smiled Vanita.

Les said goodbye then found a table amongst the other independent guests not far from the balcony. He had a look at the menu before going to the salad bar and filling one bowl with everything he could find and another with fruit. Valerie brought him a fruit drink and a pot of herb tea and Les ordered an omelette with tomato and capsicum. While he was waiting he backed up for more Bircher Muesli before polishing off his omelette. When he'd finished, Les sipped another cup of herb tea and wondered how he could put some shit on the writers in residence as they moved from the dining room into the library. If he struck now, it would probably upset the rest of their day. Les finished his cup of tea and strolled over to the library.

'Hello, boys and girls,' he said breezily as he stepped up to where they were sitting with their notebooks. 'Enjoy your breakfast?'

'Hello, Lennie,' said Tobias coolly. 'Yes, breakfast, if you could call it that, was delightful.'

'What would you give for a plate of bacon and eggs right now?' said Les. 'With toast and jam and a big frothy cappuccino? And a cigarette after?' It was more fun than dangling a vial of methadone in front of a table full of heroin addicts.

'Don't even mention fucking cigarettes,' snarled Harriet Sutton.

'Did you say jam?' gasped Danica. 'Yes. That's what I'd like. Jam. Apricot. Blackberry. Plum. Anything.'

'On a nice big crumpet dripping with butter,' proposed Les.

'Yes, yes,' squealed Danica. 'Even on a slice of toast.'

'I just want a VB,' said Benson.

'Well,' sighed Les. 'You know what it's like here. You may as well be in a Russian gulag.'

'Tell me about it,' said Harriet. 'I don't even know why my publicist got me this gig.'

I wonder if money had anything to do with it, thought Les. 'Anyway,' he said enthusiastically, 'I've got another idea for a movie. And not a murder mystery either.'

'Ohh?' said Tobias slowly. 'And exactly what did you have in mind?'

'Something like *The Three Stooges*,' gestured Les. 'Only instead of three stooges, how about four? As in, *The Four Stooges Go Writing*. We'll set it in here. And, Toby, you can be Moe. Benny, you can be Larry. Danny, with that hair, you got to be Curly. And Harry. Don't try and tell me you wouldn't make a perfect Shemp?'

Norton's suggestion went over like a banjo player at a mob funeral.

'Is this your idea of humour?' said Harriet frostily.

'My oath it is,' said Les. 'Mel Gibson's making a Three Stooges movie in America. Why don't we beat him to the punch and do one in Australia? And we toss in an extra stooge?' Les ran his eyes over the writers. 'What do you reckon, gang?'

'Len. You're about as funny as the sinking of the *Titanic*,' said Tobias.

Les pointed at Tobias and grinned. 'Nyuck, nyuck, nyuck! Oh, a wise guy, eh!' Les rubbed his hands together. 'Anyway. I have to go. I'm having a wax in ten minutes. But think it over and I'll get back to you.'

Les left the library and started back towards his villa. Love those writers, he smiled as he ambled across the grass. Lovvvve those writers.

Back in his villa Les pushed play on the ghetto blaster then sat on the balcony figuring out what to do while Marcia Ball zydecoed her way through 'Thibodaux, Lousiana'. He didn't really feel like sitting around reading because he had too much energy, he wasn't keen on a swim and he'd already had a walk. I know, I'll go down to the gym and play on the weight stations. You never know I might grow up to be big and strong like Kendrick. Les changed into his gym gear, got a sweatband and headed for the gym.

The manager was in there with a friend going for it on two cardiovascular machines and three women were into it on walking machines when Les walked in the door. He gave the manager a wave, put his towel down and wondered where to start amongst all the shiny new machines. This looks all right, he decided: seated leg presses.

Les spent the rest of the morning pushing and pulling pins and sorting out weights while he did leg curls, rear deltoid and shoulder presses and anything else that caught his fancy.

By the time he'd finished, the manager and the women had gone and Les felt as big as a dinosaur. Shit! I'd better have a walk to settle down, he thought, or I'll never get through the bloody door. Les got back on the same walking machine and did a lazy half hour watching a sports show. He finished in a lather of sweat, had a drink then picked up his towel and left for the outdoor pool.

Les walked out the door of the gymnasium to find a crowd of people on the badminton court. They were all dressed in gym gear and circled around Antoinette who was wearing a roving mike. Les climbed the stairs and as he reached the top, loud American Indian music started pounding through the badminton court. It sounded like the Sioux getting ready to go on the warpath.

'Heyyy yah, hey yah, hey yah! Hey yohh!'

'Heyyy yah, hey yah, hey yah! Hey yohh!'

Boom — boom, boom, boom! Boom — boom, boom, boom!

'Heyyy yah, hey yah, hey yah! Hey yohh!'

'Come on,' Antoinette yelled through the roving mike. 'Sing it out. Loud as you can. And stomp your feet.'

The people around her started singing and

stomping and with Antoinette leading the way, it looked and sounded sensational.

'Come on,' shouted Antoinette. 'Louder. You're going to war tomorrow. You and the rest of the braves. And you might not be coming back. Come on. Stomp and sing. Give praise to the Great Spirit.'

'Heyyy yah, hey yah, hey yah! Hey yohh!'

Les watched as the people on the badminton court yelled and stomped their feet. The Indian music stopped to be replaced by African music and with Antoinette showing the way, the people on the badminton court started dancing around and jumping up and down just having a load of fun. A movement on Norton's left made him turn around. It was Michael.

'Michael. How are you?' said Les.

'Good, Len.'

'What's going on down there?' asked Les.

'Tribal dancing,' answered Michael. 'Those people have just finished the program. Now they're all getting into a bit of bonding before they leave. Good, isn't it?'

'Reckon. If I wasn't covered in sweat and stinking of BO, I'd join in.'

Michael smiled at Norton's description of himself, but said nothing.

'That music's fantastic,' said Les. 'What's the name of the CD? Do you know?'

'It's a compilation the management had made up,' said Michael.

'Ohh.'

'But I can burn you a copy if you want.'

'Can you? Shit! That'd be unreal.'

'I'll do it for you this afternoon and leave it at your door.'

'Okay. Thanks, Michael.'

Michael ran down the stairs to the gym and Les walked across to the pool. There were two women in one-piece costumes splashing around in the outdoor pool when Les entered. So he took his smelly gym gear off and had a shower before jumping in. He exchanged pleasantries of the day with the two women, splashed around for a while, had another shower and rinsed his gym gear then left the two women to it and walked back to his villa.

After hanging out his gear, Les changed into his Levi's shorts and a blue Les Motto Fit For Life T-shirt, then got a bottle of mineral water and pondered what to do. The most sensible and enjoyable thing would be to put his feet up and have a read. By then it would be time for lunch. Les picked up *MP* and settled back on the lounge.

He got to where MP was fined $1400 in Southport Magistrates Court after he'd been busted, when Norton's stomach told him the lunch bell was definitely ringing. Les closed his book and walked up to the dining room.

The dining room was a little quiet when Les walked in and there was no sign of the writers in residence. Les found a table then walked up to the salad bar and loaded a plate with green pawpaw and celery, coating it liberally with cucumber and yogurt dressing. He ripped into that and ordered wok-seared soba noodles with chicken, mushrooms and black beans off Sandra, and while he was waiting, filled another plate with chickpeas, tomato and snowpeas, which he drowned in herb and roasted garlic dressing.

As usual the food was delicious and Les washed every last morsel down with herb tea and his ration of rye bread and hummus. As he was leaving, the writers in residence filed into the dining room like the four horsemen of the apocalypse after their horses had been shot out from under them.

'Hello, everybody,' said Les cheerfully. 'How's things?' There was a muted, mumbled reply as they walked past. 'Hey, Toby,' said Les. 'Seeing you're such a deipnosophist may I recommend the green pawpaw and celery with cucumber and yogurt dressing. It'll have you batting yourself off and doing cartwheels at the same time.' Norton left Tobias and the others to it and walked back to his villa.

So what will I do now, thought Les, after he'd seated himself back down on the lounge. It's too nice a day to be inside. But I don't feel like any more punishing exercise right now. I know. Get a bike and ride down to the front gate. Les changed into his training gear, put his cap and sunglasses on and left for the foyer.

Karla was at the desk in a crisp brown uniform. 'Hello, Mr Gordon,' she said. 'How are you today?'

'Good, thanks,' replied Les. 'I'd like to get a mountain bike, if that's okay?'

'No problem. They're down in the car park at one end. Help yourself.'

'Righto.'

'Just one thing, Mr Gordon. We'd appreciate it if you would wear a helmet. And if you leave the retreat, the management's not responsible if anything happens to you.'

'No worries. Thanks.' Les took the stairs down to the front door.

The concierge's desk was empty and there was no one around when Les stepped outside. A hundred metres to the left, the car park was built beneath the tennis court and as Les strolled down the driveway he noticed a helipad opposite the guests' car park, and the staff car park way over to the right. The field Michael spoke about was further around to the left. Les stepped inside the car park to the thumps and shouts of people enjoying a game of tennis above.

The mountain bikes were standing in a rack against the far wall where Norton's Berlina was parked between a silver Maserati and a blue Jaguar. There were six bikes with helmets hanging from the handlebars and if Les wasn't mistaken, the red one Holden had been riding was at the end. Shit! Will I or won't I? he thought. Yeah, why not? If the ghost of Alexander Holden gets me, it gets me. A black helmet hung from the handlebars. Les picked it up and strapped it down snugly over his cap. He took the red bike from the rack and, after making sure the seat was high enough, pedalled out of the garage.

The bike went well. The seat was comfortable, the brakes and gears worked perfectly and the chunky tyres bit into the driveway. Compared to his old banger at home, it was a Lexus. He pedalled past the front door, got a bit of speed up, then coasted down the steep hill.

By the time Les got to the bottom, the wind was rushing across his face and the tyres were humming on the road. He hit the brakes before he reached the gate, then cycled slowly over and sat with one leg on a pedal in front of it. It wasn't hard to see how Holden killed himself. Even wearing a helmet, if you hit the iron bar along the gate at that speed you still had a good chance of breaking your neck. Les pedalled round in circles checking out the road and the surroundings and was about to pedal back up the hill and come down again when he changed his mind. It was a beautiful sunny day and the surrounding countryside looked inviting. Les adjusted his helmet and sunglasses then pressed the button to open the gate and pedalled out.

He cycled past the two small lakes he'd seen when he drove in, before coming to the signpost at the fork in the road. What do you do again, when you come to a fork in the road? Les asked himself. You take it, don't you. Les turned left and pedalled off.

Les rode along enjoying himself immeasurably. Apart from the birds singing, there was a wonderful silence and the only sign of habitation was a rusty barbed-wire fence running along either side of the road. A pleasant breeze had picked up over the mountains and valleys and it was flicking gently at the surrounding trees as it brought the temperature down. Les cycled blissfully on till he came to a narrow road running off to the left; a battered signpost read UWORRA LANE. Yeah, why not have a look up there? he thought.

The narrow lane was red dust and gravel edged by more barbed wire fencing running in front of the trees. Hey, this is all right, smiled Les as the tyres crunched on the gravel and kicked up a little dust. This is what mountain bikes are made for. Les clicked the bike into high gear and continued on.

Les was cruising along when he came to a sagging cyclone-wire gate on the right that had been left open. Behind it a short stretch of dirt road led to a large pond in a clearing surrounded by trees. In the middle of the pond several ducks and ducklings were paddling around near the reeds on the right-hand side. I wonder if that water's fit to drink? thought Les. He went through the gate, then stopped in the shade of the trees. After leaning his bike against an old red gum, Les took his sunglasses off, left his helmet and cap on the bike and walked down to the pond. The ducks saw him, quacked a warning to each other, then backed away closer to the reeds leaving one behind as a lookout.

'It's all right, Daffy,' Les called out to the duck. 'I've only called in for a drink. You haven't seen P . . . P . . . Porky P . . . P . . . Pig, have you?'

The water definitely wasn't Mount Franklin. But it was cool and you could drink it. Les cupped a few mouthfuls up with his hand and splashed some over his face, then stood up and had a look around. It was certainly a lovely quiet spot, full of trees and birds and right out in the middle of nowhere. Les walked back to where he'd left the bike, put his cap, helmet and sunglasses back on and was about to pedal off, when he heard the sound of a car approaching. Next thing a battered yellow panel van came through the open gate and stopped near the pond. It had fat tyres, a wire grille in the back and twin aerials on the front bumper bar. The aerials stopped swaying and a moment or two later, the doors opened and two men, one shorter than the other, got out dressed in scrubby jeans, dirty white T-shirts and old trainers. The taller man had a lean, humourless face and black hair falling out from under a black baseball cap. The shorter man had a round, meaty face, covered in red stubble and ginger hair poking out from beneath a blue baseball cap.

'Hey, look at those ducks,' Blue Cap said excitedly. 'Watch this.'

Blue Cap reached into the car and came out holding an air rifle. He broke the barrel, put a slug in, then took aim and fired at the ducks. The pellet fell short and splashed into the water near the ducklings. The male ducks quacked a warning and flew off, leaving a wake across the pond, while the mother ducks stayed behind and herded the ducklings in amongst the reeds.

'Ahh, fuck it! Missed,' cursed Blue Cap. 'Wait'll I have another shot at the ones in the reeds.'

Blue Cap went to reload when his mate spoke. 'Forget the ducks,' said Black Cap. 'Let's sort this other shit out first.'

'Yeah, righto.'

Les shook his head. Why would you bother, he wondered. The poor bloody ducks aren't doing any harm. And why shoot the baby ones? What a fuckin moron.

The two blokes couldn't see Les amongst the trees and went about their business, whatever it was. Blue Cap opened the back of the panel van and behind the grille Les could see four greyhounds. Black Cap took out a wire cage covered by a small tarpaulin, dropped it on the ground and pulled the tarpaulin off. Inside the cage were four very agitated and scared brushtail possums. Three greys and an old red. A tiny black tail was poking out from one grey's pouch, showing she was carrying a baby. Les started to go red. Those rotten low cunts, he fumed. They're going to use those possums to blood their greyhounds.

Black Cap tossed his mate a pair of wire cutters. 'Here,' he said. 'Give the red one a manicure while I get some rope.'

'Okay,' nodded Blue Cap.

Ohh, fuck this, scowled Les, I have to do something. Les came out from behind the trees and strode straight up to the two men.

'Hey! What do you think you're doing?' said Les.

The two men spun around, somewhat startled. They looked at Les and saw he wasn't a ranger, then turned to each other for a moment before turning back to glare menacingly at Les.

'Who the fuck are you?' said Black Cap.

'Don't worry who I am,' said Les. 'Let those poor little possums go. You low bludgers.'

'Ohh, go and get fucked,' said Black Cap. 'What's it got to do with you?'

'Yeah. Fuck off and mind your own business,' said his mate.

Les ignored Black Cap and went to open the cage, when Blue Cap suddenly swung the air rifle down on Norton's helmet. Les felt a horrendous whack across the head and quickly brought his hands up in a defensive position. But not quick enough to stop a short right on the jaw from Black Cap and another whack with the air rifle from Blue Cap, this time across the back. The two men were tough and willing and had the jump on Les. But the big Queenslander's temper was now at boiling point and after his session on the weight stations, the two greyhound owners might as well have tried to take on the Incredible Hulk.

Les grabbed Black Cap by the front of his T-shirt and flung him against the front door of the panel van right onto the handle. It caught Black Cap in the spine, making him curse and arch his back with pain. Les turned to Blue Cap just as the hood brought the air rifle up to give him another whack, moved into him and let go a right uppercut from down round his knees that hit Blue Cap so hard, it lifted him up in the air, broke his jaw and cracked all his front teeth. Blue Cap's eyes went glassy and he dropped the air rifle before slumping down on his rump with his back against the panel van, blood trickling down his smashed chin. Les quickly spun around just as Black Cap came off the panel van throwing wild lefts and rights in all directions. Les tucked his chin in and caught all the punches either on his arms and shoulders or the top of his helmet. He waited a moment, then straightened up and let Black Cap have two quick left hooks in the face that split his lips open and made Black Cap turn his head to the right. Les planted his feet and with all his shoulder behind it, threw a short right that connected with Black Cap's exposed jaw, smashing it violently round to the other side of his face. Black Cap's eyes rolled as several teeth fell out of his gaping mouth, then his knees went and he pitched forward, face first, into Norton's right knee coming up. Black Cap gave a whimper of pain, then slumped down on his face unconscious, blood oozing out of his mouth to form a shiny dark puddle in the soil near the front tyre.

Les stepped back from the panel van and checked out the two men. They were out cold and in awful shape. But this didn't stop Norton from giving them one last serve. He picked up the air rifle by the barrel, swung it hard and gave them a few good thumps with the butt on their thighs and ribs.

Les settled down, then dropped the air rifle and stepped across to the wire cage. Possibly the possums' instincts told them they were safe now, because they appeared to have settled down also. The baby one had even come out of its mother's pouch and was clinging awkwardly to her back. Les opened the cage at the end, gave it a shake and stood away.

'Come on, you fur bearin' little varmints,' he said. 'Get going. You're safe now.'

The three grey possums didn't have to be told twice. They came out of the cage almost as one, then went for their lives round the back of the panel van and disappeared into the trees where Les had left the bike. The red one came out a little slower then and stood up on his hind legs, resting his backside on his tail, and looked up at Les with big brown eyes.

'Well, don't stand there looking at me, boofhead,' smiled Les. 'Piss off, while you're still in front.'

The red possum stared at Les a moment longer, seemed to gesture a thank you to him with one paw before scurrying off to join the others.

Les picked up the air rifle to throw it out into the pond, then stopped and changed his mind. He opened the driver's side door and, sitting in the middle of the seat amongst all the other rubbish, was a packet of Wasp pellets. Les took them to the back of the panel van and looked at the four greyhounds milling around behind the grille in the back.

'Sorry, fellahs,' said Les, loading a pellet into the air rifle. 'This is just to nark your owners. And it won't kill you.'

Les shot the first greyhound in the rump, then put a pellet into all four. The air rifle was old and not very powerful, so the dogs would still be able to get around all right. But they wouldn't race again. With the dogs yelping and licking their wounds in the back of the van, Les threw the air rifle and the packet of pellets out into the middle of the pond. He was about to walk back to his bike when he stopped and picked at his chin. I don't know, mused Les. I reckon these two hillbillies owe me a drink for all the pain and distress I've just suffered. And it's not as if it's the first time I've done it.

Les went through the two unconscious men's pockets and found their wallets. He left them with their driver's licences and credit cards and ten dollars each. But he got two hundred and ten dollars off Black Cap, and eighty-five from his mate. Les pocketed the money and put their wallets back in their pockets, then thought of another parting gift and reached into the front of the van. There was a mobile phone on the front seat. That went into the middle of the pond along with the car keys.

Les chuckled and did his best Foghorn Leghorn impersonation. 'Enjoy. I say ... enjoy the walk home, boys. Heh, heh, heh.'

Les walked back to his bike when something made him look up. The old red possum was sitting on a branch looking down at him. Les grinned and raised his arms out by his sides.

'Born free,' he sang out at the top of his voice.

The old possum took no notice. Norton left it at that, got on his bike and pedalled back towards the resort.

On the way Les thought about what just happened and if Black Cap and his mate would go to the police. It was highly unlikely. Those two morons would have that many outstanding warrants, figured Les, if they walked into a police station, they'd never get back out again. And how could they identify him? He was wearing a helmet and sunglasses. No. If anything, going for a bike ride was a good move. He'd got a little exercise, done his good deed for the day. And finished about three hundred in front. Les winked up at the sky. I can't knock that, boss. Les was still smiling when he arrived at the front gate and pressed the buzzer.

'Hello. This is Karla. How may I help you?' came the familiar voice over the intercom.

'It's Mr Gordon. Can you open the gate for me, please?'

'Certainly, Mr Gordon.'

The gate rumbled open and Les pedalled through. While it rumbled shut behind him, he stopped to have another look around and check a couple of things out. The gate closed, Les slipped the bike into low and started up the hill.

It was a bit of a grind. But by keeping the bike in low and standing on the pedals, he got to the top without killing himself. He coasted past the concierge's desk and the underground car park and stopped opposite the helipad to have a last look around before he went back to his villa. Michael was walking towards the staff car park carrying a sports bag and Peta was in the field down from the tennis court showing the Americans the finer arts of boomerang throwing. She was exceptionally good and from where Les stood he could hear the Americans commenting loudly on her skill compared to their clumsy efforts. Les watched them for a while before he took the bike and helmet back to the rack, then he walked up to the foyer and continued on to his villa.

Inside, Les got a bottle of cold mineral water, took off his T-shirt and examined himself in the mirror. He hadn't brushed up too bad. He'd have a decent bruise across his back by tomorrow and his jaw was a little swollen. But nothing to worry about. He splashed some water on his face and checked his watch. If he got his finger out, he had time for a swim before his pranic healing session at the Wellness Centre. Les finished his mineral water, changed into his Speedos and a fresh T-shirt, got a towel and headed for the outdoor pool.

Les was pleased to find he had the pool to himself again and when he dived in, the water felt glorious as usual. He flopped around, swimming and diving up and down and soon it was time for his treatment. Feeling refreshed, he got out, dried off and walked across to the Wellness Centre.

There was one woman sitting down, wearing a white robe and a towel around her head, when Les walked in, and the fair-haired girl he'd seen working at the Wellness Centre on his first day at the retreat was behind the desk. Her name tag read 'Carol'.

'Hello, Carol,' said Les. 'My name's Gordon. I'm here for some pranic healing.'

Carol looked at the ledger. 'Yes, Mr Gordon,' she smiled. 'If you'd like to take a seat, Nikki will be with you in a moment.'

'Thank you.'

Les gave the woman in the white robe a smile as he took a seat, then sat back and reflected on the day's events while the gentle celestial music wafted around the room. He was reflecting on the old red possum and trying to think of something or somewhere the possum reminded him of, when a happy faced, slightly overweight woman with lively blue eyes and short brown hair came up to him. She was wearing a black uniform with her name tag on the front.

'Hello, Mr Gordon,' she said cheerfully, offering her hand. 'I'm Nikki.'

'Hello, Nikki,' said Les, giving the woman's hand a shake.

'Would you follow me, please.'

'Sure.'

Nikki led Les round to a room down the side and opened the door for him. Les stepped into a softly lit room with a massage table in the middle and a chair in one corner. A bowl of water sat on the floor at the foot of the massage table, but apart from that the room was empty.

'You don't have to take your clothes off,' said Nikki. 'Just lie on the table face up.'

'What about my shoes?'

'No. They're all right.'

'Okay.' Les did as he was told and lay back on the table with a small pillow under his head.

'Have you ever had pranic healing before, Mr Gordon?' asked Nikki.

Les shook his head. 'No. And call me Len, if you like.'

'All right, Len. Well, what I do is utilise your life force, your prana, to re-energise your body.'

'Ohh?'

'I remove used energy with a cleansing technique. Balance your prana. Then energise your body with fresh energy.'

'In other words, Nikki, you take out the bad vibes, and put in the good vibes.'

'That's about it, Len.'

'Okay. Go for your life.'

Nikki placed her hands above Norton's chest. 'Oh,' she said, looking a little concerned. 'I'm picking up a lot of heat from the right side of your body. Especially your head and your back. Have you been in an accident very recently?'

This threw Les a little, because Nikki hadn't touched him and he hadn't taken off his clothes. 'Yeah. I fell over behind the pool trying to find a path up Meditation Hill. And bumped my head and back on that big generator. And I hurt my knee too.'

Nikki moved her hands in small circles. 'I can sense violence.'

'Yeah. Well, I swore a lot when it happened. And ... threw things around.'

'You should control your temper a bit more, Len.'

'You're right,' agreed Les. Yeah. Especially when some big goose abuses you for no reason and puts you in a headlock. You get hit across the back with a rifle butt. And some other goose belts you in the jaw. Next time I'll blow kisses. But I wonder how she picked that up?

Nikki started running her hands up and down above Norton's body then flicked her fingers at the bowl of water on the floor. Les watched her for a few moments and closed one eye.

'What sort of work do you do, Len?' asked Nikki.

'I'm a film director.'

'Ohh, you're the gentleman who found Alexander Holden's body.'

'Right on,' said Les. 'That was the first thing I saw when I drove in on Monday morning. Poor little Alexander. Lying next to his pushbike at the front gate. Garlic Bread. Dead.'

'Poor little Alexander,' echoed Nikki. 'The front gate was about as far he'd go on his pushbike.'

'Yeah?' Norton's ears pricked up. 'Why's that?'

'Somebody would be waiting for him behind a tree if he went any further. With a baseball bat or a shotgun. The little WILMA.'

'WILMA? What's a Wilma?'

'Wanking Impolite Loud Mouthed Arsehole,' said Nikki.

'Nice one, Nikki,' chuckled Les. Hello. Here we go again. 'So I gather you didn't like Alexander Holden, Nikki. Any particular reason?'

'Ohh, he came in here for a treatment,' said Nikki, furiously waving and flicking her hands over Norton's body. 'After fifteen minutes, he got up. Abused me. Told me I was a charlatan. Kicked over the bowl of water. And stormed out. And said he wasn't going to pay.'

'Fair dinkum?' said Les.

'Yeah. Fair dinkum.'

'Stanley said he was all right.'

'Yes, well that's Stanley. Stanley's not refined. I imagine he and Holden would have got on absolutely fabulously.'

'I don't know. Stanley's not a bad masseur.'

'Maybe,' said Nikki. 'But Stanley's happiest when he's sitting on the verandah with his fourteen-year-old female cousin playing a banjo.'

'Fair enough,' said Les. 'So I imagine, Nikki, if Alexander baby had come out the gate on his bike, and you were behind a tree with a shotgun, you'd have been very tempted to let him have it?'

'Both barrels, Len. I'd've utilised the little WILMA's life force.'

'And balanced his prana at the same time,' said Les.

'Yeah,' said Nikki. 'With a piece of four-by-two. Call me a charlatan. The shit of a thing.'

'I think of you more as a witch,' said Les. 'A white witch.'

'You got it, Len. That's me. Nikki the white witch of the north.'

Les lay back and closed his eyes while Nikki did her thing. She asked him a few things about directing movies. Les gave her a line of bullshit and told her he'd been shooting TV commercials. He'd just done one for Bogenhuber Chardonnay near Cessnock. Which was how he came to be at Opal Springs chilling out. Nikki told him she originally came from Taree. Now she lived on a farm at Kurri Kurri with her husband who worked at Williamstown Air Force base as a cleaner. They had six kids. Four boys and two girls. All going to school.

'All right, Len,' said Nikki. 'You're about done. You won't feel anything for the moment. But tomorrow you'll notice the difference.'

'Okay. Thanks, Nikki,' said Les.

Les half opened his eyes and saw Nikki come behind him. She placed her hands on his shoulders and Norton's eyes popped wide open. Her hands were burning hot. She left them there for a moment, then Les caught her eye as she came round and saw her smiling down at him.

'See you again, Len,' she said.

'Yeah ... right,' answered Les quietly.

Nikki left the room and Les rose from the massage table. Well, don't that beat all, he thought. She definitely didn't put her hands in hot water. And she never rubbed them together. Yet they felt like they were on fire. Alexander could have made a big mistake rubbing Nikki the white witch's prana up the wrong way. Les left the Healing Centre and walked back to his villa.

Placed against the door was the CD Michael had promised him. Ohh, what a good bloke, smiled Les. He picked up the CD, took it inside and had a look. It was just a plain CD with 'Tribal Dancing' written across the front in Texta colour. I won't play it now, schemed Les, placing it carefully in his bag. I'll wait till I get home and crank it up when Warren's got a hangover and I've hidden all the coffee. Les got a bottle of mineral water out of the fridge and although he wasn't jumping out of his skin after the pranic healing, he did feel like joining the others for the afternoon walk. He finished his mineral water and was coming back from the bathroom when the phone rang.

'Hello?' said Les.

'Hi, Len. It's Vanita.'

'Hey. How are you?'

'Fine, thank you.'

'That's good. So what can I do for you, Vanita?'

'I just wanted to say hello. And to thank you for being so discreet in the dining room this morning. It was very much appreciated.'

'Hey, Vanita,' said Les, 'discretion's my middle name.'

'It is. So are you going for mocktails tonight, Len?'

'Yeah. For sure.'

'What time?'

'Ohh. About seven-thirty.'

'Okay. And would you like me to call round to your villa later?'

'That'd be lovely,' said Les, feeling a swelling in his loins.

'Good. Well, I might be talking to someone when I see you in the library. We'll have a drink. Then go our separate ways for dinner. And I'll see

252

you afterwards. Would you like me to bring a bottle?'

'Sure. Just be careful no one sees you.'

'They won't,' said Vanita. 'Okay. I'll see you in the library. And don't forget. It's still my shout.'

'Terrific. I'll see you then.'

Les hung up the phone then looked down at Mr Wobbly. 'Behave yourself, you little monster. You were like a mad person last night. You'll end up getting us both into trouble.' Les walked into the bathroom and threw some water over his face. Now where was I? Ohh yes. The afternoon walk. Norton got his sweatband, left the villa and walked over to the Wellness Centre.

The usual team was there and by now they all knew each other. Amanda was in charge and Les was pleased to see Deliah amongst the others, looking fit and ready to rumble.

'Hello, Deliah,' said Les, 'How are you?'

'I'm great, Len. Raring to go,' Deliah replied.

'Do you mind if I join you again?' Les asked.

'Not at all. Just as long ...'

'Yeah I know,' winked Les. 'Just as long as I can keep up.'

'Exactly,' smiled Deliah.

'All right, everybody,' Amanda called out. 'Are you ready?'

'Here we go,' said Les. 'Head 'em up and move 'em out.'

As usual they started off at a leisurely pace. But as soon as they were through the gate, Deliah put the hammer down. Although the muscles in his legs felt tight from the bike ride, Les was able to keep up all right and as they motored along, he and Deliah got into a bit of light conversation. Les told Deliah about his pranic healing and how much he enjoyed tai chi on Meditation Hill with the sun coming up. And he thought he might have caught her for the early morning walk. Deliah said she had a boxercise class in the morning and besides the other activities, she went to a seminar about high protein, low carbohydrate diets. Lionel 'Don't Bore Us' kept putting his head in and they booed him out of the room. As he was leaving he said he'd like to come back and give them all poison. One of the women said if he came back they'd take it. And on the subject of food, the kids were blowing up again because all Dad gave them to eat now was TV dinners. And having to eat curried prawns and rice or roast pork and gravy with three vegetables for breakfast made them feel sick all day. Even the cat had left home. They threatened that if she didn't get back soon, they'd tie their father up in the kitchen and burn the house down.

When they reached the home stretch Deliah got into top gear. Norton's breathing was as good as gold. But with his stiff legs, Les had to push it to keep up and when Deliah beat him to the back gate by three lengths, it wasn't because Les threw the race.

'I have to commend you, Len,' said Deliah. 'You went really well today.'

'Thanks, Deliah,' said Les. 'I'm getting there. Tomorrow could be the day of reckoning.'

'I'll be here, Len.'

The others filed in through the gate then they all went their different ways. Les went straight to the pool again and jumped in wearing his T-shirt. The water felt better than ever and kicking around on his back did Norton's legs a power of good. Eventually he got out, picked up a towel from one of the cabanas, dried off and walked back to his villa.

Once inside, Les got a bottle of mineral water, dropped a cassette into the ghetto blaster and while Alabama 3 growled their way through 'Cocaine Killed My Community', hung his gear on the balcony and watched the shadows lengthen over the valley. While he was sipping his water, Les contemplated what would happen when Vanita came back to his villa. He hoped he was wrong, but something told him last night was a one off and tonight she'd play hard to get. Or even turn the old business off just to annoy him. Some women were like that. If she did and Mr Wobbly started going off his brain again, he'd boot her sophisticated arse out the door. He was in enough bother now without being charged with attempted rape or something. Les had a shower and shave, gave himself a detail then changed into his Levi's shorts and a Narooma Blues Festival T-shirt. He watched the ABC news and it was time for mocktails and dinner.

A small crowd was gathered in the library. The manager wasn't there and the writers in residence were already seated in the dining room. Max and his wife were talking to some people and Vanita was standing in the same place talking to Nerine Lushnikof. Vanita was wearing her burgundy leisure suit, with her hair pulled back in a tight ponytail. The cardiologist's wife had on a thin red dress, cut low in the front and wore her hair tied up and dumped loosely on top of her head. Vanita caught Norton's eye and motioned for him to come over. Les smiled and eased his way through the crowd.

'Hello, Vanita,' he said. 'How are you tonight?'

'I'm fine thanks, Len,' she replied. 'Len. Have you met Nerine?'

'No. Hello, Nerine.'

'Hello, Len. Lovely to meet you.' Nerine had a warm handshake, a throaty voice and definite sex appeal. Les could see why Alexander Holden had the hots for her.

'Here you are, Len.' Vanita handed Les a red frothy drink in a champagne glass. 'I told you it was my shout.'

'Thanks.' Les took the drink, clinked Vanita's glass and took a sip. 'Hey, these are all right,' he said. 'What are we on tonight?'

Nerine spoke. 'I think they're the strawberry daiquiris you have ...'

'When you're not having a strawberry daiquiri,' cut in Les.

'Exactly.' Nerine turned to Vanita. 'I wouldn't mind a blender full of the real thing right now,' she said.

'No,' agreed Vanita. 'It's going to be hard to stay on the straight and narrow when I get released tomorrow.'

'That's right,' said Les. 'You leave tomorrow. What time?'

'After lunch,' said Vanita.

Nerine downed her mocktail. 'I have to go to the loo.'

Les watched her leave and downed the rest of his drink too. 'I'll tell you what,' he said, licking his lips. 'These are delicious. I'm going to get another one. Would you like one?'

'Okay,' smiled Vanita.

Les went to the table and came back with three drinks. 'I got one for Nerine,' he said, placing a drink on the coffee table then handing one to Vanita. 'Cheers, pearlshell ears,' he smiled, clinking Vanita's glass.

'Yes, cheers,' she smiled back.

'So what's doing, Vanita? You still want to call back to my villa and keep me company for a while?' Les asked.

'Of course,' she replied.

'What time?'

Vanita looked at her watch. 'An hour from now.'

'Okay. Well when Nerine gets back, I'll stay and chat for a while. Then I'll leave you to it. And I'll see you back at my place.'

'Wonderful,' said Vanita.

Nerine came back and Les handed her the drink from the coffee table. 'Here you are, Nerine,' he said. 'Save you having to fight your way to the bar through all the drunks.'

'Ohh? Thank you, Len,' said Nerine.

They got into a bit of chitchat and had a third drink. Nerine had done funk stretch and body pump followed by Hawaiian lomi lomi treatment. Vanita did Pilates and step then had a Vichy sun shower. Les told them about tai chi and pranic healing.

'You look as if you keep yourself fit, Len,' said Nerine, giving Les a moderate once up and down.

'I try to,' said Les, finishing his drink. 'And I'll tell you what. It makes you hungry.' He placed his empty glass on the coffee table. 'I don't wish to be rude, ladies,' he said. 'But I have to go and eat. I'm starving. Nice to have met you, Nerine.'

'You too, Len,' she replied.

'I'll probably see you before you leave tomorrow, Vanita.'

'Yes. We might have lunch together.'

'I'd like that.' Les left for the dining room.

Les walked in and looked for a table. As he walked past the writers in residence, they all looked up and gave him warm syrupy smiles. 'Hello, Lennie,' they chorused.

'Hello, everybody,' replied Les.

'Have you had a nice day, Lennie?' asked Danica.

'Yes. Everything up to your film director's standards?' asked Benson.

'How's the film game going these days?' asked Harriet.

'Come across any good scripts?' asked Tobias.

'Yeah. I found a ripper down the local chemist's,' replied Les. 'It should make a great feature film.'

'How nice … Lennie,' said Harriet. She attempted a smile. But her face quickly gave up and settled back to its normal resemblance to a gargoyle with irritable bowel syndrome.

Les walked away from the writers and found a table near the balcony. The Four Stooges are in a strange sort of mood tonight, he thought when he sat down. Almost friendly. But did I perceive a hint of sarcasm there? Les picked up the menu as Valerie placed a plunger of herb tea on the table and his ration of rye bread and hummus.

Les ordered mustard-crusted chicken fillet salad with corn and pumpkin and a duo of mustard and balsamic dressing for an entrée. And baked ocean trout on soba noodles with a wasabi and coriander chutney and a red capsicum ragu for a main. Dessert? Why not the lemon and raspberry tofu cheesecake with almond angel wafer and raspberry and lime coulis? Les sipped a cup of herb tea and gave Vanita a smile as she walked in with Nerine. He glanced towards the writers in residence who were actually chuckling amongst themselves at some private joke. And Les noticed Lionel was very quiet for a change. Deliah had her back to him.

Again dinner was scrumptious; and the lime with the raspberry for dessert left a tang in your mouth that made your eyes water. Les washed it down with a cup of herb tea then got up to leave. He didn't bother waving to Vanita. But as he walked past the writers he had to have a dig at them.

'So how was dinner, Toby?' he asked pleasantly. 'Did you have the trout?'

'No,' Tobias replied. 'I chose the blue lentil timbales. They were absolutely delicious.'

'Ohh,' said Les. 'That's good.'

'And I'm off the drink for good,' said Danica.

'Same goes for cigarettes too,' added Harriet. 'Who needs them.'

'I couldn't even look at a beer,' said Benson.

'Well, that's great,' said Les. 'This healthy lifestyle gets to you after a while. Before you know it, you'll all have your youth back and you'll be writing children's books.' Les gave them a smile. 'I have to go. I'm having an early night. I'll see you tomorrow.'

'That would be marvellous,' said Tobias. 'I can't wait.'

Les left the writers in the dining room and walked back to his villa. I know what those Wallys are trying to do, thought Les, as he crossed the grass beside the Wellness Centre. They're trying the old, reverse psychology dodge. Fair enough. All I have to do now is counter with the Bugs Bunny reverse strategy dodge.

Back inside, Les went to the bathroom then blew the oil lamp out and picked up the two sheets of foolscap on his pillow. There were the usual variety of activities and he was having Watsu in the afternoon. Les turned the ghetto blaster back on and stared out at the valley while The Flaming Stars bopped their way through 'Wine Spo-de-o-dee'. I'll tell you what, thought Les, as a shooting star briefly flashed across the clear night sky, that Nerine was a horny big thing. She had a good arse under that dress. Nothing wrong with her tits either. The thought of Nerine's tits and bum had no sooner entered Norton's mind, when Mr Wobbly snapped to attention, ram-rod straight, and started going crazy again. Holy mother of the lord, Les blinked down. What's going on? I've only got to think of women and I turn into a sex-crazed

Mr Hyde. All I need is some face fur, a top hat, a cape and a cane.

Les turned the ghetto blaster off, splashed some water over his face then got a cold bottle of water from the fridge. God almighty, Les thought as Mr Wobbly started thumping his chest and howling like Tarzan under Norton's shorts. I hope Vanita wants to be in some porking tonight. She'll only have to look at me when she walks in the door and I'll be all over her like ants at a picnic. A second later, there was a soft knock at the door. Les adjusted himself and opened it. Vanita was standing in the shadows, holding another plastic bag.

'Hello,' she said. 'We're canvassing the area. Do you know about Jesus?'

'Yeah. He's a Mexican welterweight. Come in.' Les closed the door behind Vanita as she stepped into the villa. 'What's in the bag tonight?' he asked.

'This.'

Les opened the bag. 'Wow! Pellegrino. I don't know what to say.'

'Just pour a couple of glasses, handsome. You'll think of something.'

Les unscrewed the cap and poured two glasses of mineral water. He handed one to Vanita and clinked her glass, spilling some on the carpet.

'Well. Here's looking up you old address,' he sweated.

'Yours too.' Vanita drank some mineral water then immediately placed her hand on Norton's pulsating rod. 'Ooh, Len,' she said. 'What's the matter with you? I walk in here wearing this old leisure suit and you're like a man possessed. What would happen if I walked in wearing a see-through nightie?'

'What would happen?' croaked Les. 'Vanita. You'd never get out of here alive.'

Les put his glass down, took hold of Vanita and started kissing her passionately. Vanita put her glass down and kissed him back, then undid the front of her leisure suit. Les moaned and ran his hands up her ribcage before placing them on her ample breasts. He rubbed them till the nipples firmed beneath the black lace then started easing her pants off. Underneath Vanita was wearing a black G-string that could have doubled as a postage stamp. Les moved her back to the bed, lay her on it, then slid Vanita's G-string off and pushed his face into her ted while he got his clothes off.

Les got into Vanita's business like it was a huge bowl of delicious wine trifle and ice cream. Vanita bucked, kicked and sighed. Les lasted as long as he could before he had to bury the bone. Frothing at the mouth, he got between Vanita's legs, ready to mount her, when she unexpectedly pushed him away.

Shit, I knew this was going to happen, cursed Les. 'What ... what ... What's the matter?' he said desperately.

'Nothing,' said Vanita. 'Put this on.' She reached over to her leisure suit and took out a fat iridescent pink rubber ring with tiny knobs on it. 'It's a cock ring.'

Les looked at it. 'A cock ring? How am I going to get my knob into that?'

'Easy.'

Vanita slipped her mouth around Norton's dick and gave him a polish that rattled his brain then took the cock ring and slid it over his knob. It was surprisingly soft and stretched easily.

'Okay,' said Vanita, lying back on the bed and putting her knees up. 'Let's go.'

'Yeah, let's,' enthused Les.

Les buried Mr Wobbly wearing his new pink jabot into Vanita. Vanita shuddered and howled then grabbed hold of Les and started going off her brain.

After that it was nothing more than a two-person orgy. Les pumped and bashed away, and the harder he shoved, the more Vanita liked it, digging her nails into Norton's back, tearing at his hair and spitting obscenities into his ear. The cock ring didn't affect Les. If anything, it made Mr Wobbly swell up bigger and harder than ever. And every time Les blew, it seemed to last a light year. They sucked and fucked and had the time of their lives. If it wasn't the best sex Les had ever had, it was that close it didn't make any difference. They'd stopped for some water and were getting into it again when the phone rang.

'Shit!' cursed Les, looking up at Vanita who was going up and down on top of him like a fiddler's elbow. 'I'll bet I know who this is.' He picked up the phone. 'Hello,' he snapped, as Vanita kept grinding away, her ponytail spinning round like a tail rotor.

'Mr Gordon. I'm sorry to disturb you. But it's the desk again. Would you please turn your TV down? We've had another complaint.'

'Listen,' fumed Les, 'I keep telling you. I haven't got the TV on. I've got a friend around and we're talking.' He held the phone out. 'There. Can you hear a bloody TV?'

'No.'

Les put the receiver in front of Vanita. 'Hey. Have we got the TV on?'

'No,' she barked. 'We haven't got the bloody TV on.'

'There. Are you happy?'

'Sorry, Mr Gordon.'

Les slammed the phone down and gripped Vanita around the waist as she kept bouncing up and down.

Just before midnight, Vanita decided to call it quits and so did a very battered, very shiny Mr Wobbly. She slipped the cock ring off, placed it back in her top and cuddled up to Les.

'I have to go,' she said. 'I'm checking out tomorrow. And I'm having a couple of treatments early in the morning.'

'Okay,' said Les. 'Do you still want to join me for lunch?'

'Of course. In fact we'll hold hands across the table this time. How does that sound?'

'Very romantic,' said Les.

Vanita kissed Les, then got up and put her clothes on. Les got into his jox and saw Vanita to the door.

'Well, goodnight,' smiled Les. 'I'm glad you came around.'

'So am I,' Vanita smiled back.

'Hey tomorrow, while we're having lunch, all right if I bring my camera? And we get a photo?'

'That would be lovely. Make sure you send me a copy.' Vanita gave Les a gentle kiss on the lips. 'Goodnight, Len.'

'Goodnight, Vanita.' Les closed the door and went to the bathroom.

And I thought she was going to play hard to get, thought Les as he splashed some water over his face. Christ! She came on like Attila the Hun. Les winked at himself in the mirror. Of course you didn't have anything to do with it. Did you? Super screw.

Les rubbed some hemp cream into poor Mr Wobbly then turned out the lights and flopped onto what was left of the bed. His last thoughts as he pushed his head into the pillows were: absolutely nothing. The big Queenslander yawned once and blacked out.

After another sensational night's sleep, Les bounced out of bed early the next morning, feeling lighter, fitter, stronger, and more clear-headed than he'd felt in years. He put the kettle on, cleaned his teeth then made a pot of herb tea and took it out onto the balcony to study the activities sheet while he greeted the start of another beautiful day. He'd missed the tai chi class. But he still had time for the morning walk. After doing the herb tea two-step, Les got into his training gear and, whistling happily, walked down to the Wellness Centre. Antoinette was in charge and Deliah was missing. But standing tall amongst the others, wearing a loose white top and knee-length black lycra shorts was Nerine. She saw Les and walked over.

'Len,' she smiled. 'How are you this morning?'

'I'm good thanks, Nerine,' replied Les. 'How's yourself?'

'Great.'

'Lovely morning for a walk,' said Les.

'It is,' agreed Nerine. 'Do you mind if I join you?'

'No. I like a bit of company.'

'All right, everybody,' called out Antoinette, checking her watch. 'Let's go.'

'Come on, Len,' said Nerine. 'Last one home's a rotten egg.'

As usual they started off slowly then once they were through the gate everybody set their own pace. Les felt that good, it was all he could do to stop from bursting into a run. But he kept near the front of the field, alongside Nerine, who wasn't setting a bad pace with her long legs. He dropped back a couple of times to check out her arse and it looked good; firm and neat and with a very nice motion under the lycra shorts. It wasn't quite as good as Antoinette's. But the instructor was giving Nerine a few years. Les and Nerine fell into a bit of chitchat, the weather, the food, movies, life in Bondi and on the lower North Shore. Then Nerine swung the conversation around to current events.

'So what did you end up doing last night?' she asked.

'Last night?' said Les. 'Nothing. Had dinner. Then went back to my villa. Watched TV and had an early night.'

'Ohh yeah?'

'Ohh yeah?' repeated Les. 'What do you mean by ohh yeah?'

'Well. You and Vanita gave me the impression you're on good terms, Len,' said Nerine. 'Very good terms, actually. And although I haven't seen Vanita this morning, yesterday she had a glow on her face you don't get from the facial a-la-carte at Opal Springs.'

'Really,' said Les, as they strode along in the morning sun. 'Maybe she's using a new French moisturiser,' he suggested.

'I don't quite think so,' smiled Nerine.

'Think what you like,' said Les. 'Besides. Even if I was, I wouldn't tell you.'

'Why not?'

'Because I wouldn't.'

'I'll take that as a yes,' said Nerine.

Les shrugged and kept walking. 'Anyway, if it comes to that, you malicious old gossip, I heard you and the late Alexander Holden had a few extra activities of your own going on.'

'Ohh, did you now?' said Nerine.

'Yes I did. I also heard you gave him the old see you later alligator, and Alexander went into a tail spin.'

'God! And you've got the hide to call me a malicious gossip,' said Nerine.

'I'm only going on what I heard,' said Les.

Nerine gave a toss of her head. 'Well, you could have heard right.'

'So what happened?'

'What happened? Let's just say Alexander bit off more than he could chew.'

'Well, you're a big girl, Nerine.'

'And Alexander was a little man, Len. I would have had more fun if Bugs Bunny had raped me with a baby carrot.'

'Nerine. Please,' said Les. 'You're disgusting.'

'Thanks,' smiled Nerine. 'I like to think so. Put me in one of your movies.'

'What about the R rating?' Shit! All this talk about porking, thought Les. I'd better watch myself, or I'll end up finishing the walk on three legs.

But apart from a passing interest, Mr Wobbly behaved himself and Les finished the walk in good shape. In fact, Les could have streeted the field easily when they got to the last hill. Instead he went up step for step with Nerine and waited at the gate with her for the others.

'You're a big old healthy girl, Nerine,' said Les. 'I'd hate to fight you when I'm drunk.'

'I wouldn't like to tangle with you either, Len,' said Nerine. She gave Les a sultry once up and down. 'Then again, I might,' she smiled.

Les looked shocked. 'Madam. I'll have you know I was raised in a good Christian family.'

'I can imagine,' said Nerine. 'Are you going for mocktails tonight?'

'Probably,' replied Les.

'All right. If I don't see you before, I'll see you then.'

'Righto. That'd be nice.'

Antoinette arrived to open the gate. Everybody filed through, then said goodbye and went their separate ways. Les went straight to the outdoor pool and jumped in wearing his sweaty T-shirt.

Well, what a dirty old thing that Nerine is, thought Les as he leisurely swum around and cooled off. Not only is she not backwards in coming forwards about her and Alexander, if I'm not mistaken, she just dropped the weights on me at the gate. I've half a mind to take Stanley's advice and drag her back to the villa and give her a good cock whipping. Les spurted some water up into the air. As well as Vanita. I'll get a photo of her too. Between those and the ones of Alexander, I'll certainly have some good stories to tell Warren when I get home. Les wallowed happily around enjoying himself then looked at his watch. Shit! I'd better make a move or I'll miss out on the hash browns and bacon. Les got out of the water, picked up a towel and left the pool area.

Back at his villa, Les drank some mineral water and hung his wet gear out on the balcony. He gave himself a squirt of Lynx under the arms and a quick detail, then tucked his Blues Festival T-shirt into his Levi's shorts and left for the dining room.

The writers in residence were seated in the library with their notepads looking very scholarly when Les walked past. They were talking animatedly amongst themselves and appeared to have put aside their mutual hatred for each other.

'Hello, everybody,' said Les cheerfully. 'Another lovely day out there.'

'Ohh, good morning, Lennie,' said Tobias Monk amicably. 'I say, Lennie. Would you happen to have a minute?'

'Only a minute, Toby. I'm running late.'

'Lennie. Will you be having mocktails in the library tonight?' asked Tobias.

'Probably. Why?'

'We insist on having a drink with you,' said Harriet Sutton.

Les thought for a moment. 'Okay,' he said. 'If you put it like that, Harry, why not.'

Harriet managed to ooze out a horrible, oily smile. 'Wonderful.'

Les gave the writers a brief smile. 'Anyway, I have to go. I'm starving.'

'You'll find the breakfast selection particularly scrumptious this morning, Lennie,' said Danica Bloomfield.

'Yes. Absolutely first class,' added Tobias Monk.

'Good. Cause I'm that hungry, I could eat a dead cane toad between two slices of burnt toast.'

After finding a table amongst the remaining independent guests, Les filled two bowls with fruit and cereal and ordered a tomato and zucchini omelette when Sandra placed a pot of herb tea and a fruit juice on the table. Les polished all that off and had some more Bircher

Muesli, fresh figs and papaya, then, ignoring the writers when he left the dining room, strolled back to his villa to work out what he was going to do with the rest of the morning.

As he was walking across the grass, Les noticed Nurse Judy in her white coat, talking to the two cleaners outside a villa several down from his. They were all having a good laugh at something, so Les thought he might see what the joke was.

'Hello, ladies,' he said brightly. 'What's the big joke? Or should I mind my own business?'

'No. Not at all, Len,' chuckled Judy. 'Hey, Len. Do you want something for your next movie?' she asked.

'Always, Judy,' said Les. 'Why? What have you got in mind?'

'This.'

Nurse Judy handed Les a small blue and white packet. Printed on the front was PHYSICIAN SAMPLE PACK. NOT FOR SALE. LIBIDENEX. 20MG. Les looked the packet over then handed it back to Nurse Judy.

'What is it?' he asked.

'You don't know?' said Nurse Judy.

Les shook his head. 'No.'

'You've heard of Viagra?'

'Yeah. It's a sex pill for blokes or something.'

'Well, this is the next one up,' said Nurse Judy. 'Pop one of these. Wait an hour. Next thing you'll be rooting like a plague of rabbits.'

Les studied Nurse Judy for a moment. 'Where did you find that?' he asked her.

The fair-haired cleaner looked at Nurse Judy. 'Is it all right to tell him?'

'Sure. Why not?' Nurse Judy turned to Les. 'If the cleaners find any drugs or booze and that in the villas, they have to inform me. Go on. Tell him, Tracey.'

'We found two empty packets in Mrs Raquelme's villa,' said Tracey.

'Mrs Raquelme. The dark-haired woman from Melbourne?' said Les.

'That's her.' Nurse Judy started to laugh. 'She's certainly been having a fine old time with someone while she was here.'

'And it's a sex drug?' said Les.

'Sure is,' smiled Nurse Judy. 'Works like a charm, so I've been told.'

'I wonder who the lucky man was?' giggled the dark-haired cleaner.

'Yes. I wonder,' said Les.

'So you think that would go all right in a movie, Len?' asked Nurse Judy.

'I'm sure it would,' said Les. 'Anyway. If you'll excuse me, ladies, I have to go. I'm expecting a phone call. Nice talking to you.'

The three women chorused a goodbye, then started laughing again.

Les walked stiffly back to his villa, shoved the door open then slammed it shut behind him. He strode across the kitchen, tore the flyscreen open then stormed out onto the balcony and glared out at the valley.

'You rotten bastard,' he bellowed. 'I've been date raped.'

So that's what the filthy old toad was up to. Don't forget, Les, it's my shout. The rotten moll. She was slipping those things into my mocktails. Timing it to the minute. Then coming round to my villa and porking me into the next postcode. I'm a very sophisticated woman, Len. Yeah. So's Linda fuckin Lovelace. Les spun around angrily. Where's the bloody phone?

'Hello, reception.'

'Yes. It's Mr Gordon. Could you put me through to Mrs Raquelme's villa please? I'm not sure of the number.'

'I'm sorry, Mr Gordon. Mrs Raquelme checked out earlier.'

'She what?'

'A driver called at seven-thirty, and Mrs Raquelme left for Sydney to catch her flight to Melbourne.'

'Did she leave a message?'

'No, Mr Gordon. There was no message.'

'Thanks.'

'You're welcome.'

Les hung up and stared sourly at the phone. The low dropkick. Not only is she a rapist. She's a two-faced bloody liar. Yes, Len, I'd love to get a photo. We can hold hands across the table. Make sure you send me a copy. I know what I'd like to send her. Les got up then went into the bathroom and splashed some water over his face. Hello, super screw, he scowled at himself in the mirror. Give me an L. Give me an E. Give me an S. What's that spell? Mug. Les looked down at his groin. Sorry about that, mate. Next time, keep your eye on your drinks. Les dried his face then walked out onto the balcony and stared across the valley again. Despite his anger at being used and abused and left to dangle, the corners of Norton's eyes slowly started to crinkle. I have to admit something though, he smiled to himself, what a fantastic two nights' porking. How would you go mixing those things with Warren's pot and a few nice delicious? What were they called again?

Despite everything, Les was still jumping out of his skin, so he decided to change whatever anger was left into energy. Another session on the weight stations, followed by a long, leisurely swim would sort that out. Then a nice healthy lunch. Les went inside and changed into his gym gear. As he was lacing up his trainers, Les suddenly remembered that this was his last day at Opal Springs. Tomorrow morning he'd be on his way back to Sydney. After all that had happened, why not go out in style? Les found a dry sweatband, got a towel and headed out the door to the gymnasium.

Amanda had a pump class and Michael was in charge of a stationary bike session when Les took the stairs down to the gym. Inside the manager and a friend were going for it on two cardiovascular machines and several women in leotards were sweating it out on the rowing and walking machines. Les gave the manager a wave then placed his towel on a bench and started doing chest presses.

An hour flew by as Les pushed and pulled while he plotted and schemed. The manager and his friend left, then the women on the walking machines, who were soon replaced by another three women. Les finished with a series of leg extensions then looked at himself in the mirror.

Shit! I look like a two-hundred kilogram mudcrab. To settle himself down, Les joined the women on the walking machines and strode along watching half an hour of a good movie, *Sexy Beast*. While he was watching it, Les couldn't believe how much the leading actor, Ray Winstone, reminded him of a forger he knew from the Kelly Club. And he couldn't believe Ben Kingsley was able to play such a reprehensible dropkick as Don Logan. When Les switched off the machine, he made a mental note to buy the film or hire it and see it right through. Norton left the women to the rest of the movie, had a drink, then picked up his towel and walked across to the indoor pool.

There were two women happily splashing about when Les walked in. Les returned their smiles then got out of his sweaty gym gear and found the same flippers as before. After slipping them on, he dived in, adjusted his goggles and started backstroking up and down the pool. After ten laps Les had pretty much worked out his Bugs Bunny reverse strategy and exit plan. After ten laps freestyle and two backstroking, he had it down to the last detail. Les got out of the pool, wrapped a towel around himself and walked back to his villa.

Inside, Les drank a cold bottle of mineral water while he changed back into the same clothes he wore at breakfast. He gave his hair a quick run through with a plastic bug rake, finished his mineral water and left to have lunch.

The dining room was almost full when Les walked in and the same faces were seated at their usual tables. Lionel Bouris and Deliah were amongst the people on the program. The writers in residence were hunched at their regular table. Nerine was seated with Max and his wife, and the manager was at the end of the captain's table talking with the Americans and several newly arrived guests. Although the novelty had diminished slightly, Les was still the centre of attention when he entered and he exchanged several glances as he found a table and sat down, two across from John Reid and his guests. Les glanced at the menu then went to the salad bar and loaded a plate with Mediterranean salad, with grilled polenta and eggplant, which he smothered with seeded mustard, yogurt dressing. Sandra brought him a plunger of herb tea and a fruit drink and Les ordered wholemeal spaghetti with low fat goat's cheese, bechamel, cherry tomatoes and spinach. With an edge on his appetite from all the exercise, Les quickly finished his first plate of salad and while he was waiting on his main, backed up for another; chickpeas, tomatoes and snowpeas coated in herb and roasted garlic dressing. Les polished that off and his main arrived.

The main was delicious. Les finished every morsel and poured another cup of herb tea. He drank half then decided it was time for action. After carefully wiping his mouth, Les placed his napkin on the table then rose to his feet and tapped the side of his glass with a spoon, loud enough to be heard in every corner of the dining room.

'Ladies and gentlemen,' he announced. 'May I have your attention please. There is something I wish to say.'

An abrupt silence settled over the dining room as everybody stopped eating to stare at Les and exchange puzzled looks with each other. The staff stood where they were and one of the chefs poked his head round from the corridor near the salad table.

'Thank you.' Les placed his glass on the table then looked back at the faces in the dining room. 'As most of you are aware,' he said solemnly, 'there is a rumour going round that the late Alexander Holden was murdered.'

The manager's jaw dropped. 'No. No. It's not true,' he said glancing nervously at the newly arrived guests.

Les turned and narrowed his eyes at the manager. 'If you will kindly allow me to continue.' The manager gave Les a double blink and remained silent. 'As most of you are also aware,' continued Les, 'my name is Leonard Gordon. Aimh a fill-um di-recht-torrh. I was the person who found Mr Holden's body at the front gate. Subsequently, I was vociferously interrogated by the local constabulary. Because of this interrogation, I am now led to believe there is another rumour going round. A rumour. That I. Am a murderer.'

A subdued muttering spread around the dining room while the manager's face contorted with anguish.

'Mr Gordon. Please,' said the manager. 'I've heard of no such thing.'

Les raised his hand for silence. 'Since then, I have made some investigations of my own. And through the consequences of my investigations, tonight in the library I will announce the circumstances and the identity of the person responsible for the untimely demise of the late Alexander Holden.'

'The murderer,' gasped Lionel Bouris.

Les filled his nostrils deeply with air and stared imperiously across at Lionel's table. 'Tonight. In the library,' reiterated Les. Les squared his shoulders and raised his chin then, to the gobsmacked stares of the entire dining room, strode stiffly towards the door, stopping at the writers' table on the way. 'Be there. Or be square,' he told them.

'Ohh, don't worry, Lennie,' said Tobias Monk. 'We'll be there all right.'

'With bells on,' said Harriet Sutton.

'Big silver ones,' added Benson Gritt.

'Oh, this is so exciting,' beamed Danica Bloomfield. 'I can't wait.'

Norton left the writers and everybody else to it and continued on to his villa.

Once inside, Les stepped out onto the balcony and sat down with his feet up. Well, that certainly caught their attention, he smiled. And what about the writers in residence. Toby and the gang are keener than ever. Les chuckled to himself as he watched a small flock of galahs screeching at each other in a nearby gum tree. Love those writers. Lovvve those writers. The galahs flew off and Les absently drummed his fingers on the chair. So what will I do now? I've had enough exercise for the time being. And I'm too full to go for a swim. Why not kick back and have a read before I go for my Watsu? If I'm going to play Hercule Poirot in the library tonight I'll need to bone up on waxing eloquent. Les went inside and picked up *The World's Best Mystery Stories* then made himself comfortable on the lounge and gave himself another mental battering at the hands of Ashton Wolfe and 'The Knights of the Silver Dagger'.

After wading through that and a story by Sir A.T. Quiller-Couch, Les was that glad when the time came for his Watsu, he could have burst into song. Putting the book down was like dragging his brain out of quicksand. For all Les cared in the end, François Sarzeau could have stuck the Druid monument up his arse. And he would have laughed out loud if Father Brown had fallen under a penny omnibus and broken every bone in his body. Even if it did mean being viewed with universal distaste and punished with universal execration. Not knowing what Watsu was and imagining he'd probably feel like a swim afterwards, Les changed into his Speedos and gym gear, got a towel from the bathroom and left for the Healing Centre.

There were two women seated in chairs and Carol was back behind the reception desk when Les walked in.

'Hello,' said Les. 'It's me again. Mr Gordon. I'm here for my Watsu.'

'Certainly, Mr Gordon,' smiled Carol. 'Please take a seat and Robyn will be with you shortly.'

'Thanks.'

Les settled back on one of the lounge chairs listening to the gentle celestial music and it wasn't long before a blue-eyed woman wearing a white robe came up to him. She was barefoot and had her dark hair pulled back in tight ponytail.

'Hello, Mr Gordon,' she said softly. 'I'm Robyn. I'll be taking you for your Watsu.'

'Okay, Robyn,' said Les, rising to his feet.

'Are you wearing a swimming costume?'

'Yes. I am actually.'

'Good. Follow me, please.'

Robyn led Les back past reception to a door in the corner that opened into a large, softly lit, tiled room, taken up mostly by a heated indoor pool. There was a shelf full of towels and robes when you walked in and a bench to place your clothes on. A few floats lay on a narrow walkway round the pool and that was about it.

'You can place your clothes on the bench,' said Robyn, taking off her robe to reveal a black one-piece swimming costume underneath. 'Have you ever had Watsu before, Mr Gordon?' she asked, as Les got out of his gym gear.

Les shook his head. 'No. I haven't.'

'Well. What happens is, I'll put a pair of floats on your legs, then you float in the pool while I hold you in my arms and you completely relax. Then I work your spine and muscles in ways that are only possible in water.'

'Sounds good.'

'It is. Come on. Let's get in the pool.'

Les followed Robyn down a set of steps leading into the water and was surprised how pleasantly warm it was. He waded to the edge of the pool and Robyn picked up a small pair of green floats from the walkway.

'Lift your legs up,' she said.

'Okay.' Les did as he was told and watched as Robyn attached the floats just above his ankles. 'Have you been doing this long, Robyn?' he asked.

'About five years. But I only started here yesterday,' she replied.

'Then you wouldn't know anything about the bloke that got killed in a bike accident.'

'Only what I read in the papers,' Robyn answered.

'Right,' said Les. Well that counts you out.

'Okay,' said Robyn. 'Now close your eyes and relax in my arms. I'll have hold of you. So totally relax. Listen to the music and let your mind drift back to when you were little.'

'Righto.'

With only his face out of the water and Robyn cradling him in her arms, Les did as he was told. Robyn began slowly moving him around and soon Les was amazed how relaxed he'd become. He felt like he was floating in space. Beautiful warm space. And being gently massaged at the same time. Les kept his eyes closed while the celestial music softly filled the room and soon his mind began to fill with happy scenes from his childhood. Visiting relatives, birthdays, school. Watching corny TV shows with mum and dad in the old wooden house in Dirranbandi. Stealing fruit and catching yabbies with his brother. Sneaking a kiss with Mrs Southern's daughter behind the classroom. Taking it a bit further and copping a boot up the arse from Mr Southern. Copping a couple from his father as well. Then one funny little scene played out in his mind as clear as a bell.

Les and his brother were no more than four or five. They'd just come home with Mum after visiting Aunty Janey in Goondiwindi. There was a small hole in the back flyscreen and they had an old red possum used to hang around the house called Smitty. That night when they came home, Smitty had forced his fat arse through the hole in the flyscreen and helped himself to the fruit bowl on the dining room table. There were pieces of chewed fruit and little turds all over the table when Mum switched the light on and right in the middle of the mess was Smitty, gorging himself on the last banana. Les and his brother started laughing. But Mum didn't see the joke. She abused Smitty and Smitty ran out through the hole in the flyscreen, splitting it wide open. Once he was out, Smitty ran right up to the top of a tree and sat there looking at them. Mum was furious. She picked up a piece of wood and flung it at Smitty. Les could clearly see the piece of wood turning round and round in the air in slow motion, like the bone in *2001: A Space Odyssey* before it hit Smitty in the head. The piece of wood fell to the ground and Smitty ran down a branch and jumped into another tree. Anyway, it couldn't have done too much damage, because Smitty was back the next night as if nothing had happened and Mum gave him some grapes. But Les remembered it was a great shot, because it was dark and Smitty was at the very top of the tree.

'Mr Gordon. You can open your eyes now. I'm finished.'

'Huh? What?'

'You can open your eyes,' said Robyn. 'We're finished.'

'Ohh, please,' said Les. 'Just let me stay here a little while longer, will you? This is fantastic.'

'It's lovely, isn't it?'

'You've got no idea.' Les felt Robyn take the floats off then opened his eyes as his feet sank slowly to the bottom of the pool. 'That was unbelievable,' he said when he stood up. 'I've never felt so relaxed in my life.'

'I know,' said Robyn. 'I'm really pleased you liked it. Can I get you a robe?'

'Yeah. Yeah, that'd be nice.'

Les got out of the pool and put on a robe. 'Honestly,' he said. 'I went right back to when I was a kid.'

'That's what it's all about,' smiled Robyn. 'How's your back? Have you got any aches and pains?'

'No. Not a thing.'

'Good,' said Robyn. 'Come on. I'll see you out.'

Les picked up his clothes and followed Robyn out the door. He thanked her again, said goodbye and walked back to his villa.

Still in his robe and feeling like he'd come out of a mild hypnosis, Les spread himself back on the lounge and put his feet up on the coffee table. After a while the feeling wore off and Les went to the bathroom and splashed cold water over his face. He dried off then got a bottle of mineral water and took it out onto the balcony.

As he sipped his water and stared out over the valley, Les started thinking. He kept thinking till he finished his mineral water, then he went inside and changed back into his gym gear. He got his cap and sunglasses, left the villa and walked back towards the Healing Centre.

Les went past the indoor pool and kept going round the back, till he came to the work station he'd found when he was looking for a path up Meditation Hill. It didn't take him long to find what he was looking for. A short length of pipe lying amongst several others next to the resort's generator. Les tucked it up under his arm then walked back around the pool and followed the path to the foyer. Several people were reading in the library and a staff member was dusting when Les took the stairs down to the front door. Outside there were no cars or people on the driveway; Les turned right and followed the road down to the front gate.

There was no one around when Les got to the bottom of the hill and the only sound was a crow circling in the distance and the afternoon breeze moving gently through the trees. Les took the piece of pipe over to the gate and compared it to one of the bars. Then a few metres back from the gate he took the piece of pipe and pressed one end against the road. He checked everything again then, satisfied with what he'd found, started back up the hill. When Les reached the top, he left the piece of pipe under some bushes at the edge of the driveway then took the stairs to the foyer and walked back to his villa.

Les took himself out onto the balcony then sat down and quietly watched the clouds pushing over the surrounding hills. Although he was satisfied with what he'd found, he wasn't pleased and would just as soon preferred he hadn't. It certainly gave him no joy. But, no matter what, tonight in the library the show had to go on. Les gazed at the trees and the sky a while longer then looked at his watch and decided to join the others for the afternoon walk.

Michael was in charge and Deliah was standing amongst the others outside the Wellness Centre when Les strolled up. Naturally after his announcement in the dining room all eyes were upon him when he joined the group.

'Hello, Len,' said Michael. 'How are you?'

'I'm good, thanks, Michael,' replied Les.

'I can't wait for tonight,' said Michael. 'All the staff are going to be there. John's not too happy, though.'

'Well, I can't help that,' shrugged Les.

'Are you really going to expose the murderer, Mr Gordon?' asked a dark-haired woman in a grey tracksuit.

'Can you give us a clue who it is?' said her dark-haired friend wearing blue shorts and a white top.

'All I can say at this stage,' smiled Les, 'is, you two are definitely in the clear.'

Deliah came over from amongst the others. 'Hello Len,' she said. 'How's things?'

'Pretty good, thanks, Deliah,' said Les. 'How are you?'

'Good.' She looked directly at Les. 'That was a nice little hand grenade you lobbed into the dining room at lunchtime today.'

'Well. All this gossip and innuendo going around, Deliah. A man's just got to do what a man's just got to do. Hasn't he?'

'I don't know about the manager not liking it,' said Deliah, 'but Lionel is absolutely shitting himself.'

'Gone a bit pale, has he?' said Les.

'You could say that. Was it him?'

'You'll find out tonight, Deliah.'

Two more joined the group and Michael checked his watch. 'All right, everybody,' he called out. 'Let's go.'

They started off in their usual leisurely fashion till they got to the gate, then as soon as they were outside Deliah shot to the lead and stepped up the pace. This time, however, Les decided to put a little pressure on as well. He didn't get in front of Deliah. But kept by her side, sneaking in that extra zing every now and again as they went along, so that if Deliah didn't want to fall behind, she had to push herself hard to keep up. Consequently, the conversation, which was limited to begin with, fell away to nearly nothing.

'You're going extremely well today, Len,' puffed Deliah as they went past a row of trees alongside the golf links.

'You think so, Deliah?' replied Les indifferently. 'I just looked at my watch, and we're not going any faster than normal.'

'It doesn't seem like it,' said Deliah.

Les smiled at her. 'Are you sure you haven't been sneaking a few meat pies in with your broccoli florets and toasted sesame seeds, Deliah?'

Michael suddenly jogged up alongside them. 'What's going on?' he said with a smile. 'Are you two trying to break the record today?'

Les turned to Michael and without breaking his stride had a quick peek behind them. They were a hundred metres or more in front of everyone. 'No. Not at all,' said Les, very nonchalantly. 'I'm just trying to keep up with Deliah. That's all.'

'Yeah. All right.' Michael turned and jogged back to the others.

A hundred metres further on, Les turned the screws a little more and Deliah's arms started pumping like steam pistons. They kept going along the flat, then the road curved round and next thing they were approaching the final hill.

'Here it is, Deliah,' said Les. 'Heartbreak Hill.'

Deliah sucked in air and with a look of steely determination in her eyes, set her jaw. She knew Les always faltered on the hill and she was determined to beat him to the gate. She dropped back a gear and gave it everything she had. Les kept with her then, halfway up the hill, turned around and walked the rest of the way backwards.

When they got near the top he slowed down and let Deliah beat him to the gate by two lengths.

'Fair dinkum, Deliah,' said Les. 'I try and I try. But you always beat me on the hill. You're a deadset legend, mate.'

Deliah's chest was heaving and her face looked like an eggplant as she rested with her hands on her knees while the others came straggling up the hill.

'That was hard enough as it was today,' she puffed. 'Without doing it backwards. And you look like you wouldn't blow out a candle.' Deliah looked up at Les. 'I don't know about you, Len.'

Les gave her a wink. 'There's a lot of things you don't know about me, Deliah.'

Michael arrived to open the gate and they all filed through. Les said a quick goodbye to everyone, then instead of going straight to the pool as he normally did, walked round to the foyer.

Karla was behind the front desk looking her efficient best when Les walked up. 'Hello, Mr Gordon,' she smiled. 'How can I help you?'

'Karla,' said Les, 'would it be possible to have dinner delivered to my room tonight?'

'Not a problem, Mr Gordon,' replied Karla. She reached under the desk then handed Les the dinner menu. 'Just ring the kitchen and tell them what you want.'

Les took the menu. 'Thanks,' he said. 'And Karla. Could you loan me a clipboard?'

'Certainly.' Karla reached back under the desk then handed Les a plastic clipboard with several sheets of Opal Springs stationery on it. 'Getting ready for the big one tonight, are we, Mr Gordon?'

Les pinned the menu to the clipboard. 'Yes I am,' he smiled. 'Are you going to be there?'

Karla shook her head. 'I have to work. But I can listen from over here.'

'Good.' Les thanked Karla again and left for the outdoor pool.

Careful not to get the clipboard wet, Les placed it on a cabana with a towel over the top and jumped into the pool wearing his T-shirt. He dived up and down, swum a few laps then as the shadows got longer and the pool area was in complete shade, floated around thinking things over.

It was no good letting his findings change his present mood. Besides, he might still be wrong. And tonight in the library could turn out to be a hoot. Whatever the result, his few short days at Opal Springs had definitely been an eye-opener. All that coffee and eating almost anything that came along wasn't where it was at. And the treatments he got were fabulous. He definitely owed Warren a big one for the favour. Les looked at his watch. It was time to get cleaned up, order dinner then get his shit together and do his thing in the library. Les got out of the pool, dried off and with the clipboard under his arm, walked back to his villa.

The first thing Les did after hanging his wet things on the balcony, was ring the kitchen and order steamed scallops in their shell with rice noodle salad and saba vinegar dressing for an entrée, pan-seared Atlantic salmon with roasted lemon, sweet potato and skordalia for a main, and baked mango topped with meringue cloud, with saffron custard and berry coulis for dessert. It would be delivered in about half an hour. Les thanked the girl in the kitchen then switched on his ghetto blaster and with Red Rivers taking his guitar to 'Heart of Honky Tonk', got under the shower. By the time he got out, had a shave, dabbed his craggy moosh with Lomani and changed into a pair of black cargo shorts and his favourite white Led Zeppelin Stage Crew T-shirt, freshly washed and ironed, a knock on the door told him dinner had arrived. Les thanked the fair-haired young girl that delivered it and ate in the lounge room.

As far as Les was concerned, his last supper at Opal Springs would have made a Christian rock band smash their guitars on stage and kick in the drum kit. And when he left the tray outside his door, the plates shone in the dark. He let the meal settle down while he sat in the kitchen going over the notes he'd taken down after his lymphatic massage with Harold then, after adding some of his own, fastened them onto the clipboard. Satisfied he had all the ammunition he'd need, Les switched off the ghetto blaster and with the clipboard under his arm, left the villa.

The library was packed when Les arrived; the management had even supplied herb tea and nibblies for the occasion. Any noise quickly settled down and turned into an expectant silence when Les appeared at the entrance, where he stopped to see who was there. John Reid was seated with the Americans and Dallas was missing, but Michael, Peta, Amanda, Rita and Nikki were seated with Nurse Judy near the writers in residence, where Benson Gritt actually had on a clean white T-shirt, half tucked into his grubby jeans. Wearing her apple green leisure suit, Nerine Lushnikof was seated with Max and Hannah. Lionel Bouris and Deliah were seated with several other guests on the program. With every eye watching him, Les stepped across to the marble table and placed his clipboard next to a half empty tray of yeast muffins. He then looked up, raised his chin and stonily returned the stares of the people seated or standing around him.

'Thank you,' said Norton. 'If I might have silence and your full attention. This should not take long.'

John Reid, the manager, rose from his table and stepped trepidatiously over to Les. 'Mr Gordon,' he said quietly. 'May I have a quick word with you?'

'You may,' nodded Les, raising his voice. 'But make it quick.'

'Mr Gordon. You do know this is highly irregular, don't you?'

'I do, Mr Reid,' replied Les. 'But in this instance, sir, my good name and reputation has been called into question and vile imputations have been cast against my character which I consider to be a felonious affront upon my person. Therefore, if you would be so courteous as to allow me the correctitude to continue, sir, I will disseminate my address and we can all be on our way.'

The manager gave Les a double blink. 'I'm sorry, Mr Gordon.'

Les waited till the manager was seated then continued. 'As I was saying. We all know why we're here. To clear my name and get to the bottom of the inauspicious death of Alexander Holden. And it is not beyond my pertinacity,' said Les, 'to believe the person responsible for his untimely demise is in this room.'

There was a flurry of movement throughout the library and a buzz of muted conversation as people whispered to each other and surreptitiously ran their eyes over the people around them.

'There are many suspects assembled here,' continued Les. 'People who would gladly have done such a foul deed. So without any further procrastination, I will endeavour to expose the person accountable for this iniquitous act.' Les gave the crowd time to settle down then pointed an accusing finger at the man sitting behind John Reid. 'Was it you? Lionel Bouris?'

'Me?' squeaked the albino.

'Yes, you,' Les nodded slowly. 'Is it not a fact that Alexander Holden reduced you to tears in front of the guests one night in this very library? Did he not say you were a fat, useless, blabber-mouthed mummy's boy who should wear a dress if they could find one to fit you, and if you wore a brassiere it could double as a hammock for a jockey? You'd talk under two metres of hot tar and the guests only put up with you out of politeness? Your name is Lionel Bouris. But the guests now refer to you as Lionel Don't Bore Us. Is this not a fact?'

'Well ... yes,' piped up Lionel.

'And did Alexander Holden not also refer to you as a walking blancmange? And said you looked like a ghost who'd been rolled in self-raising flour? You came here to lose weight, and all they could do was rearrange it? Not only that, you have been passing yourself off as French, when all the time you're a New Zealander. In fact, you're a Maori. An albino Maori. A man of two tribes. Wanted by neither. You sit down to pee, you drink your milk out of a saucer and you threatened to poison everybody in the conference room. And I also have it on excellent authority, when Alexander Holden exposed you and you exited the library, that if looks could kill, Alexander Holden would have been dead before he made it to the front gate.' Les glared menacingly at Lionel. 'Answer me, sir. True or false?'

Lionel stared helplessly at Les for a moment. 'Yes, it's all true,' he wailed. 'But I didn't kill him.'

'So you say.' Les ignored Lionel and turned to the staff seated behind the manager. He paused for a moment then pointed. 'Or was it you — Nurse Judy?'

'Me?' said Nurse Judy. 'Get out. You're off your bloody head.'

'Possibly,' agreed Les. 'But is the death of Alexander Holden's on yours? In your office on my first day at Opal Springs, did you not refer to Alexander Holden as a WOLF?' Les briefly turned to the manager. 'Yes, I know all about your staff's usage of acronyms to describe various guests. BERTs. LOMBARDs. WILMAs and the like. A WOLF is a Whingeing Obnoxious Little Fart.' This brought a gasp from some of the guests. 'And, Nurse Judy, did you not say to me, put me in your next movie — as a murderer? Was this a subliminal reference to a part you may have had in the death of Alexander Holden? Was it a cry for help? Answer me, woman.'

'I'll answer you all right,' said Nurse Judy. 'Go and get rooted.'

'And look like you for the rest of my life?' answered Les. 'I think not, madam.' Les pointed to another staff member. 'Or was it you, Nikki? Pranic healer.'

'Me. Ohh give me a break, you dill.'

'Give you a break? Hah! Did not Alexander Holden kick over your bowl of water, call you a

303

charlatan and refuse to pay?' Nikki went silent. 'And did you not refer to him in front of me as a WILMA? A Wanking Impolite Loud Mouthed Arsehole? And did you not say to me, if you were behind a tree with a shotgun, you would have given him both barrels? And also said — quote — you would have utilised the little WILMA's life force and balanced his prana at the same time with a piece of four-by-two. Well, did you or did you not, woman?'

'So what if I bloody did?' said Nikki. 'He was a prick with ears.'

'A prick that helped pay everyone's wages,' said Les. 'Which brings me to my next suspect.' Les pointed to another staff member. 'Yes, you. Rita. The hot stone masseur.'

Rita looked shocked. 'Me? I had nothing to do with it,' she insisted.

'Indeed?' said Les. 'Did you not refer to Alexander Holden as a BERT — A Boring Extremely Rude Turd? Well. Did you?'

'I might have,' admitted Rita.

'And did Alexander Holden not call you a stupid bitch and walk out in the middle of his treatment?'

'He might have,' shrugged Rita.

'And when I was getting a treatment from you and we discussed your short stories, and I jokingly said you had a way with words, you'd be a killer as a writer, did you not say, you never know, Mr Gordon? Was this another subliminal reference to your involvement in his death? Another cry for help? Same as Nurse Judy?'

'Ohh blow it out your arse,' said Rita.

'Yeah. You're up yourself, fellah,' sneered Nurse Judy.

'I'd rather be up at six in the morning than up you, bag lady.' Les poured himself a glass of water from a jug on the table and took a sip while he checked out the faces in the library.

Except for Lionel, the guests appeared somewhere between shock and enjoyment. Michael was quietly chuckling to himself. Amanda and Peta weren't doing anything. Nurse Judy and the others were looking at him like he'd been left in the library by grave robbers and John Reid was in a state of embarrassed disbelief. The writers in residence were staring at Les like a row of statues on Easter Island. Les put his glass down and continued.

'Which now brings me to my next list of suspects,' said Les, pointing an accusing finger at a table near the staff. 'The writers in residence.'

'Us? This is preposterous,' declared Tobias Monk.

'How dare you,' said Harriet Sutton.

'What's he on about now?' queried Danica Bloomfield.

'Silence,' commanded Les. He moved the papers on the clipboard and turned to the guests. 'I have it on excellent authority that one night here in the library, Alexander Holden picked out the writers for a particularly vitriolic diatribe. Inciting any one of them to cause him injury. Or worse. Starting with you — Tobias Monk.'

'What? Why you vilipendious slubberdegullion,' fumed Tobias Monk.

Les raised his chin. 'Is it not a fact, Tobias, that Alexander Holden called you a writer for the ages? The ages between four and seven. Your last book, *Chained to Destiny*, was that dull one critic read the last page first in case he died before he finished it. You're that slow, if you were a lift they'd show movies between floors. You couldn't write a shopping list. Couldn't write your name on a shithouse door. Couldn't write clean me on a dirty windscreen. And as for your book winning a literary award, your writing wouldn't win a loaf of bread at a bakers' picnic. Plus you're that mean, you had a hip transplant and asked the surgeon if you could have the bone for your dog. Is this not true?' demanded Les.

'You insulting brigand,' thundered Tobias Monk.

Les held the clipboard up to the crowd. 'I'm only going on what I was told,' he said. Les put the clipboard down and turned back to the writers. 'Which brings me to you, Danica Bloomfield.'

'Now just a minute, Lennie,' said Danica.

'Silence, you stupid woman,' commanded Les. He glared at her before starting again. 'Is it not true that Alexander Holden said you don't write books, you knit them, and compared to you, Barbara Cartland sounds like Madam Lash. Your nickname is Oil Well, because you never stop gushing, you open every conversation with a corkscrew, and you'd be one of the nicest women on two legs, if you could stand on them. You wear all grey when you drink in bars, so you match the footpath when they throw you out, you're the good time that was had by all and you divorced your last husband because he had a sobering effect on you. He hid all your bottles.'

'You insidious swine,' said Danica.

Les held up the clipboard. 'Ms Bloomfield, if Alexander Holden said anything to insult you, I'm sorry. But he was doing his best.' Les put the clipboard down again. 'Which brings me to you, Benson Gritt. Grunge writer.'

'What?' said Benson. 'There's nothing wrong with my books.'

'No? Well for starters,' said Les, 'according to Alexander Holden, they're full of single entendres, your writing in general is epitomical feculence and you wouldn't know the difference between a semi-colon and a semi-trailer. Reading your material is like bathing in somebody else's bathwater and none of your books should be taken lightly. They should be flung into the nearest garbage bin with great force. You'll never eat your words, because they'd taste like shit. And talking about shit. Your last book, *Rat Sandwich*, should have been called *Shit Sandwich*. The only rap one critic gave it was, the first capital letter wasn't too bad, and the last full stop was half all right. But anything in between wasn't worth reading.' Les looked pleadingly at Benson Gritt. 'Should I go on?'

'In your arse,' scowled Benson Gritt.

'I wish you were, kid. I'd shit all over you.' Les tapped on the clipboard. 'Which brings me to my last suspect,' he said, then pointed once more to the writers' table. 'Harriet Sutton.'

'Bastard,' hissed Harriet.

'Illegitimacy is in the eye of the beholder, madam. Love child is the correct term.' Les drew a deep breath as total silence descended on the library. 'Alexander Holden,' stated Les, 'did he not say you can always tell your books by the hair under the covers. And your last book, *The Fruits of My Labia*, was aptly named because it was an absolute cunt of a book.' Les held the clipboard up to the guests. 'Alexander Holden's words. Not mine.' He turned back to a fuming Harriet Sutton. 'You've been over that many carpets, your nickname in literary circles is Godfrey's. You've pirated more work than Henry Morgan and your idea of originality is undetected plagarism. You don't bother with re-writes because you haven't even got re-reads, the shelf life of your books is somewhere between milk and yogurt. And a publisher would rather see a werewolf in his office during a full moon than you. Did Alexander Holden say that in the library or not? Answer me. You wretched excuse for a woman.'

'Alexander Holden wouldn't know shit,' spat Harriet Sutton.

'He knew a malicious old carpet muncher when he saw one,' said Les. 'Which now brings me to my last question.' He narrowed his eyes at Harriet Sutton. 'When Alexander Holden was forced to leave the library in fear of his life at the enraged hands of you and your fellow writers, did you not say to him, I'd like to break your neck?' Les stared directly at Harriet Sutton. 'Yes, you did, madam. And what did Alexander Holden die from?' Les turned to Nurse Judy. 'Would you be so kind as to answer that please, Nurse Judy.'

Nurse Judy looked at Les for a moment. 'Cervical fracture of the fourth vertebra. With spinal cord compression.'

'Exactly,' said Les. 'In other words, a broken neck. Thank you, Nurse Judy. Your expertise is greatly appreciated.'

'That's absolutely ridiculous,' shouted Harriet Sutton, over the noise in the library. 'I was nowhere near the bastard when he was killed.'

Les stared impassively at Harriet Sutton then turned to the rest of the library and held up his hand for silence. 'So there you have it, ladies and gentlemen,' he said. 'My deductions, my list of suspects. And their motives for wanting to despatch the unfortunate Alexander Holden.' Whispering amongst themselves, the guests turned to the people Les had named; in particular, the writers in residence. Les put his clipboard down and ran his gaze round the library. 'So who was the murderer?' he asked. Les waited a moment then smiled and gestured magnanimously. 'It's simple,' he said. 'There was no murderer. Alexander Holden commited suicide.'

There was complete silence for a moment before the library burst into a hubbub of astonishment and conjecture.

'Suicide?'

'What was that?'

'Suicide?'

'That's ridiculous.'

'Suicide? I don't believe it.'

'Impossible.'

'Yes,' said Norton. 'Suicide. And the blame lies squarely at the feet of the woman over there in the green leisure suit.' Les pointed, his arm as rigid as a steel rod. 'Nerine Lushnikof.'

Nerine's nose wrinkled. 'Me?' she said. 'How do you figure that out?'

'Mrs Lushnikof,' said Les directly. 'Were you or were you not having an affair with Alexander Holden? Come on, woman. The truth.'

Nerine thought for a moment. 'All right,' she admitted. 'We could have been having a bit of a fling.'

'And did Alexander Holden not fall madly in love with you?'

Nerine shrugged. 'Yes. He was a bit my way, I suppose.'

'And for his trouble, you gave Alexander Holden an ignominious rebuttal. Is that not also true?'

'Well he didn't bring much to the party,' said Nerine airily. 'So I sort of told him to … get on his bike. No pun intended,' she added.

'No pun taken,' said Les. 'And did you not say to me during the walk this morning, as far as sex with Alexander Holden went, you would prefer to have been raped by Bugs Bunny with a baby carrot? And you'd find more meat on a vegetarian's toothpick, than you would on Alexander Holden's wozzer? Well, did you?'

Nerine ran a delicate finger across her bottom lip. 'Words to that effect,' she conceded.

'Thank you, Mrs Lushnikof,' said Les, with a polite nod of his head. 'At least you're honest.' He then turned to the others in the library. 'So there you have it, ladies and gentlemen. Alexander Holden died not only of a broken neck. But also of a broken heart. He fell deeply in love with Mrs Lushnikof. Which is quite understandable, I might add. She is an exceptionally attractive and charming woman. Who nonetheless spurned Holden's affections. And suffering from both emotional torment and penile inadequacy, Alexander Holden pedalled his bike down the hill at literally breakneck speed. And deliberately slammed his head into the front gate. Ending his life.' Les gave his last words a moment to sink in. 'I will now leave it at that. Thank you.' A ripple of applause suddenly ran through the library and Les took a bow. 'Thank you,' he repeated. 'Thank you.'

Les had another drink of water and was about to pick up his clipboard and leave, when Tobias Monk rose grandly to his feet, adjusted his reading glasses and cleared his throat.

'Ladies and gentlemen,' he said eloquently. 'May I ... have your attention please?'

'Hey, Toby. It's all cool, baby,' said Les. 'You don't have to congratulate me. I might be a genius. But I am modest.'

Tobias ignored Les. 'On behalf of myself and the other writers in residence, there is something I would like to say.'

'Very well,' said Les breezily. 'If you insist.'

'We have been making some enquiries ourselves. And in front of the assembled guests and staff, I would like to state unequivocally,' Tobias stopped to point Les out, 'that this man is an imposter.'

'What?' said Les. 'How dare you, sir. Why, I've never been so insulted in my life.'

'Ohh I don't know, Lennie,' said Harriet Sutton. 'Think back. You must have been.'

Tobias produced a fax. 'I have here a photo of Leonard Gordon, the film director.' Tobias held the fax up to the library. 'As you can see, the real Leonard Gordon is a short dark-haired man with glasses. And he is currently in America. Los Angeles to be exact. Filming a TV commercial for Coors Beer.' Tobias turned haughtily to Les. 'You, sir, are not the man you claim to be.'

'Not the man I claim to be?' Les gave Tobias an indignant once up and down as a whisper of suspicion ran round the library. 'That's absolutely ridiculous,' said Les. 'Why, only this morning I saw myself in the mirror. And I said, hello my fine fellow, and how are you today? And I replied, I'm quite well thank you. How's yourself.' Les gave Tobias another once up and down. 'Upon my soul Mr Monk. I think I know myself when I see me.'

Egged on by the other writers, Tobias put down the fax and picked up two pages from the Sunday papers. 'Not only are you not Leonard Gordon,' he declared, waving them in the air. 'You are this man here. Les Norton. Currently out on bail for assault. Parading amongst us under an assumed name.' Basking in Harriet Sutton's evil, twisted grin, Tobias narrowed his eyes at Les. 'So. Len Gordon. Alias Les Norton. What do you say to that, sir?'

Les tried to look both incensed and offended. But it was no good. His cover had been blown. 'Why, I ...' he hesitated.

'As I suspected,' huffed Tobias. 'A prevaricator and a simulacrum.'

'Pooh! You big fizz,' said Danica Bloomfield.

'Some bloody film director,' laughed Benson Gritt.

'You couldn't direct anyone to the nearest post office, you turd,' said Harriet Sutton.

John Reid stared suspiciously at Les. The staff members started laughing amongst themselves as a buzz of suspicion swept through the library. Les picked up his clipboard and turned to the crowd.

'This is absolutely preposterous,' he said. 'I don't have to stand here and be insulted by fools and faineants who don't know what they're talking about.'

Les was about to leave when half a blueberry yeast muffin, thrown from the writers' table, hit him in the face. This was followed by a small tub of yogurt, another of fruit compote and a handful of salmon in aspic.

'Well, go somewhere else and be insulted. You mug,' cackled Harriet Sutton.

Trying to salvage what little pride he had left, Les flicked the food from his T-shirt, and contemptuously faced his accusers. 'You miserable, odious rabble,' he sniffed. 'Well may you deface me with cake, jam, custard and jelly. But mark my words. I'm not a man to be trifled with.' Les turned on his heel and leaving the uproar in the library behind him, strode back to his villa.

Well, that didn't quite turn out as I expected, thought Les as he wiped the food off him in the bathroom. Somehow or other, those bloody writers tumbled me. No wonder they were looking forward to tonight. The bastards.

Anyway I asked for it. And they got me fair and square. Writers might be dumb and boring. But they're intuitive. Les took his white T-shirt off and folded it away. He put his Blues Festival one back on then kicked off his trainers, turned on the TV and lay back on the bed. Despite having just been pissed on from a great height, Les couldn't help a tiny smile forming on his craggy face. Breakfast should be interesting in the morning, he imagined.

Les was getting into a weird American show on SBS about sex machines, when there was a knock on the door. Shit! I wonder who this is? Les hauled himself off the bed and opened the door to find Nerine standing there.

'Nerine,' said Les. 'What do you want?'

'This.'

Nerine hauled off and slapped Les hard across the face. It hurt. But Les shook his head and copped it sweet.

'Thanks,' he said. 'At least you didn't hit me in the face with a custard pie.'

Nerine smiled at Les. 'And at least you did refer to me as an exceptionally attractive and charming woman.'

Nerine suddenly flung her arms around Norton's neck and started kissing him like she was a boa-constrictor trying to swallow him whole. Les kissed her back while he tried to breathe and fight her off at the same time, when Nerine kicked the door shut behind her.

'Come on,' she growled, and pushed Les back towards the bedroom.

'Yeah, okay,' said Les, a little nonplussed.

Les fell back on the bed with Nerine on top, grinding herself against him. She moaned and groaned as she kissed him and Les did his best to return her kisses, except it was like kissing a German Shepherd. He ran his hand across her boobs and found them reasonably firm. But when he placed his hand between her legs, it was like grabbing hold of a huge, steaming meatloaf. Moaning louder, Nerine stuck her hand inside his shorts and started pulling and yanking away at Mr Wobbly like she was trying to start a lawn mower. But whether it was a come-down from the Libidenex or he'd just taken enough of a battering over the last two nights, Mr Wobbly didn't seem all that interested. Finally Nerine gave up and stared daggers at Les.

'What's the matter with you?' she demanded.

'I don't know,' said Les. 'It's never happened before. Maybe it was something I ate.'

Nerine placed his hand back between her legs. 'Why don't you eat some of this?'

Les shook his head. 'Sorry. I'm not that hungry.'

Nerine glared at Les then got up and stood at the side of the bed. 'Anyway,' she sneered. 'You haven't got much more to offer than Alexander bloody Holden.'

'Yeah?' replied Les. 'Well, Nerine, even a Jumbo Jet'd look small if it landed in the Great Dividing Range.'

'Fuck you!'

Nerine tossed her head back then stormed out of the villa slamming the door behind her. Les wiped the lipstick and saliva off his face and went back to watching TV.

The strange, semi-pornographic show on SBS ended and Les was about to switch the TV off when the phone rang. His eyes narrowed as he picked up the receiver.

'Hello.'

'Mr Gordon. It's the desk again. Look, we're terribly sorry. But we've had another complaint.'

'Yeah, I know,' said Les. 'Would you turn the TV down?'

'Would you mind, Mr Gordon?'

'No,' replied Les sweetly. 'Not at all.'

Les switched the TV off then went to his bag and took out the CD Michael had burnt for him. He switched the stereo on, found the track he wanted and turned the stereo up full volume.

Heyyy yah, hey yah, hey yah! Hey yohh!

Heyyy yah, hey yah, hey yah! Hey yohh!

Boom — Boom, boom, boom!

Boom — Boom, boom, boom!

Les opened the flyscreen door and stood out on the balcony while inside the Sioux got ready for battle. The villa had a good stereo and the drumming and chanting pumped right through the building and well out into the valley.

'How's that?' yelled Les. 'Is that too loud? You whingeing fuckin pricks.'

Heyyy yah, hey yah, hey yah! Hey yohh!

Heyyy yah, hey yah, hey yah! Hey yohh!
Boom — Boom, boom, boom!
Boom — Boom, boom, boom!

'I'm Len Gordon. I'm a fill-um di-recht-torrh,' shouted Les. 'And don't you ever fuckin forget it. You miserable — fucking — cunts.'

Les let the track run out then went inside and switched off the stereo. He put the CD back in his bag, stripped off then cleaned his teeth before turning out the lights and climbing into bed. Les stared up at the ceiling for a short while then closed his eyes and pushed his head into the pillows. Before he dozed off, his last thoughts were that even though he'd brought himself undone in the library, he'd still done the right thing.

Les had a sleep-in the next morning and when he got out of bed he felt great. He cleaned his teeth, gave himself a big smile in the mirror then made a pot of herb tea and took it out onto the balcony. The sky was thick with clouds pushing in over the valleys from the surrounding mountains. But it was still quite warm and if the clouds lifted it would be another beautiful day.

Lès sipped his herb tea and watched a pair of magpies whistling happily to each other as they searched for worms on the dew laden grass below his balcony while he figured out what he should do first.

Although he was going to feel like a nice dill when he walked into the dining room, he was starving hungry and he wanted two last bowls of the retreat's sensational Bircher Muesli before he left. So too bad. But first he'd pack his gear. That wouldn't take long. Then as soon as he had breakfast, he'd settle his account and get out while he was in front. Les watched the magpies a while longer then did the herb tea tango and packed his bag. After making sure he'd included some of the retreat's choice toiletries, Les tucked his Les Motto T-shirt into his Levi's shorts, adjusted his sunglasses and with his camera in his hand, went to have breakfast.

The dining room was half full when Les walked in and naturally he was once again the centre of attention. Although there was a little bit of nudge-nudge wink-wink, the reception was better than he'd expected and Les returned a few smiles as he found a table. The writers in residence were nowhere to be seen and neither was Nerine. But Deliah was seated with the others on the program and gave Les a smile and a wave before Les walked across to the salad bar and loaded two bowls with cereal and fruit. Sandra brought him a plunger of herb tea and Les ordered poached eggs.

'I heard you went really well in the library last night, Mr Gordon,' said Sandra.

'I did my best, Sandra,' Les assured her.

'I'd've loved to have been there,' she said. 'John was a bit funny. But Peta and Michael were still laughing when I arrived this morning.'

'That's good,' said Les.

'When are you leaving?'

'Today, Sandra. As soon as I finish breakfast.'

'Ohh,' said Sandra. 'Well anyway, Mr Gordon. It's been really nice meeting you.'

'You too, Sandra,' smiled Les. 'Thanks very much.'

That made Les feel better and he got into the Bircher Muesli with gusto before backing up for more. His poached eggs arrived and Les was enjoying the last of them when he looked up to find Deliah standing at his table.

'Hello, Len,' she said. 'How are you this morning? It is Len — isn't it?'

'It might be, Deliah,' said Les. 'But what's in a name anyway?'

'True,' she replied. 'But you're definitely a strange man.'

'I'm just a good Queensland boy, Deliah. That's all.'

'Fair enough,' smiled Deilah. 'Did you hear what happened after you left last night?'

'No. What happened?' asked Les.

'The writers finished up in a big fight with each other. Harriet Sutton punched Tobias Monk in the face and broke his glasses. And the manager and some of the staff had to forcibly eject them from the library. Danica Bloomfield was drunk. Apparently they've been asked to leave.'

'Fair dinkum?'

'Whatever it was you said to them, it sure struck home.'

'Ohh, Deliah,' laughed Les. 'That's made my day.' He looked at her and picked up his camera. 'Deliah, do you mind if I get a photo taken with you?'

'No. Not at all, Len,' said Deliah.

Les stood up and got Sandra to take a photo of him with Deliah. And one more for safety. He shook Deliah's hand then said goodbye and Deliah left for a pump class. Les finished his breakfast and there was a spring in his step when he left the dining room for the foyer to settle his account.

Karla was behind the computer and gave Les a friendly smile when he walked up to the desk.

'Good morning, Mr Gordon,' she said. 'How are you today?'

'Good, thanks,' replied Les. 'Except I have to leave.'

'Yes. It's your last day. Did you enjoy your stay with us?'

'Karla, it was sensational.'

'That's good,' said Karla. 'If you'll give me a couple of minutes, I'll have your account ready.'

'Thanks.'

Les waited with his Visa card while Karla itemised his account when the manager appeared at his side wearing a crisp white shirt tucked into a pair of blue slacks. In his hand was a sheet of paper.

'Mr Gordon,' he said, quietly. 'Do you mind if I have a word with you?'

'No,' said Les. 'Go ahead.'

'I have here the fax Mr Monk had sent to him. And after what happened in the library last night, I'm afraid I'm going to have to ask you for some identification.'

'Some ID?' said Les.

'Yes please.'

'What for?'

'Because if you're not really Mr Gordon,' said the manager, 'you'll have to pay the account yourself.'

'But it's already been paid for in advance,' said Les. He nodded to Karla working on the computer. 'I'll pay for my massages and whatever. And we're all square.'

The manager shook his head. 'I'm sorry, Mr Gordon. But it doesn't work like that.'

Les looked directly at the manager for a moment. 'Okay,' said Les. 'You want some ID. Here you are.' Les switched his camera on and brought the screen up on the back. He flicked past the two photos of him and Deliah and started slowly flicking through the photos of Alexander Holden's body at the front gate, stopping on the close-up of the motivational speaker's lifeless face. 'How's that for ID, Mr Reid? Recognise anyone you know?'

The manager swallowed hard. 'What . . . exactly do you intend to do with those?'

'I don't know,' shrugged Les. 'Maybe sell them to *People*, *Hustler*. One of the papers. Get a journo to write a beat-up saying Alexander Holden was murdered and there was a cover-up. I'll have to figure my options.'

The manager paled. 'Mr Gordon ...'

'But,' interrupted Les. 'If you behave yourself, I'll send you the card after I get home. I'd give it to you now, but there's some other photos on there I want. You're going to have to trust me. That's all.'

The manager gave Les a double blink then turned to Karla. 'Don't worry about Mr Gordon's account. I'll take care of it.'

'Very well, Mr Reid,' said Karla.

'I say,' said Les. 'That's rather sporting of you, John.'

'You will send me the card?'

'I promise,' said Les honestly. 'And I keep my promises.'

'All right,' nodded the manager.

'Then I'll be off,' smiled Les. 'But before I go, Mr Reid, there is something I'd like to say.'

'Yes, Mr Gordon. What's that?'

'This place is deadset unbelievable. The food. The staff. The facilities. The treatments. I just spent five of the best days I've ever had in here. I feel fantastic and I learnt a few things too. So thanks.'

The manager studied Les for a moment. 'Thank you, Mr Gordon,' he said. 'I'll have Michael take your bag down to your car.'

The manager went behind the desk, Les gave Karla a wink, and walked back to his villa for the last time.

Well, that all turned out absolutely delightful, smiled Les as he checked his bag to make sure he had everything. I'll send John that card too. Because I wouldn't mind coming here again. I can't see how they can knock me back as long as I pay in advance. Les zipped up his bag and got a bottle of mineral water from the fridge. He was drinking it, staring out the flyscreen door, when the phone rang.

'Hello?'

'G'day, mate, it's Eddie.'

'Eddie,' said Les. 'How are you? I was just about to leave.'

'I'm all right. Listen. I won't talk long. But everything's sweet down here. I've spoken to Big Arse. And I rang our mate Caccano. All charges have been dropped and the homeboys are in the shit. I'll tell you all about it when I see you.'

'That's unreal, Eddie. Good on you, mate.'

'When will you be back?'

'Before lunch.'

'Ring us when you, get home.'

'I will. See you, mate.'

Well, how about that, grinned Les after he hung up. It gets better by the minute. He put his camera in his bag and finished his mineral water when there was a knock on the open door. It was Michael.

'Hello, Michael,' said Les. 'How's it going, mate?'

'Pretty good,' replied Michael. 'So what do I call you, Len or Les? Or what?' he smiled.

'Mate,' said Les, 'grab my bag, and I'll tell you all about it on the way.'

As they were walking along the path to the foyer, Les filled Michael in. He kept some things back. But by the time they were outside the front door Michael knew pretty much what had been going on.

'So that's the story, Michael,' said Les. 'Warren got me the gig. And I just went along for the ride. And had a bit of fun at the same time.'

'I had an idea you weren't really a film director, Les,' said Michael.

'Yeah. Why's that?' asked Les.

'You're too down to earth. And the way you obliterated Kendrick in the gym that morning.' Michael laughed. 'I don't think there'd be many film directors can fight like that.'

'Maybe,' shrugged Les.

'So I imagine my part in your next movie's still on hold?' said Michael.

'I'm afraid so, mate,' smiled Les.

Michael turned around at the sound of a car approaching from the garage. 'Here's Peta with your car,' he said.

Peta pulled up alongside them with the window down. She smiled at Les then switched the engine off and got out wearing her brown uniform just as Michael's pager went.

'Wouldn't you know it,' he said. 'They want me in the gym.' He offered his hand. 'I'll see you again, Les.'

Les gave the young trainer's hand a warm shake. 'See you, Michael. Thanks for everything, mate. Especially that CD.'

Michael disappeared inside the front door and Les turned to Peta who was wearing her brown uniform.

'So it is Les,' she smiled.

'Yes, Peta,' replied Les. 'It sure is.'

'Where would you like your bag, Les?'

'On the back seat'll do.'

Peta placed Norton's bag on the back seat, then closed the door and smiled at him. 'I have to give it to you, Les,' she said. 'That was a great turn you put on in the library last night. Suicide. Sounds good to me.'

'I'm glad you liked it,' said Les.

'So you're not a film director after all?' said Peta.

Les shook his head. 'No, I'm not.'

'Ohh well,' said Peta. 'It doesn't matter.'

'No. It doesn't. But, Peta,' said Les, looking directly at her, 'say I was a film director or a writer, how's this idea sound? Say for a film or a story?'

'Go on,' said Peta.

'This big goosey bloke we'll call George arrives at a health resort posing as a film director. The first thing George sees when he arrives is a body at the front gate. It's a motivational expert. We'll call him Harry. George recognises him and takes a few photos then drives up to the front door where the concierge is a girl. We'll call the girl Jill. Jill acts nervous when she takes George's car. And George, being a bit of a dill, imagines this is because he's a film director. So rather than say anything about Harry and making Jill even more nervous, George waits till he checks in. Am I making sense, Peta?' asked Les.

'Sort of,' she replied.

'Okay. So then the shit hits the fan. The police arrive and interview George because he found the body. Funnily enough, George knows one of the cops from Sydney. And he's one of the dumbest cops in New South Wales. The cop doesn't blow George's cover and the cop's convinced Harry's death was an accident. George knows how dumb this cop is and later George comes across all these people who absolutely hate Harry. Harry's not only an obnoxious little prick by nature. He's also sent a lot of people to the wall. He's even caused a few deaths. So George wonders if Harry might have been murdered. George has got nothing much to do while he's at the retreat. So he starts playing Horatio Cain.' Les smiled at Peta. 'How am I going now, Peta?'

'Keep going, Les,' answered Peta.

'Early one morning, George does tai chi and Jill's the teacher. She quietly tells George she used to do tai chi with her brother. In tai chi there's a movement, "Man paints a rainbow across the sky". George finds out there was a band called Painted Rainbow who used Harry's services. And because of Harry the band broke up and one of the members hung himself.' Les gave Peta a soft smile. 'Does that sound right, Peta?'

'Keep talking, Les,' said Peta.

'George is no rocket scientist. But he thinks he knows a way someone could have killed Harry.

George looks around and finds this. Wait there a minute, Peta.'

Les crossed the driveway and picked up the piece of pipe from where he'd left it under the bushes. He carried it back and showed the short length of pipe to Peta, who looked at it impassively.

'George believes,' said Les, 'that someone was waiting at the bottom of the hill, and when Harry came racing down on his bike, threw a piece of pipe at Harry hitting him in the forehead. Then when Harry fell off his bike, that same someone broke Harry's neck and dragged both his body and the bike over in front of the gate to make it look like an accident. Someone who knew Harry's movements and knew he didn't wear a helmet. Someone who'd have time to run down the hill while Harry went to the garage and got the bike. Wait for him at the bottom, do the business and run back up again. Someone who knew the gate was obscured by trees. And knew they'd have a good window of opportunity, because the retreat didn't take deliveries before ten in the morning. And the only person checking in that morning was silly big George, the would-be film director. That someone would also have to be fit, strong and a bloody good shot.

George wonders if the killer might be Jill, the concierge? Jill can lift bags and teach women how to use weight stations. So she's got the strength. She can throw a boomerang as good as any Aborigine. So she'd be a good shot. And when George checked in, Jill wasn't nervous because he was a film director. Jill was nervous because he didn't say anything about Harry's body down by the gate. Not even when she asked him in a roundabout way if everything was all right. Plus, if the bloke that hung himself in the band Painted Rainbow was Jill's brother, who she no doubt loved very much, Jill might have a reason to kill Harry.' Les smiled at Peta. 'It wouldn't be hard for George to find out if the bloke in the band was Jill's brother. Would it, Peta?'

Peta kept looking at Les but remained silent as Les slowly moved the piece of pipe around with one hand.

'I'm not saying this is the piece of pipe that struck Harry,' said Les. 'But if you take it down to the front gate, Peta, you'll find it's exactly the same diameter as the bar across the gate Harry was supposed to have hit his head on. You'll also find a half-circle in the driveway the same diameter. It was hot the day Harry got killed. And when the piece of pipe landed on the driveway, it left a distinct indentation in the soft bitumen. Not far from some scratch marks on the driveway made by the pedals when the bike was dragged over in front of the gate.' Les toyed with the piece of pipe in his hand. 'Anyway,' he said, looking up. 'Thanks to some clever planning, a dumb cop and good fortune, it all panned out okay. And Jill got away with murdering the man responsible for her brother's death.' Les smiled at Peta then flung the length of pipe down the hill into the bushes. 'So what do you reckon, Peta?' he asked her. 'Would that make a good story? Or a movie?'

Peta looked evenly at Les for a second or two. 'How come you never brought this up in the library last night?' she asked him.

'How come?' replied Les. 'Because Alexander Holden was such an arsehole, Peta, and caused so many good people grief, that if he was murdered, and I ever met whoever did it, I'd be the first person to shake their hand.' Les smiled warmly at Peta and offered her his hand. 'Goodbye, Peta.'

Peta stared at Les then shook his hand with a firm, warm grip. 'Goodbye, Les,' she said softly. 'It was nice to have met you. You're a good man.'

'Thanks, Peta,' said Les. 'And you're a good woman.' Les went to open the car door and stopped. 'Besides that,' he added, 'you're a greenie. And I like people who are into the environment.'

Peta looked at Les curiously. 'A greenie?' she said.

'Yeah.' Les pointed to the badge next to Peta's name tag. 'That's a greenie badge, isn't it?'

Peta shook her head. 'No.'

'It's not? Well, what's SOFA stand for?'

'Stamp Out Fuckin Acronyms. Why? What did you think it stood for?'

Les looked at the young woman in the brown uniform for a moment then shook his head. 'I think I'll leave you to it, Peta,' he said. Norton got into his car, started the motor and headed for home.

THE END.

TRIFECTA

The Ultimate Robert G. Barrett Collection
Mud Crab Boogie
The Wind and the Monkey
So What Do You Reckon?

ROBERT G. BARRETT

Two classic Les Norton adventures in one volume, plus Robert G. Barrett's outrageous columns on life in Australia plus the ultimate Les Norton trivia challenge.

Mud Crab Boogie Oogie oogie oogie, do the Mud Crab Boogie. Look out Wagga Wagga — Les Norton's in town and he feels like dancing …

The Wind and the Monkey A week in Shoal Bay, and all Les has to do is help Eddie get rid of a crooked cop. But then he meets Digger, and finds Elvis …

So What Do You Reckon? The master of the politically incorrect on everything from duck-shooting to punting to the republic …

Trifecta It's a sure bet.

ISBN 0 7322 8081 8

ROSA-MARIE'S BABY

ROBERT G. BARRETT

If it wasn't for a letter lost in the system for decades landing in his lap, Les would never have known he wasn't the only Norton to gain notoriety thanks to Kings Cross. There was another — Rosa-Marie Norton, the Witch of Kings Cross. Rosa was so bad that the police arrested her for lewd behaviour and obscenity and the customs department burnt her paintings. Paintings now worth thousands of dollars.

Yet according to the lost letter, a bundle of her paintings had been secreted at an old church in Victoria. By sheer coincidence, Eddie needs Les to help him with a hit in Melbourne on a shonky art dealer named 'Latte' Lindsey. After the hit on Latte, Les decides to take a trip down the Great Ocean Road, call in to the Church of the Blessed Madonna, and see if he can find 'mum's' paintings.

Does Les find the missing paintings? Along with plenty of trouble, he finds sexy Sonia, and staunch Stepha. Les also finds there's a lot of déjà vu getting around in Victoria. And when it comes to violence south of the border, there's no Mexican stand-offs.

Robert G. Barrett's *Rosa-Marie's Baby* is action, *l'amour*, and intrigue with a diabolical twist. Set in Melbourne, Lorne and Apollo Bay, Victoria, it proves once again why Robert G. Barrett is called the king of popular Australian fiction.

ISBN 0 7322 7818 X

MYSTERY BAY BLUES

ROBERT G. BARRETT

Just when everything was going so good, Les slips a disc in his back. He can't run, he can't train. He can't do anything much. But he can still drive his car. So it's down to Narooma for the South Coast Blues Festival and a bit of R and R. Thirty bands and three days and nights of non-stop rock'n'roll. Which would have been great, only Les has to have a slight altercation with four fishermen on his first night in town. Now the toughest, meanest, horriblest bloke on the south coast is after his blood.

Then Les met Amazing Grace. Add some magic mushrooms, a dancing bear and Jerry Lee Rat. It all made for an interesting time at the Blues Festival.

Robert G. Barrett's *Mystery Bay Blues*, set in beautiful Narooma on the New South Wales south coast, is non-stop action spiced with humour, mystery and romance. And proves once again why Robert G. Barrett is the king of popular Australian fiction.

ISBN 0 7322 7560 1

THE ULTIMATE APHRODISIAC

ROBERT G. BARRETT

'Leave it with us, sir,' said the Secretary of Defense. 'We'll have Operation Jaws organised and ready to rock'n'roll before you know it.'

'Operation Jaws?' queried President Clooney.

'Yessir,' said the Director of the DEA. 'We feel the name gives a definite veracity to the exercise.'

The President looked at Abelard Sisaric for a moment. 'By golly! It sure does,' he agreed. 'and anybody'll tell you, ol' CC doesn't veracitate unless he has to.'

Aussie Vietnam veteran Ron Milne was on a good thing growing hemp on the tiny Micronesian island on Lan Laroi. Besides being President, the natives treated him as a god. To the American DEA he was a dangerous criminal. President of the United States Clifford J. Clooney decides to invade.

All Lan Laroi wanted to do was sit peacefully in the sun away from everybody. The little island had absolutely no intention of starting a third world war. But if Lan Laroi had to fight a world war, the little island had absolutely no intention of losing.

Robert G. Barrett's *The Ultimate Aphrodisiac* moves away from Les Norton. However, it still has all the action and humour you would expect from the king of popular Australian fiction.

ISBN 0 7322 7168 1